THE GUARDIAN

HERD

LANDFALL

D1056057

JENNIFER LYNN ALVAREZ

HARPER

An Imprint of HarperCollinsPublishers

FOR CRYSTAL, THE GIRL WITH THE CHESTNUT HAIR

The Guardian Herd: Landfall

Text copyright © 2016 by Jennifer Lynn Alvarez

Interior art © 2016 by David McClellan

All rights reserved. Printed in the United States of America.

No part of this book may be used or reproduced in any manner whatsoever without written permission except in the case of brief quotations embodied in critical articles and reviews. For information address HarperCollins Children's Books, a division of HarperCollins Publishers, 195 Broadway, New York, NY 10007.

www.harpercollinschildrens.com

Library of Congress Control Number: 2015940698

ISBN 978-0-06-228613-0

20   BRR   5 4

❖

First paperback edition, 2016

TABLE OF CONTENTS

1	DESTROYER	1
2	SHOOTING THE STARS	10
3	THE WEANLING ARMY	17
4	SLEEP	24
5	CALL OF THE OVER-STALLION	34
6	THE TRAP	41
7	NEWS	50
8	THE ANCESTORS	62
9	DECOY	67
10	AWAKE	75
11	SEA OF RAIN	82
12	LOOSE FEATHER	90
13	CLOSE CALL	98
14	CONFESSION	104
15	STRENGTH	110
16	THE UNITED ARMY	117
17	THE SOUTHERN NESTS	123
18	TRAINING	132
19	THE SWAMP	142
20	DANGERS BELOW	150

21   HERD SECRETS   157

22   OUTBURST   164

23   THE SWALLOWS   170

24   FRIENDS   179

25   TO FALL IS TO DIE   184

26   ADVICE   195

27   MISSING   203

28   REVELATIONS   210

29   CELEBRATION   216

30   DOOMED   226

31   STARWING   235

32   FEAST   243

33   PROMISE   251

34   BONE BREAKER   256

35   COUNTING THE ENEMY   265

36   WARRIOR BLOOD   272

37   THE WOUNDED   279

38   HEALER   288

39   NIGHTFALL   294

40   UNITED   302

41   DEATHBLOW   308

42   SURVIVAL   313

43   CRY OF THE WOLF   320

Do not go gentle into that good night,
Rage, rage against the dying of the light.

—Dylan Thomas

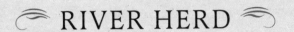 RIVER HERD

The black foal:

STAR—solid-black yearling colt with black feathers, white
   star on forehead

Under-stallions

THUNDERSKY—dark-bay stallion with vibrant crimson
   feathers, black mane and tail, wide white blaze, two hind
   white socks. Previously Thunderwing, over-stallion of Sun
   Herd

HAZELWIND—buckskin stallion with jade feathers, black
   mane and tail, big white blaze, two white hind socks

SUMMERWIND—handsome palomino pinto stallion with
   violet feathers. Deceased

ICERIVER—older dark-silver stallion with powder-blue
   feathers, white mane, white ringlet tail, blue eyes, white
   star on forehead. Sire of Lightfeather. Previous over-
   stallion of Snow Herd. Deceased

GRASSWING—crippled palomino stallion with pale-green
   feathers, flaxen mane and tail, white blaze, one white
   front sock. Deceased

CLAWFIRE—white stallion with blue-gray feathers, jagged scar on face, gold eyes. Born to Snow Herd, joined River Herd

Medicine Mare:

SWEETROOT—council-mare. Old chestnut pinto with dark-pink feathers, chestnut mane and tail, white star on forehead

Mares:

SILVERLAKE—light-gray mare with silver feathers, white mane and tail, four white socks. Previously Silvercloud, lead mare of Sun Herd

CRYSTALFEATHER—small chestnut mare with bright-blue feathers, two front white socks, white strip on face

DAWNFIR—spotted bay mare with dark-blue and white feathers, black mane and tail. Deceased

ROWANWOOD—blue roan mare with dark-yellow and blue feathers, white mane and tail, two hind white socks

DEWBERRY—battle mare. Bay pinto with emerald feathers, black mane and tail, thin blaze on forehead, two white hind anklets

LIGHTFEATHER—small white mare with white feathers, white ringlet tail, white mane. Star's dam. Born to Snow Herd, adopted by Sun Herd. Deceased

MOSSBERRY—elderly light-bay mare with dark-magenta feathers, black mane and tail, crescent moon on forehead and white snip on nose, two white hind anklets. Deceased

Yearlings:

MORNINGLEAF—elegant chestnut filly with bright-aqua feathers, flaxen mane and tail, four white socks, amber eyes, wide blaze

BUMBLEWIND—friendly bay pinto colt with gold feathers tipped in brown, black mane and tail, thin blaze on face

ECHOFROST—sleek silver filly with a mix of dark- and light-purple feathers, white mane and tail, one white sock

BRACKENTAIL—big brown colt with orange feathers, brown mane and tail, two hind white socks

FLAMESKY—red roan filly with dark-emerald and gold feathers

SHADEPEBBLE—heavily spotted silver filly with pale-pink feathers, black mane and tail, thin blaze, three white socks. Born a dud and a runt to Mountain Herd, joined River Herd

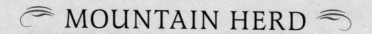

MOUNTAIN HERD

ROCKWING—over-stallion. Magnificent spotted silver stallion with dark-blue and gray feathers, black mane and tail highlighted with white, one white front anklet. Deceased

BIRCHCLOUD—lead mare. Light bay mare with green feathers, two white front socks

HEDGEWIND—flight instructor. Bay stallion with gray feathers, black mane and tail, thin white blaze

FROSTFIRE—captain. White stallion with violet-tipped light-blue feathers, dark-gray mane and tail, one blue eye. Born to Snow Herd, adopted by Mountain Herd

LARKSONG—sky herder. Buckskin mare with dark-blue feathers, white snip on nose, black mane and tail

DARKLEAF—sky herder. Dun mare with black dorsal stripe, purple feathers, black mane and tail, white snip on nose, golden eyes

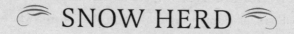

SNOW HERD

TWISTWING—over-stallion. Red dun stallion with olive-green feathers, black mane and tail

PETALCLOUD—lead mare. Power-seeking gray mare with violet feathers, silver mane and tail, one white sock, wide blaze on face

STORMTAIL—gigantic dapple gray stallion, purple feathers, black mane and tail, black eyes

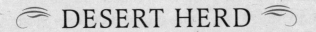 DESERT HERD

SANDWING—over-stallion. Proud palomino stallion with dark-yellow feathers, wide white blaze, one white sock

REDFIRE—captain. Tall copper chestnut stallion with dark-gold feathers, dark-red mane and tail, white star on forehead

SUNRAY—spy. Golden buckskin mare with light-purple feathers, black mane and tail, white star and snip on face

RAINCLOUD—legendary mare. Fine-boned palomino. Deceased

JUNGLE HERD

NIGHTWING—solid black stallion. Four hundred years old. Immortal

SMOKEWING—over-stallion. Speckled bay stallion with

brown and white spotted feathers, black mane and tail,
white snip on nose

ASHRAIN—battle mare. Wiry dark-bay mare with yellow
and green feathers, one white sock, snip on nose

SPRINGTAIL—battle aide. Light-bay skewbald mare with
dark-blue feathers

SPIDERWING—legendary over-stallion. Deceased

HOLLYBLAZE—legendary sister of Spiderwing. Spotted bay
weanling filly with gold-tipped emerald feathers, two front
white socks, light-brown eyes, black mane and tail, wide
blaze on face. Deceased

THE
GUARDIAN
HERD

LANDFALL

Ice Lands

Hoofbeat Mountains

Ice Caves

The Trap

WESTERN ANOK

Blue Mountains

Black
Lake

Wastelands

Canyon
Meadow

MOUNTAIN
HERD

Interior
of
Anok

→

Vein

Canyons

Vein

Lower
Grasslands

Tail River

Valley
Field

Feather Lake

DESERT HERD

Red Rock Mountains

Cloud
Forest

Turtle Beach

SEA of RAIN

Vein

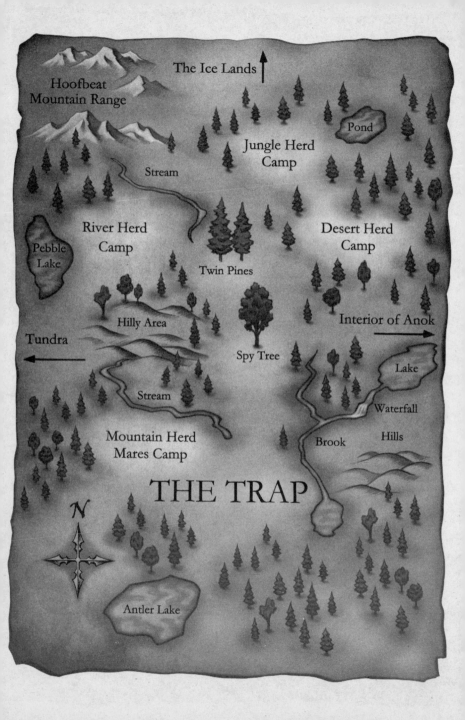

1

DESTROYER

THE SUN HERD LANDS WERE ON FIRE, AND NIGHT-wing the Destroyer reared in the center of the flames, facing Star, his hollow eyes gleaming silver. He'd landed in Anok just moments ago, and surrounding him were Hazelwind's warriors and Mountain Herd's army. Nightwing had arrived during a battle between the two, but the fight was forgotten when the Destroyer's hooves touched the soil. In a hushed voice, Hazelwind ordered his steeds to retreat, but Nightwing kept his eyes trained on his rival. He had not risen from a four-hundred-year hibernation and crossed the Great Sea to jump into a war between herds. No, he had come for Star.

Star advanced toward the Destroyer, his ears pinned,

his posture wary. "Why have you returned?" he asked. "What do you want?"

Nightwing's eyes darted to Star's dull hooves and flattened ears, and Star could imagine what Nightwing was thinking—that Star was an inexperienced yearling, not yet a warrior.

Nightwing kicked off and flew a lazy circle around Star, examining him, looking fearless. He reminded Star of the orcas that swam in the ocean, carefree yet deadly. "I want you," he said, flashing the sharp rims of his hooves and snapping his yellow teeth.

Star's heart stalled, but he wasn't surprised. He'd awakened the Destroyer on his first birthday, when he received his power from the Hundred Year Star. On that night he became Nightwing's rival—the only living pegasus who possessed the starfire besides Nightwing.

Star flared his wings, shielding his best friend, Morningleaf, who stood near him. "Stay back," he whispered to her. She edged closer to her dam, Silverlake.

"What are you going to do?" Morningleaf asked Star, panting, still out of breath. She'd just escaped from the Mountain Herd captain, Frostfire, who'd been holding her captive in the lava tubes beneath a volcano in the south.

Star glanced at her fluttering aqua wings, wishing she

hadn't arrived in the Sun Herd lands at the same time as Nightwing. How could he keep her safe and battle Nightwing at the same time? "I'm going to fight him," he said, and Morningleaf gasped.

The Destroyer hovered overhead, taunting Star, but with the flat expression of a snake. "Come fly with me, black foal; show me your powers." He panted, drawing his silver starfire, and his black hooves glowed silver.

All around Star, the Mountain Herd warriors who'd flown here to fight folded their wings and retreated toward the woods. Their leader, Rockwing, was dead. The first thing the Destroyer had done was to kill the over-stallion with a breath of starfire, turning him immediately to ash. Only Hazelwind's herd and Star's friends from River Herd remained close to Star, crouching and coughing on the smoke. Star's fear bubbled up from the depths of his mind—not for himself, but for his friends, and all of Anok. Nightwing was powerful. Star felt the energy blazing out of him, and maybe he was too powerful to beat, but Star had to try.

He charged Nightwing, hooves splayed and tail lashing as he leaped into the sky. Nightwing dodged him and struck Star's shoulder, slicing it open and leaving a trail of blood. Star tucked, tumbled through a cloud, and came up beneath Nightwing, biting his leg and tugging him off balance.

Nightwing rebounded and sank his incisors into Star's neck. Star gasped as Nightwing ripped out a hunk of mane, then let go and pummeled Star with kicks to his back and wings.

Star fluttered, absorbing the blows in silence, trying to get his bearings. Nightwing's front hoof struck Star's jaw, causing his brain to rattle. He whirled and double-kicked Nightwing with his rear hooves.

Nightwing's body, thin from hibernating, somersaulted backward. Star pinned his ears and followed. The rain had lessened, but now it picked up again, and the drops splattered the grass like tears. Nightwing spun out of the mist and dropped onto Star's back, driving him toward the ground. Just before impact, Nightwing darted away, and Star slammed onto the grass, blood spilling from his nose.

Thundersky, the past over-stallion who'd once threatened to execute Star, galloped to his side. "Use your starfire."

Star wiped his muzzle, pointing. "But *he's* not."

Thundersky shook his head and shot out of the grass, springing like a puma and smashing into Nightwing.

Thundersky's adult colt, Hazelwind, followed, and they flanked the ancient black stallion.

"No! Stay back," whinnied Star. He rocketed off the grass, hurtling forward to protect them.

Nightwing circled the three of them, glaring at Thundersky, and Star recognized the short, fast breaths he was taking. He was drawing on his starfire, the immortal power they'd each inherited on their first birthdays from the Hundred Year Star. He was going to kill Thundersky.

Star pinned his wings and dived into the Destroyer, slamming into his back while drawing on his own starfire from deep within.

Nightwing flung him off and blasted Star in the side, scorching the skin over his ribs. Star bit back the pain and dived at him again. Nightwing flipped around and exhaled, dousing Thundersky in a burst of silver light.

"No," Star neighed, but he was too late.

The bay stallion's crimson feathers curled into black ash and his hooves melted, dripping like sap onto the grass.

"Father!" screamed Morningleaf. She stared at the sky, out of breath, watching her sire fall.

As Thundersky dropped through the clouds, he flung back his head and trumpeted the call to battle, but it was for the last time. The silver flames engulfed him as his regal voice carried across Anok, rebounding off the trees, skipping across the lakes, whispering over the grasses, and then wafting up into the sky—touching all the places Thundersky had lived and loved and fought to protect.

Nightwing closed his mouth, and Thundersky's lifeless body crashed onto the meadow.

Sorrow blasted Star, crippling his thoughts. Thundersky's family galloped to him, fanning his sizzling flesh with their wings, but the mighty stallion was dead.

Nightwing landed in the meadow, smoke billowing out of his nose, sparks crackling between his teeth, his wings spread wide. The steeds who'd fled to the woods in fear of Nightwing gaped at Star in desperate silence, waiting to see what he would do.

Star ransacked his mind for his worst memories— focusing on the feelings that turned his golden fire silver, and deadly. He arched his neck, drawing on the hot embers in his belly and turning them cold. His muscles tightened, and untold power flowed through him. He would show Nightwing. He could destroy too. "Over here," he said.

When Nightwing turned, Star roared silver fire at him. The Destroyer evaded it, but the grass burned where the fire landed, quickly spreading across the field in spite of the rain. The mothers and newborns who Hazelwind had brought with him when he split from River Herd in the north took to the sky and flew away. The rest pranced in place, unwilling to draw attention. But Nightwing didn't follow the mares. He let them go.

Star tucked his wings, dived toward Nightwing, and found Hazelwind flying by his side. "Go," said Star. "He'll kill you too."

The young son of Thundersky set his jaw. "We're warriors, Star. We fight together, and we die together."

Star met his gaze, surprised. Hazelwind had abandoned Star in the north because he viewed him as weak, lacking leadership ability. He'd said Star couldn't protect a herd. But now he'd taken a place by Star's side and called him a warrior. Star nodded, and the two raced toward their enemy.

As they swooped over Nightwing, Star pelted him with exploding bombs of light, but Nightwing dodged them. The blazing starfire seared the soil, scarring it in long, black streaks. Nightwing whirled and smacked Hazelwind; sending the buckskin careening, hoof over wing.

Hazelwind's best friend, the Sun Herd yearling named

Echofrost, charged after him. "Hazelwind," she whinnied, and her dark eyes blazed with fear.

Star reared and clashed with Nightwing in midair.

Nightwing kicked, and Star rolled sideways, gasping and grunting. The blow had cracked several of his ribs. With every breath, throbbing pain shot from his sides to his tail. Then Star saw Nightwing flex his gut. He ducked as Nightwing's silver fire grazed the tips of his ears.

Star whirled and slammed Nightwing in the chest with his hooves.

Hazelwind returned, rocketing from the heights, and he kicked the Destroyer in the back. Nightwing rolled, recovered, and lit after Star, ignoring Hazelwind, who was followed by Echofrost. Nightwing flew over Star's head, striking the crest of his neck and cracking his other hoof against Star's skull.

Stunned, Star tumbled toward land. Nightwing flapped his wings, rearing to strike again, but Hazelwind intercepted, taking the blow and tumbling across the sky, shrieking in pain. Hazelwind crashed onto the grass, and Echofrost landed next to him, whispering into his ear.

Star regained his altitude and took a breath. He needed more power, more anger. He needed a horrible memory, and one came to him quickly. It was about Crabwing, the young seagull he'd befriended on the coast of Anok many moons ago. A cruel over-stallion had crushed the bird. Star remembered Crabwing's tiny gray body split open on his flat feeding stone, and fury like lightning pulsed through Star's veins. He drew all his starfire into his gut, turned on Nightwing, and blasted him with blinding silver light.

2

SHOOTING THE STARS

STAR'S SILVER FIRE SHOT ACROSS THE SKY. BUT HE watched, incredulous, as Nightwing puffed up his chest and projected a silver sphere, like an air bubble, around his body. The starfire streamed around it, leaving Nightwing unharmed. Nightwing clacked his teeth and tore after Star, dropping his shield and hurling bolts of light that slammed Star in waves. He stifled a groan as his feathers caught fire and he began to fall. Nightwing followed, spewing sparks.

"Stop it, please!" Morningleaf screamed at Nightwing from the ground.

Star stared at the Destroyer, dumbfounded. He didn't know anything about a shield. What else didn't he know about their power? Star hovered over the grass, breathing hard, his mind rattled by pain and confusion. He couldn't beat Nightwing, not if the ancient stallion had a shield. Star hadn't realized his eyes had filled with tears until he blinked, and the tears rolled down his cheeks, soaking into the scorched grass. Fresh white flowers erupted in the ashes.

But Star's reprieve was short-lived. Nightwing flew toward him, shooting a stream of fire like lightning, and Star's reflexes jolted his body out of the way. It was just the two of them now, and Nightwing was quick. He shot a burst of starfire that missed Star and exploded against a tree. When the branches ignited, Star's adopted dam, Silverlake, rushed to the pegasi who were too terrified to flee and herded them into the woods.

Nightwing kicked Star's chest and knocked him into the clouds. Star's skin sizzled where the silver hooves had struck him.

"Come on, black foal, what do you have for me?" Nightwing asked, taunting him.

Star flew beneath Nightwing and attempted to grab the stallion's legs, but Nightwing projected his shield immediately, and Star's teeth knocked against the silver orb that protected the stallion. It looked like a bubble but was as hard as a rock.

Nightwing nickered, amused, and then attacked with new fury, retracting the shield so he could pummel Star with fiery explosions.

Star's black hide smoldered, and his bones splintered. He glanced at Morningleaf far below. She looked so small, so scared. He gathered the cold starfire, and his mood blackened like a storm.

Star wanted to land in the field, to regroup, but at least two of his legs were broken and so he hovered and took short, fast breaths, drawing the silver fire into his throat. Perhaps he could scorch the Destroyer while his shield was down. Star circled Nightwing, and the four-hundred-year-old black stallion faced him, unprotected by the silver orb.

Star blasted Nightwing in the face, but Nightwing deflected the fire with his own. Over the heads of the watching pegasi, silver clashed against silver, and sparks showered the grass. More fires erupted on the ground, and more pegasi spooked into the smoke-filled sky and flew away.

Star took a breath, and Nightwing launched his starfire so hard and so fast it hit Star square in the chest and tossed him past the clouds toward where the blue sky turned black. Star screamed as the pain blazed up and down his spine and the planet shrank beneath his hooves. The high, cold winds buffeted his face, freezing his lips. Star tucked his tail and shook his head, but his wings stuttered, giving out on him.

Below, Morningleaf's desperate scream rattled like it was being ripped from her throat. "You're killing him!"

Star's chest heaved. His smoldering tail was broken, and his mane had caught fire. He struggled in the wet clouds as he fell back toward land, gnashing his teeth. Nightwing flew up to meet him, and they traded shots, blast for blast, but each time Star thought his starfire would reach Nightwing, the ancient stallion threw up his shield, blocking it.

Nightwing whinnied. "Haven't you figured it out yet? You can't hurt me, black foal."

Star choked on the smoke that filled the air. Nightwing hurled another fireball at Star, breaking another leg. Desperate, Star trumpeted a plea to the Ancestors for help.

It was a slaughter, not a fight. Star glided below the clouds now and noticed more steeds slipping away from both herds. Nightwing noticed them too and became distracted. Star lunged at him, exhaling a massive burst of fire; he hurled it straight at the stallion's head while he was looking away.

But Nightwing sensed it coming. He whipped his head around, his mane flowing in a black arc, and he sprang his shield. The starfire encompassed the sphere and then seconds later it flamed out. Nightwing remained untouched.

Star reeled. He needed the golden fire to heal his wounds. He tried to shake off the darkness that gripped his soul, to reach the warm embers that would save him, but they were out of reach.

Tired of the battle, Nightwing sighed. "Fly straight and find your rest, Star." He drew up a colossal silver flame and shot it in a thin, destructive beam.

Star flailed, trying to dodge it, but Nightwing flew toward him, redirecting the beam as Star ducked and twirled. Nightwing galloped across the sky, his silver fire sparking, his power electrifying the atmosphere around him. But still Star refused to flee. He met his enemy head-on. He had to beat Nightwing. Every steed in Anok was counting on it. And then Nightwing's starfire found its mark, and the ancient black stallion's eyes glowed with victory as his silver beam of light pierced Star's chest and then sizzled into his heart.

Star's wings went slack and he fell, upside down, toward the field, the wind whipping his feathers. He blinked at the black smoke drifting across the beautiful, stormy sky. His broken body felt no pain. He might as well have been floating. He plummeted toward the field, picking up speed, his wings useless.

Star didn't see the ground coming, but he felt it when he struck the grass. Star recognized the shrill whinny of Morningleaf, and his heart filled with sorrow.

Driven by terror, the remaining steeds of Anok, save his closest companions, stampeded into the sky. Star watched them scatter like frightened birds. And then he felt the hot, familiar breath of his best friend on his muzzle and her tears dropping onto his cheeks. "Don't leave me, Star," Morningleaf nickered, her voice wavering.

Star opened his mouth to answer, but he couldn't form words or starfire or draw breath. He wished he could unwind the planet, spin it backward to another day. He wanted to play chase with his friends one more time, or fly through the clouds, or nap in the sun. He wanted to tell Morningleaf he was sorry he'd failed her. In agony, Star experienced the excruciating weight of things unfinished. As Morningleaf cried over him, shedding her aqua feathers, one of them drifted over his head and he watched it, transfixed, noticing that his body felt as weightless as the feather.

I can't let it end this way, he thought.

As the triumphant cry of Nightwing echoed throughout the vast, empty plain, Star's smoldering heart thumped weakly, desperately, and then his mind slid, helpless and unwilling, into darkness.

3

THE WEANLING ARMY

MORNINGLEAF SWEPT HER WINGS OVER STAR'S body. "No, no," she cried, her lips quivering. Nightwing landed in the distance and stamped the soil, causing more flames to erupt and feed the existing fires that would soon reach the woods. She stood and whirled, facing Nightwing, her voice rasping. "Look what you've done!" Tears filled her eyes, and her view of him blurred.

He blinked at her. "I've seen you before. . . ."

She wiped her eyes and advanced on him. "Star was good and brave. He's everything you're not!" Morningleaf's heart felt like it had been sliced in half. First Nightwing had killed her sire, Thundersky, and then he'd attacked Star and maybe killed him too. He'd destroyed everything.

Dusk had fallen, and she stared up at the sky and bleated her sorrow into the clouds. Nightwing watched her with his head cocked, looking smug and enraging her further. "Ancestors, help me!" she whinnied, locking her gaze on the Destroyer.

Morningleaf's mother, Silverlake, reared, guessing her filly's intentions. "Don't do it, Morningleaf!"

Morningleaf charged Nightwing, her head low and teeth exposed.

Echofrost and the new River Herd yearling, Shade-pebble, galloped across the meadow to stop her.

Morningleaf knew she should stop, but Star lay on the ground in a heap, his body broken. Her throat squeezed shut; her heart hardened into an aching ball. She focused on Nightwing.

"Look!" whinnied Echofrost. She and Shadepebble dug in their hooves and slid to a halt.

Morningleaf was ten wing lengths away from striking the Destroyer, but she glanced upward because of the strange tone in Echofrost's voice—a mixture of awe and wonder.

Above them the bright lights that migrated across the sky of the north descended—the Ancestors. Morningleaf's jaw dropped and she halted, staring. The colorful lights swirled through the clouds, the white mist reflecting all the colors. The pegasi who'd fled into the woods returned, chased out by the flames, and they paused, stunned. Nightwing watched the lights too, his amused expression gone.

The Ancestors swarmed the meadow and took the shape of living pegasi. Their hides glowed with a reflective sheen, and their feathers glittered, each one refracting light, creating prisms of color that surrounded their bodies. Around the meadow, pegasi lowered their heads, their tails swishing nervously. Morningleaf bowed her head too, but noticed something unusual. These visiting Ancestors were weanlings—all of them, which meant they'd died as weanlings and had never grown up. There were at least a thousand of them.

A spotted bay filly took the lead, and the weanlings lined up behind her in battle formation. They surrounded Star's body in a defensive spiral. The spotted filly raised her wings, and all murmuring from the watching pegasi ceased. She stepped away from her army and floated across the smoking grass, landing near Nightwing. "I knew you'd return to Anok," the spirit filly said to him.

He stared at her with rounded eyes.

Morningleaf glanced at Echofrost, who had sidled next to her. "Did you hear her speak?"

Echofrost nodded, her eyes bulging.

"I hear them too," said Shadepebble.

Nightwing flared his nostrils, showing the deep-red color inside. "Hollyblaze?"

The filly buzzed her wings, and rapid bursts of gold and emerald light erupted from her feathers. "Don't say my name."

Morningleaf exhaled, whispering to Echofrost and Shadepebble. "Hollyblaze is an ancient filly. She was Nightwing's best friend four hundred years ago—they were raised together."

"What happened to her?" asked Echofrost.

"She was murdered. The legends say Nightwing caused her death."

Nightwing stared at Hollyblaze with longing and dis-belief. A single tear formed in his eye and rolled down his cheek. When it hit the ground, a black flower sprang from the soil.

"Don't cry for me," the filly spat at him. "Go. Leave Anok. Let my brother's descendants live in peace."

"Who is her brother?" asked Shadepebble.

"Spiderwing, the founder of the five herds, the most beloved stallion of all time."

"Oh, I didn't know he had a sister."

"She died so young, she's rarely remembered in the stories," whispered Morningleaf. The legends she'd heard from the elders surfaced in her mind, but a lot about Hollyblaze was unknown, like how she died and why Nightwing had spared her brother's life.

Nightwing pricked his ears, responding to Hollyblaze. "But the pegasi don't live in peace; they're always at war." His rumbling voice shook the filly's transparent body, making it glimmer.

"You're still a coward," neighed Hollyblaze. She glanced behind her. "Charge!"

She and her weanling army rattled their feathers and marched toward Nightwing. He backed away from them. Lightning crackled across the sky, but there was no storm, and the rain had ceased. Hollyblaze flared her wings, sending bright light into Nightwing's eyes. "Destroyer. Killer. Coward," she cried, and her army chanted with her.

Nightwing cringed, ducking behind his wings.

The remaining pegasi fled, this time for good, leaving Morningleaf alone with her friends. The weanling Ancestors marched toward Nightwing, flinging blinding lights into his eyes and chanting. "Destroyer. Killer. Coward."

The lightning dropped from the clouds and struck the land near his hooves.

Nightwing blasted them with silver starfire, but it passed through them without causing harm or slowing them down.

Morningleaf and her friends galloped to the rear of the weanling army to avoid being blinded by the sharp lights. The Destroyer backed away from them, snorting, the whites of his eyes flashing. "Leave me alone!" He hurled starfire at them and staggered when he stepped on his own tail.

"He's afraid of them," said Shadepebble. "Why?"

Morningleaf thought she understood. "Because he can't hurt them and because they know what he did. They're haunting him. No wonder he slept so long."

Shadepebble shook her head, overwhelmed by the thousand dead weanlings who quivered with rage as they faced Nightwing. "That's horrible."

"It's good for us," said Morningleaf. "Come on." She galloped to Silverlake and Hazelwind. "This is our chance to get Star out of here."

"Morningleaf, he's . . ." Silverlake struggled to finish her sentence.

Morningleaf stamped her hoof, refusing to believe

Star was dead. "I won't leave him, and we have to go now, while Nightwing is distracted. This isn't over." Hope and anguish blazed in her expression.

Silverlake nodded reluctantly. "All right, let's move him."

4

SLEEP

MORNINGLEAF'S OLDER BROTHER, HAZELWIND, and her friend Bumblewind each gripped one of Star's wings in their teeth and lifted him. "He's heavy," said Hazelwind through a mouthful of Star's feathers. Morningleaf's brother was injured and bleeding, but his sharp eyes glinted with energy.

"I'll get his tail," offered Clawfire. Morningleaf exhaled, grateful for the big Snow Herd captain who'd joined River Herd after being banished from his own herd. He'd inadvertently stolen Rockwing's filly in a raid on Mountain Herd. That filly was Shadepebble, and when Clawfire returned to Snow Herd with her, the leaders had banished them both to avoid a war with the filly's sire. But

Clawfire had befriended Shadepebble, and the pair had joined River Herd together. They'd both become Morningleaf's good friends.

"Thank you, Clawfire," Morningleaf said. His added strength enabled them to lift Star off the ground. "Fly low, and be careful with him," Morningleaf said, grimacing at the sight of Star's limp body.

"Where to?" asked Shadepebble.

Morningleaf glanced at the weanling army; they were driving Nightwing east, away from Star. "Let's fly west."

The group hovered over the grass and darted forward, flying toward the ocean. As they disappeared over the foothills, Morningleaf looked back and saw that Nightwing had turned from the weanling army and fled. The army's leader, Hollyblaze, lifted her eyes and seemed to look toward Morningleaf, who dipped her head to the ancient filly, a gesture of respect and thanks. The filly dipped her head too.

Morningleaf's broken heart thumped hard. The Ancestors had protected Star from Nightwing. She was encouraged but saddened too. What peace was there in the golden meadow if the dead were still haunting, and haunted by, their enemy? She flattened her ears; Nightwing needed to be destroyed—for everyone's sake.

Morningleaf flew with her friends for many hours. She sobbed freely, letting her tears soak the soil until she arrived at the coast and soared over the cliffs.

"There's the cave where I hid Star when he was a weanling," said Silverlake.

Morningleaf saw the dark maw carved into the cliff. Her dam had hid Star there so that he wouldn't be executed before he received his power on his first birthday. Silverlake had lost her position as lead mare of Sun Herd and was banished for hiding Star, but it had saved his life. And Morningleaf knew Star had hated living alone, which was unnatural for a pegasus. He'd survived by eating sea kelp and befriending a lazy bird, a seagull that he'd named Crabwing. She exhaled, long and slow. His stories about Crabwing were some of her favorites, and now, looking at Star's beaten body dangling between the three stallions, she dissolved into fresh sobs.

The group landed on the beach. Hazelwind, Clawfire, and Bumblewind laid Star gently on the sand. Bumblewind brushed Star's forelock out of his eyes, which were closed.

Silverlake trotted to Morningleaf and nudged her away from the others. "Now is not the time for tears," she said quietly. "Wipe your eyes and tuck your wings."

Morningleaf sucked in her breath, but her dam was

right. Now was not the time to break down, and Morningleaf had to remember that Silverlake, Hazelwind, and Shadepebble were grieving too. Besides murdering Thundersky, Nightwing had also killed Shadepebble's sire, Rockwing. Morningleaf wiped her tears.

"That's better," said Silverlake, and Morningleaf noticed that her mother had aged into an old mare in the span of a day. "Why don't we bury Star here," Silverlake suggested.

"*What?*" Morningleaf sputtered. "Bury him? No!"

Silverlake stared at her. "Why not?"

"He's . . . he can't be . . . gone. We need to get him to Sweetroot." Sweetroot was their medicine mare, and she was hiding in the Trap, the thick northern forest at the base of the Hoofbeat Mountains. It's where Star had asked the herds to hide after he became aware that Nightwing was returning to Anok. Snow Herd had refused him, but many steeds from the other herds had come and were hiding there, and with them was Sweetroot.

Silverlake trotted to Star and nosed his chest, then licked his ears, gentle and loving, like he was a newborn. "Nightwing stopped his heart, Morningleaf."

The others watched Morningleaf, their agonies flickering in the depths of their eyes, and she felt their pity for her. "Look," she said to them, imploring. "Star's magical. He has healing power, and he's immortal. We can't give up on him."

Bumblewind glanced at Star, who was his best friend, his expression forlorn. She could guess what he was thinking, that Star didn't look immortal, not right now.

"He won't die of old age, Morningleaf, but he can be killed," Hazelwind reminded her softly.

"Yes, but we don't know for sure if he's dead. We need Sweetroot to examine him. I won't bury him until she says."

Hazelwind glanced at the western horizon. The setting sun streaked pink rays across the ocean. "No one knows where we are. Let's rest awhile. Tomorrow at sundown we'll head northeast to the Trap, to the hiding herds and to Sweetroot. She can examine him there. Agreed?"

Morningleaf and Bumblewind lashed their tails. "We can't wait until tomorrow," they said in unison.

"Well, we can't travel in daylight; it's too risky," said Hazelwind. "Nightwing could be anywhere. We have to wait until tomorrow after dark, to give Star his best chance."

"It's almost dark now. Let's go tonight," urged Morningleaf.

Hazelwind stared at her, his cuts from the battle with

Nightwing still dripping blood, and her ears grew hot with shame as she realized what Hazelwind was unwilling to admit. *He* needed rest. He couldn't carry Star another mile. "You're right," she said quickly. "It's best to go at sundown tomorrow."

Hazelwind nuzzled her. "Thank you."

The group drifted apart, each steed lost in exhaustion or grief or both.

Morningleaf and her brother trotted to the edge of the sea and let the gentle breakers splash against their hooves. Morningleaf's breath hitched, and she fought back more tears, thinking of Thundersky, the mighty sire they'd lost.

"I know," Hazelwind said, wrapping his wing over her back. "I'm going to miss him too." The two stared at the setting sun, thinking of their sire—the magnificent crimson-feathered over-stallion who'd given up his power to follow Star. Silverlake trod across the sand and joined her adult colt and her filly.

"Oh, Mama," cried Morningleaf, and she buried her muzzle deep into her mother's soft mane.

Silverlake wrapped her wings around her. "Shh," she whispered, and Morningleaf's body trembled, seeming too small to hold her pain.

Hazelwind stepped closer, and Silverlake included him

in her embrace. "He was so proud of you both," she said to them. "So proud."

Hazelwind blinked rapidly, and silent tears rolled down his cheeks. The three of them stood on the beach, leaning against one another, until the red sun vanished into the sea.

Morningleaf woke at dawn and stretched, feeling hungry but enjoying the warm sunshine on her chestnut coat. Maybe she'd take Star to the lake to swim and graze on reeds. Her hooves dug into the grass, sinking deep. *Wait, this isn't grass; it's sand.* Morningleaf jolted upright. She'd been dreaming of Dawn Meadow, where she'd been born. In the dream she was playing with Star, tugging on his tail and chasing him, wishing she were as fast as her long-legged friend. She rubbed her eyes with her wings, confused. She was not home in Dawn Meadow, and there was Star, resting on a beach, and he was a yearling, not a foal.

No.

She reeled.

Remembering.

The shocks of the day before slammed her: Nightwing

killing her father, Nightwing fighting Star, Star hitting the ground, and Hollyblaze's weanling army. Her head throbbed—was yesterday the dream?

She walked slowly to Star, lifting each hoof with precision, terrified to reach him, to find out the truth.

"There's no change in him," said Bumblewind, who'd guarded Star's body throughout the night.

Morningleaf rushed the rest of the way to Star's side. She felt his chest, but it was cold and still. She placed her muzzle against his, feeling for breath, but none came. And yet he did not look dead to her.

"It's like he's sleeping," said Bumblewind. "But I can't wake him up." His sudden tears splashed onto Star's hide, and Bumblewind quickly wiped them off. He'd arranged Star in a natural position and preened all his feathers. His eyes traced Star's battered body, hunting for signs of life, but Bumblewind himself was haggard, his skin thin from dehydration.

"Have you eaten?" Morningleaf asked him.

"I don't need food."

She didn't want to eat either. Her hunger had quieted as soon as she remembered where she was and what had happened. She peered down the beach to where Silverlake and Hazelwind had found a bed of kelp. They were dragging it back to share with the group. Clawfire, Echo-frost, and Shadepebble floated in the waves, cleaning their bodies. It appeared Hazelwind had bathed too; his cuts were clean and beginning to close.

"I'll watch Star," Morningleaf said, nudging Bumblewind away. "Clean up and eat so we can get back to Sweetroot quickly."

"I'm fine," said Bumblewind.

"I said I'd watch him." Morningleaf's sharp tone snapped his focus, and he took his eyes off Star long enough to look at her. "The food will give you the strength to carry him," she added.

Bumblewind nodded and trotted toward Silverlake and the kelp. Morningleaf noticed how muscular he'd become since they'd all turned one year old. As a foal, he'd been chunky, always hungry. Well, now she knew why—his body had been building the foundation of a very large stallion.

After everyone had eaten, Morningleaf took her turn, forcing down bites of the fibrous green kelp. "We're exposed out here on the beach," she said. "Why don't we shelter in Star's cave until dark?"

Her friends agreed and they moved Star's body into the cave, where Morningleaf curled by his side. "Look!"

she said to her friends. "Seagull feathers." The small gray and white feathers adorned a circle of dried seaweed. Inside the circle were shiny rocks and empty oyster shells. "It's Crabwing's old nest," she said, her voice rising with excitement.

"Who's Crabwing?" asked Shadepebble.

Echofrost nickered. "He was the over-stallion of birds."

As Echofrost retold Star's funny stories about the seagull, Morningleaf touched his delicate nest with her wingtip, imagining Star shucking oysters for Crabwing and letting the little bird eat bugs out of his mane. She inhaled deeply, marveling at the evidence of Star's gentleness. But the contrast of Star's love for Crabwing to his present condition, injured so badly that he'd retreated into death or something else—an infinite sleep—ripped at her heart.

Morningleaf rested her head over Star's neck and whispered into his ear. "We need you, Star. Please come back."

5

CALL OF THE OVER-STALLION

THE GROUP LIFTED OFF AT DUSK AND FLEW north, following the shoreline and gliding like bats, fast and silent except for the whooshing of wings. The heavy clouds shielded the moon and stars, making the night darker than most. They passed out of Crabwing's Bay, the brackish inlet Star had named after his bird friend, and veered east. They journeyed in the Vein, the neutral zone that existed so pegasi could travel through Anok without crossing into one another's territories. It would protect them from foreign pegasi, but not from Nightwing. None of them believed the Destroyer would respect the sanctuary of the Vein.

"The sun is rising," said Silverlake. They had flown all night, stopping only twice to give Star's carriers rest and water. "We'll land there for the day." Silverlake banked and dropped toward the base of the Blue Mountains. Morningleaf and the others followed her, landing near a gully in a forest of redwood trees. The gully was thick with plants and creeping vines. "We can dig into these and cover ourselves," said Silverlake.

Hazelwind and Clawfire cleared a space for Star, laid him down, and then covered him with the pliant shrubs. A shallow creek fed by snowmelt trickled nearby. Each pegasus drank and then burrowed into the plants just as the morning sun ripped across the sky.

Morningleaf meant to stay awake, but in seconds she was fast asleep. When she woke, it was midday. The sun blazed overhead, and the clouds had vanished. She was glad for the shade and the cool soil under her hooves. She checked on Star, who was curled beside her, but he was unchanged from the day before. She nibbled on the nearest leaves. They were bitter, but edible.

A figure flew high overhead, a pegasus, and she startled. The Blue Mountains guarded the northwestern edge of Mountain Herd's territory. She squinted. The sun shone behind the pegasus, making him look black. "No one move," she whispered to the others.

The pegasus in the sky trumpeted the call of an over-stallion. It thundered across the airy plain like the roar of a lion. But this stallion's voice was different from most. His call vibrated at multiple frequencies, slipping into the air currents and whipping across the planet, carrying far-ther than was natural. And she recognized the voice from the other day. "It's Nightwing," she told her friends.

"But he's calling a herd," said Shadepebble. "He doesn't have a herd."

Morningleaf remembered Rockwing, the deceased over-stallion of Mountain Herd who'd wanted to make a pact with Star, and then with Nightwing, to rule Anok. "He doesn't have a herd . . . yet," said Morningleaf, listen-ing. "He's calling for followers."

"But who would follow Nightwing?" whispered Echo-frost, who was tucked next to her twin brother, Bumble-wind.

"We'll see," said Morningleaf, feeling angry. With Night-wing present in Anok, every over-stallion stood to lose his power, and the pegasi who had chosen not to hide in the Trap would be restless, fearful. She wouldn't be sur-prised if they followed Nightwing to protect themselves from death, or to try and share in his victory. Obedience to authority was built into their bones like the urge to fly—and it helped keep peace within the herds, to have only one pegasus in charge of each—but it worked against them when the leader was ruthless, like Rockwing, or evil, like Nightwing.

She watched the Destroyer circle overhead, braying, and then he moved on, but his distant calls continued to disturb her. Eventually, he was quiet.

Shadepebble gave Star's body a sorrowful glance. "How are we going to stop Nightwing now?"

Morningleaf lifted her chin and spoke so her mother and brother and friends could hear her. "We aren't going to stop him. We can't. All we can do is hide Star and get him to Sweetroot. If it takes days, moons, or years—it doesn't matter—we will protect Star until he wakes up . . . or flies to the golden meadow. We are his guardians."

Bumblewind edged closer to her. "But you saw what happened in the fight. Nightwing is stronger."

"Maybe, but Star is better," said Morningleaf, her tone firm. "And he has help. You saw the Ancestors; I don't think they would have shown themselves to all of us, and protected Star, if they didn't believe in him. Star can defeat Nightwing. I know it, I just don't know how, but I'm not giving up. There's a way. There *has* to be a way."

Clawfire agreed. "Star lost a battle, not a war."

"Exactly," said Morningleaf.

"At dark we'll continue on," said Silverlake. "Let's try to sleep."

But Echofrost stood and shook herself. "I agree with Morningleaf, but I can't just wait. We're going to need information about Nightwing."

"What are you talking about?" asked Hazelwind, rising.

"I'm going to follow him to see who answers his call."

Morningleaf gasped. "You can't. He'll kill you."

"Not if he doesn't see me. Anyway, he's calling for followers. If I'm captured, I'll join him and spy on him from the inside." She shook the dirt out of her feathers and flared her wings. "But don't worry; I won't be captured. Not again."

Morningleaf understood her fear. Echofrost had been captured by a Mountain Herd patrol when she was a weanling. A colt named Brackentail had lured Star and his friends into Mountain Herd's territory and attempted to kill Star in a canyon run, a game played in flight school where instructors tricked their trainees into galloping off cliffs at full speed. Regular pegasi unfurled their wings and flew to safety, but since Star couldn't fly, the drop would have killed him. Morningleaf had stopped the race, saving Star, but Mountain Herd steeds had spotted her and the others in the canyons, and had captured Echofrost and Brackentail. Echofrost was tortured and then eventually released, but she'd never forgiven Brackentail for it.

Echofrost's foalhood dream had been to become a spy, and she would get her wish today, but to begin by spying on Nightwing the Destroyer—that was ambitious. "I *am* worried," Morningleaf said to her friend.

Bumblewind rose and trotted to his twin. "I'm going with you."

"No, stay with Star. I'll go," said Hazelwind.

Echofrost glanced from her brother to her dearest friend, Hazelwind. "Spies are safest when alone," she said. "Besides, you're both needed to carry him." She nodded toward Star's heavy, lifeless body buried in the leaves.

"No, I can help," said Silverlake.

"It's not just Nightwing out there," Morningleaf added, thinking of predators.

Hazelwind trotted close to Echofrost and dropped his muzzle next to hers. "Let me go with you," he whispered. "I'll watch your back, and—and I need something to do."

Echofrost blew into his nostrils in a long exhale. "All right, but when we get close to Nightwing, you have to let me do my spying on my own. I'll find out what I can and get back quickly. I promise."

He nodded and turned to his dam, Silverlake. "When we're finished, we'll meet you back at the Trap."

Silverlake rushed to her son and embraced him in her wings. The twins rubbed muzzles and then Hazelwind and Echofrost trotted into the redwoods, kicked off, and coasted through the trees.

When darkness fell, Silverlake, Bumblewind, and Clawfire lifted Star's body; and the group flew all night toward the Trap, and their medicine mare, Sweetroot.

6

THE TRAP

THEY ARRIVED THE FOLLOWING MORNING AFTER sunrise, landing at the base of the Hoofbeat Mountains. The trees that formed the Trap lifted out of the melting snow like an army, so tall and tight that once inside the forest, a pegasus couldn't fly up and out of it. This is why they called it the Trap, because it confined them to the ground. They would have to flee from predators, fires, and enemies by hoof. But the Trap was also secure because the pegasi couldn't be seen from the sky.

Star had chosen the Trap as the place to hide from Nightwing. It was after Star received his power that he'd become aware of the Destroyer. Their minds had linked through the starfire they'd each inherited, and

Nightwing, who had been hibernating in the Territory of the Landwalkers, woke up when he also became aware of Star. In a series of visions, Star realized that Nightwing was returning to Anok to kill him. The River Herd council had agreed with Star's choice to hide in the Trap, and they'd sent messengers to all the herds, inviting them inside. About half the pegasi in Anok accepted; the rest stayed in their territories, unwilling to abandon their homelands.

Silverlake had sectioned the massive forest into separate encampments to keep the peace between the foreign herds while they waited for Nightwing to arrive. The steeds who'd accepted the invitation were inside, waiting for news about the Destroyer.

Now Morningleaf stared at the silent trees with dread. When the pegasi saw Star's broken body dragged in like a carcass, would they abandon him? Would they lose hope?

"Follow me to River Herd's camp," said Silverlake. She released Star's tail and let Clawfire and Bumblewind carry him the rest of the way. Star's hooves dragged across the lichen, carving long grooves into it. Morningleaf and Shadepebble followed.

The forest was dark, and a layer of wispy fog drifted above the animal paths. Narrow stripes of sunlight pierced the leaf cover at the tops of the trees and struggled through the mist, spotlighting the soft soil and the blooming wildflowers. Morningleaf thought the Trap would be cold, but it wasn't. The ceiling of branches overhead locked in the hot breath of the forest's inhabitants, and the rays of light caused moss and plants to grow. Morningleaf tread softly, feeling frightened by the darkness and the enclosed space. If trouble came, she could not fly away.

"See the animal paths?" said Silverlake, pointing. "They lead to each herd's camp, and to streams and ponds. Use them and you won't get lost."

Morningleaf hadn't flown over the Trap, but her sire had, and he'd told her it was the largest forest in western Anok. If she lost her bearings, she could gallop for weeks without ever finding the end of it. He'd said it was important to always have in mind the borders, so she could exit quickly. Morningleaf's throat tightened as she remembered him. Thundersky had fought so hard to protect her since the day she was born, and he'd been so strong and powerful. She'd never imagined losing him.

"The herds have formed a United Council made up

of pegasi from each herd," Silverlake explained as they moved slowly toward River Herd's camp. "I represent River Herd, and I report back to our council. The other steeds on the United Council are Ashrain of Jungle Herd, Redfire of Desert Herd, and Birchcloud of Mountain Herd."

"My mother is here?" cried Shadepebble, referring to Birchcloud. Morningleaf knew Shadepebble hadn't heard news of her dam since she'd been stolen by the Snow Herd captain, Clawfire, and taken to the north.

"Yes. When she learned that your sire, Rockwing, planned to claim Star's birthland, no matter what the cost, she left him. Many of her mares followed."

Shadepebble's hooves lightened as she walked, and her eyes shone with excitement. Morningleaf glanced at her own mother, feeling grateful they were still together.

"Look, there's Dewberry," nickered Bumblewind.

The pinto battle mare heard Bumblewind's voice and cantered toward him, whinnying to the rest of River Herd that Star had returned. But the joy in her eyes evaporated when she drew closer and saw Star's body hanging between Clawfire and Bumblewind. "Oh no," she said, covering her muzzle with her wing.

"We need Sweetroot," said Silverlake.

"I'll get her." Dewberry galloped back the way she had come.

Silverlake led them into River Herd's camp of trampled soil and sunken depressions in the moss where pegasi slept at night. Morningleaf glimpsed the flutter of Sweetroot's dark-pink feathers as she trotted toward Star.

"Lay him there," she ordered, taking charge. "Dewberry, bring me the vandal roots I stored in that aspen grove yesterday. Remember?"

Dewberry nodded and trotted to get the roots.

"Do you already know what's wrong with him?" asked Silverlake, looking surprised.

"The roots are for you," said Sweetroot. "You're exhausted. All of you are."

Silverlake's legs trembled, and her back had curved into a sway. She didn't argue with the medicine mare.

Sweetroot knelt beside Star, pressing him gently with her wings and assessing his wounds. She paused near the burned flesh on his chest, and her lips tightened. "I've never seen a wound like this. What happened?"

Morningleaf, Silverlake, and the others collapsed, lying in the moss as Dewberry returned with the calming roots. Silverlake told the story, telling Sweetroot everything that had happened since Nightwing had landed in Anok. All the while, Sweetroot worked, packing Star's wounds with yarrow leaves, straightening his broken legs, wrapping them with flexible branches, and massaging his cold chest.

All around them, River Herd steeds gathered, trotting out of the mist as the news spread that Star was back. They stood in quiet circles, listening. When Silverlake finished the story, she asked Sweetroot the question they were all too scared to ask. "Is he alive?" Silence dropped on the pegasi like a deathblow, and their ears twisted forward as they waited.

"I think he's alive," she answered.

"You *think* so?" Silverlake sounded disappointed.

Sweetroot stood and folded her wings. "The truth is, I can't hear a heartbeat, but if this happened when you say it did, then his body would have begun to . . . you know . . . to decay."

A collective gasp coursed through the watching pegasi.

"But there's no sign of that happening to Star," she assured them. "He seems asleep, but it's so deep I can't wake him."

"Like he's knocked out?" asked Shadepebble.

"No. He's deeper than that. Whatever it is, it's not natural, but then, neither is he." Sweetroot wrung her feathers, distressed and unsure. "I'll do what I can for him. He might wake up. We'll have to wait and see."

Silverlake turned to Dewberry. "Please inform the other herds and call the United Council to meet tonight, at the twin pines."

Dewberry nodded, trotted down an animal path, and disappeared.

Later that evening, Silverlake left River Herd's camp and followed a trail to the twin pines—two massive coniferous trees that were identical in shape and size. The trees were so large, they impaired the growth of smaller trees, and it was one of the few places in the Trap where pegasi could gather in numbers. The United Council met there, with each herd sending a representative.

After several hours, Silverlake returned and reported the discussion to River Herd's council, and to all the River Herd pegasi who'd gathered to listen. They were curious and on edge, as was Morningleaf.

"We've decided we have no choice but to continue hiding

in the Trap," she said. "Sweetroot doesn't believe Star's body should be moved again unless it's an emergency. And with Nightwing hunting for followers, the sky isn't safe."

The gathered pegasi glanced upward and tensed. The sky had never been a domain they feared.

"There are thousands of pegasi out there who chose not to hide with us," Silverlake added, nodding toward the vast space outside the Trap. "Those steeds could become . . . quite dangerous to us if they join Nightwing. We need to know what they're doing, which side they are taking."

"What do you mean 'which side'?" asked Dewberry. "We're all against Nightwing, aren't we?"

Clawfire interrupted. "You haven't seen Nightwing yet. His power surpasses what I imagined. It will be difficult for pegasi to resist his authority."

"We can't live here forever," said Bumblewind.

Silverlake flicked her tail nervously. "We won't. We will act, but not until we have more information."

"Echofrost and Hazelwind are spying on Nightwing," explained Morningleaf to the River Herd steeds.

"Yes, and until they return, we'll wait." Silverlake clapped her wings. "That's it for now."

The pegasi dispersed, and Morningleaf trotted back to

Star, falling asleep by his side.

Six days later, Echofrost and Hazelwind returned, streaming blood and galloping through the trees like they were on fire. "Gather!" neighed Hazelwind. "We bring news."

7

NEWS

"CALL THE HERDS TOGETHER," HAZELWIND CRIED as he dropped his haunches and skidded to a halt.

"This news is for everyone," Echofrost added, sliding up beside him.

Morningleaf trotted close to her brother and Echofrost. "You're hurt," she whinnied.

"It's nothing," said Echofrost. She shook her head. "It doesn't matter."

"Follow me," said Silverlake. She whirled around and cantered east. Echofrost and Hazelwind followed, along with Morningleaf and the River Herd stallions and mares who'd been grazing nearby.

Morningleaf examined her brother and Echofrost

closely, noticing they cantered without limping; their breaths were fast but normal for galloping steeds. Their hides were scratched up as if by thorns, but they weren't as injured as they appeared.

When they reached the twin pines, Silverlake called for the other three herds. Soon, all pegasi within earshot had gathered, including Ashrain, Redfire, and Birchcloud from the United Council.

Echofrost wasted no time. "I've been following Nightwing," she began, still panting. "He's been trumpeting for followers across Anok. A few times I lost him, and I think he was riding the jet streams. But his voice—it carries like no other; it's powered by starfire. Every steed in Anok has heard him by now."

Ashrain nodded. "His call reached us here."

"The herds are hiding from him, right?" asked Bumblewind, his eyes trained on his twin sister.

She snorted. "It's the opposite." Echofrost took a gulp of air, staring at the pegasi around her, waiting for all mumbling to cease. Then she spoke. "They've answered his call. All of them."

The gathered pegasi shrank from her words. "No," whispered Bumblewind. "That can't be."

"It's worse than that," she said. "Nightwing knows he

injured Star, that his body is so damaged he's dead, or as good as dead. He says his connection to Star's mind has been severed, and he . . ." Echofrost glanced at Morningleaf, grimacing.

"What is it?" breathed Morningleaf.

"He's offered to make a pact with the first steed who"—Echofrost lashed her tail and tears raced down her cheeks—"who brings him Star's head."

"His head!" Morningleaf staggered sideways, and Bumblewind caught her in his wings.

Echofrost nodded. "Yes, to ensure that Star can't heal himself, that he's truly dead."

Her words stunned the gathered pegasi. Morningleaf sobbed, but it was wrath that fueled her tears. Her belly churned like the sea, and the forest floor swayed beneath her hooves. She covered her face with her aqua feathers, her heart wilting like a severed rose. *His head?* A battle cry bubbled deep within her chest and surged toward her throat. She gritted her teeth and tamped it down, saving her anger for the Destroyer. Morningleaf vowed in her heart to defy him.

As she collected her emotions, Redfire, the tall, copper-colored captain from the Desert Herd camp, spoke. "Did any steeds accept this offer?"

"Yes," said Hazelwind. "Petalcloud and Frostfire, and they've already formed two armies to destroy us if we try to stop them."

Morningleaf flattened her ears, controlling her breathing. She was not surprised to hear Frostfire's name. He was the Mountain Herd captain who'd volunteered to hide her from Nightwing, at Star's request, but then he'd killed her personal guards and stolen her, holding her hostage in the lava tubes of the volcano Firemouth. Frostfire and his over-stallion, Rockwing, had planned to use her to control Star, but that plan had failed when she'd escaped. She blanched at the memory of the horrible black tubes beneath the belching volcano in Jungle Herd's territory.

But Morningleaf was also not surprised to hear the name of the Snow Herd mare, Petalcloud. She was Frostfire's dam, and she'd traded him, her first and only colt, for her freedom from Mountain Herd. She would never lead there as long as her sire was over-stallion and her mother was lead mare, but Rockwing wouldn't let Petalcloud join another herd until she met his condition: a weanling colt. All his foals had been born dead, save his two fillies, Petalcloud and Shadepebble, but he was willing to give Petalcloud up in exchange for Frostfire. And now mother and son were seeking to enhance their power.

Redfire rattled his feathers. "They will rush the Trap. They know we're hiding here."

Morningleaf lifted her head, looking at Echofrost. "Are Frostfire and Petalcloud working together or against each other?"

Echofrost twisted her ears, listening as always for danger. "Against each other."

"Of course," hissed Morningleaf.

Echofrost continued. "Nightwing allowed them to select warriors from the thousands of pegasi who answered his call. Petalcloud chose the biggest, nastiest steeds, and she calls them her Ice Warriors. Frostfire chose smaller, highly skilled warriors, and he calls them his Black Army. The rest of the pegasi, the elders, and new mothers, are living in the Blue Mountains with Nightwing."

Brackentail, the big brown yearling who'd once tried to kill Star but then had been accepted by him, stepped forward. "But why would they join Nightwing? What about their territories and their over-stallions?"

Redfire startled. "Yes, what happened to Twistwing, Sandwing, and Smokewing?"

"Sandwing is here," said Bumblewind, interrupting.

Redfire shook his dark-red mane. "No, he's not. Not anymore. He returned to Desert Herd when he'd heard that Nightwing had made landfall in Anok. He left me in charge of our herdmates here."

Echofrost watched them, her eyes glowing. "Sandwing is dead. Nightwing used the jet streams to fly to each territory, where he executed the over-stallions. All of them. And then he took their steeds. The territories are empty."

Morningleaf gasped, and her heart ached afresh for her sire, and for all the mighty pegasi who were now gone. "He's killing his rivals," she whispered.

Echofrost heard her. "Yes. And Star is the last one."

Brackentail flattened his ears. "But he knows Star's badly injured. Why doesn't Nightwing come after Star himself?"

Morningleaf's muscles twitched at his words. She wanted to fight the Destroyer, though she knew he'd kill her in a breath.

"I don't think Nightwing wants another run-in with that army of weanling Ancestors that came down and protected Star," answered Echofrost. "And he's still recovering from his hundreds of years of hibernation, and his recent battle with Star. It hurt him more than he let on. Nightwing's starfire might be strong, but his body is weak. And by offering a pact, he's testing the pegasi, finding out who's loyal to him."

"Where are these two armies now?" asked Redfire.

Echofrost raised her voice so all could hear. "Petalcloud took the Ice Warriors to her home in the north to train. Frostfire took the Black Army to the empty Sun Herd lands to strengthen and train them. Both are preparing to attack, but they aren't sure where Star is." Echofrost glanced at Silverlake. "Nightwing saw you all flying west with Star, toward the coast. As far as the armies are concerned, he could be anywhere, and Petalcloud doesn't think you'd be . . . stupid enough to hide him in the Trap. Sorry, those were her words."

Silverlake huffed but looked pleased that she'd fooled Star's enemies.

Hazelwind glanced at Morningleaf. "Nightwing has given them two clues: that you flew west, and that Star's body is with the 'blue-winged filly.' He told them that if they found her, they'd find Star."

Morningleaf reeled at this news. How did Nightwing know that she wouldn't leave Star's side? Had his connection to Star's mind shown him the depth of her devotion?

Echofrost continued. "Before Frostfire and Petalcloud left to prepare their armies, they each dispatched scouts across Anok—they're flying through the territories and searching the Vein, the coast, and they're coming to the

Trap. Once Star or Morningleaf are spotted, they will report back and then the armies will move out in force."

"What are we going to do against two armies?" asked Bumblewind.

"When they come, we'll unite our forces," said Hazelwind, filling his voice with the rumbling timbre of an over-stallion to catch the attention of every steed. The pegasi turned to him, listening.

"We're Star's guardian herd," Hazelwind neighed. "It's our duty by the Hundred Year Star to protect him or kill him." He glanced at each steed, many who came from foreign herds. "Don't make the mistake I made. I thought following Star meant that he would keep *me* safe. No!" Hazelwind stamped his hoof. "Following Star means that I keep *him* safe. That is what a guardian does, and I failed Star once, when I abandoned him to start my own herd. I won't do it again." He arched his neck, making eye contact with each steed he could. "Today, right now, you will commit your lives to Star, to protect the black foal to his death or yours, or you will leave the Trap."

The pegasi listened to him, their silence heavy, their breath steaming, and then Brackentail spoke. "I vow my life to Star."

And then Redfire from Desert Herd, and Ashrain from

Jungle Herd, and Birchcloud from Mountain Herd vowed the same, and from there the pegasi raised their voices in a cheer, each and every one vowing to protect the black foal. Star, oblivious to all of them, rested in the moss, too damaged to breathe.

Morningleaf broke into fresh sobs, shedding tears of gratitude, and chaos erupted. The herds were going to war. The newborns bleated, hovering over their mothers like anxious birds. Battle mares and stallions lashed their tails, feathers buzzing, and the elderly steeds flexed their wings. War. They understood it. It focused them, gave them a purpose.

But fear needled at Morningleaf. If Petalcloud's and Frostfire's scouts searched the Trap, it would only be a matter of time before they discovered her presence or Star's body. And Sweetroot didn't think it was wise to move him again. Morningleaf swiveled her ears, her senses thrown into high alert. She was a target, she was the hunted; and her heart thudded against her ribs.

Shadepebble nuzzled her. "We won't let them get Star," she said. "And we can hide you too, to keep you safe."

If the armies find me, they'll find Star. Morningleaf's thoughts tumbled through her head, and an idea formed. "Come here!" She snatched Shadepebble's wing and drew her away from the group. "Hide me? No. I need to be seen!"

"What? I don't understand."

"It's simple. I can lure the armies away from the Trap."

"Like a decoy?" Shadepebble's pulse raced in her neck as she thought about Morningleaf's words. "It's dangerous, but it's not a bad idea."

Morningleaf studied the pegasi around her who were already arguing about the best way to join their separate herds into one army. "They need time to organize."

"And Star needs time to heal," said Shadepebble. Her eyes shone against the bleakness of the Trap. Night had fallen, and only thin rays of moonlight leaked between the branches overhead. "I'm going with you."

"No."

Shadepebble set her jaw. "Star saved me from drowning and healed my wounds from that ice tiger that attacked me and Clawfire. I'm going. I can keep you safe."

Her tone was resolute, and so Morningleaf reluctantly agreed.

"I heard you talking," said Brackentail, trotting closer to them. "I owe him too. Star accepted me when no one else would. Without him, I would be banished, living alone. Please let me come. I can help."

Brackentail was strong, that was evident from looking

at him. And he owed Star his life, Morningleaf knew that, but he'd once betrayed his herd—*her* herd. She'd accepted him because Star had, but she still didn't trust him. She was about to say no when Silverlake approached. "What are you three plotting?" she asked, her gaze boring into her filly.

Morningleaf nickered; her dam knew her well. "I'm leaving, to draw the armies away from Star."

Silverlake exhaled in a long, soft breath. Morningleaf lifted her head, preparing her arguments, but Silverlake hushed her with a word. "Go," she said.

"Mama?" Morningleaf could not believe her ears.

"I'll gather some River Herd warriors to protect you. Wait here. But I won't stop you. I can't stop you." Silverlake trotted away.

Morningleaf glanced from Shadepebble to Brackentail. "They'll need every warrior they have in case we fail," she said.

"Are you thinking what I'm thinking?" asked Brackentail.

"If you're thinking we should leave before she gets back, then yes," said Morningleaf.

"I think we're thinking too much." Shadepebble spread her wings. "Let's go!"

The three yearlings turned and bolted, galloping south to the edge of the Trap. Morningleaf wondered at her two companions—they were brave to follow her, and gratitude sent fresh energy through her muscles. Star's friends were devoted to him, and the steeds in the Trap had decided to defend him, not abandon him, and this gave her hope—not just for Star—but for all the pegasi of Anok.

8

THE ANCESTORS

"IT'S TIME TO ROLL HIM OVER."

The medicine mare's voice seeped into Star's mind like rain through dry soil. He latched on to her words and tried to follow them up and out of the black pit of sleep.

Sweetroot continued. "You grab the hooves; I'll pull the wing. Bumblewind, you turn his head."

"Got him," said Bumblewind.

Star heard their words, but he couldn't open his eyes, or move his body at all. He felt heavy and cold, like he was buried in snow. *Where am I?* he wondered. *What happened to Nightwing?* Star remembered battling the Destroyer and then nothing but pain—pain that shred his heart and crushed his thoughts—and then blackness. But now he heard voices, and he began to be aware that days were passing and that he was not dead, but he was stuck. He tried, but he couldn't wake up.

"Ready?" Sweetroot asked.

"Ready," three voices responded.

And then they shoved Star, and his body rolled like floating driftwood, tipping, tipping, and then falling to the other side, dragged by the weight of his limbs. Sweetroot rolled him three times a day, so this was nothing new, but every time he hoped to get her attention, to escape the blackness surrounding him.

Sweetroot's voice wafted through the dark. "Echofrost, rub that tree sap on his hooves so they don't dry out. Bumblewind, press these mint leaves in his nostrils. The scent is strong; it might awaken him."

Star knew he was being rubbed and prodded, and he was grateful but embarrassed for the help. His starfire had gone dormant in his belly, withdrawing into a tiny, latent ember. Star relived Nightwing's final blow often in his dreams—the silver beam of fire that had pierced his chest and caused him to fall from the sky, the swirling aqua feather, and Morningleaf's hot tears on his face. His guardians had hidden him; he was glad to know that. It meant they still believed in him, in spite of his overwhelming failure to destroy Nightwing.

Sweetroot often spoke directly to him, and she encouraged others to do the same. Once, she'd spoken to him like she understood his predicament. She'd said, "Star, I know you're alone and its dark, but you must not follow the Ancestors if they come to take you away."

What she didn't know was that the Ancestors had already visited him, an army of them. Star thought back to that day, remembering.

They'd invaded his dreams, bringing light and joy, and he'd whinnied with pleasure. The Ancestors were transparent and brilliant, their feathers refracting light, their eyes glowing with love, and their bodies strong and muscular.

They flew around him in circles, dazzling him. He'd wanted to join them, but they wouldn't let him. His mother was there, and Grasswing, and ancient pegasi from the legends. There was no mistaking the bay pinto Spiderwing, the founding sire of the modern herds, or Raincloud, one of the bravest mares who'd ever lived. Detailed descriptions of the pair had been handed down for centuries, and they were so accurate that Star recognized them immediately.

But they were elusive, flying just on the edge of his thoughts. It was a beautiful spotted filly who finally spoke. She hovered upright with her back legs dangling, and at least a thousand weanlings surrounded her in the formation of an army. "You're not finished here," she whinnied.

Star struggled to answer, but he couldn't form words. *Who are you?* he wondered.

"I'm Hollyblaze, Spiderwing's sister, and I will not rest until the Destroyer is defeated," she answered. "All our hope is in you, Star."

But you're dead, Star thought.

"That's true," she answered, and Star realized she could read his thoughts. "But we're alive in the golden meadow, where every pegasus goes when they die; but Star, not all of us have made it here. The steeds murdered by the silver starfire are trapped. Their souls are stuck in a dimension we call the Beyond because we cannot travel there; no steed can. Thundersky and many others are caught in the Beyond, and the only way to free them is to destroy their killer: Nightwing."

Star's mind reeled at her words. *Thundersky was not in the golden meadow? He'd seen Nightwing destroy the stallion; and Silverlake had galloped to his side, sobbing with grief. Her solace was that her mate was now safe and living with the Ancestors. But this filly said Thundersky's soul was trapped? How could Star free Thundersky and the other souls when he couldn't wake up?*

Hollyblaze angled her brilliant gold-tipped emerald feathers and cruised close to him, and he was struck by the sadness in her eyes. "You must destroy Nightwing; it's the only way to free the souls."

I tried that. He's stronger than me.

Hollyblaze charged toward him, her bright wings making a whoosh of noise. She narrowed her eyes, not angry, but determined, and she said, "You must try again."

Star's helpless heart thudded in response, just once, but it pushed some blood through his veins, giving him hope.

Hollyblaze gestured with her wing, indicating all the Ancestors who'd come to visit him. "Nightwing has caused grief in the golden meadow, and grief doesn't belong there."

Star understood. They missed their loved ones who had died but were trapped in the Beyond.

"My army drove the Destroyer away from you, Star, after he pierced your heart, and your guardians have hidden your body. Now it's time for you to wake up."

Hollyblaze shot upward, followed by the Ancestors, and then they vanished in a burst of light, leaving Star in darkness that felt blacker and colder than before.

9

DECOY

MORNINGLEAF SKIDDED ACROSS THE WET ROCKS and dived into Desert Herd's Tail River. Her thumping heart rushed the blood through her veins, giving her energy and erasing all thoughts but one: *Escape!* She paddled her legs and angled her wings, swimming deeper into the channel and away from Petalcloud's scouts who, like her, were so far from their home.

She cruised to the very bottom of the Tail River. Morningleaf and her friends had arrived in Desert Herd's territory three days ago, and this morning two of Petalcloud's Ice Warriors, who were scouts out searching for Star, had spotted her and were now chasing her. She flapped her wings, straining the warm water through her feathers. It was like flying, except her lungs were hot, throbbing for air.

After several minutes Morningleaf breached the surface like a crocodile, allowing only her nostrils and eyes above water. She circled slowly, peering at the shore, and her eyes widened when she spotted the two warriors standing in the reeds nearby; the taller one was white, and the other was a gray pinto.

"She lost us," the pinto said.

"No. She can't be far."

Morningleaf was afraid to slip back under the water in case she created ripples, so she held still and willed the stallions not to see her.

"I don't see hoofprints." The pinto glanced at the sky. "She took off, I think."

The other warrior wiped the sweat rolling down his brow. "If Morningleaf is here, Star's body must be close. This is good news."

Morningleaf held her breath at the mention of Star's name. Her plan to lure Star's enemies away from him was working.

"Getting his head off will be tricky," said the gray pinto. "I don't see why Nightwing wants it. Everyone who was there saw what happened. Nightwing destroyed his heart. Star is surely dead."

"Maybe," the other said. "But Star's magical. We all saw that chestnut filly die too, and now here we are chasing her."

The pinto snorted. "True, but there's nowhere to hide in this territory except the Red Rock Mountains just southeast of here. I'll check it out. You fly back to the patrol and send a messenger to Petalcloud. She'll want to know that Morningleaf is here and not in the Trap." The two warriors kicked off and flew in opposite directions.

Morningleaf ducked under the surface. It was springtime, so the river water was clear and deep. It didn't rain in the desert, not often anyway. This water came from fresh snowmelt in the higher elevations. It filled Black Lake and then spilled into the Tail River, which led all the way to the Sea of Rain.

Morningleaf spiraled through a collection of tall reeds, scattering black-bellied fish, and let the currents push her south ever faster, toward her friends Shadepebble and Brackentail.

The land bordering the Tail River was lush with tasty coyote willow and flowering arrowweed shrubs. The ancient waterway carved through solid bedrock, creating a deep channel that traveled through canyons, flat deserts, and wide basins. The rest of Desert Herd's territory was desolate and hot, dotted with cacti and shrubs, and crawling with poisonous snakes and scorpions. During the peak of the afternoon, the hard ground was too hot to walk on, and the air blistered her lungs, making breathing and flying difficult. Morningleaf and her companions learned quickly to travel in the early morning and the early evening.

Morningleaf coasted with the current, gently paddling her legs and steering with her wings. Her eyes drooped as the soothing water lulled her. Early this morning, Morningleaf had left her friends to graze on the coyote willow when two of Petalcloud's scouts had spotted her. She hadn't realized they were so close, and getting chased by the stallions had taken a huge toll on her. Now her eyes closed, just for a second it seemed, and she fell asleep.

The sound of rushing water woke her.

Morningleaf blinked, feeling confused by the frantic roar of the rapids. The stallions who'd chased her into the Tail River were gone, and she remembered falling asleep in the gentle current, but now the river's surface was fast and frothy. She lifted her wings and tried to fly, but her heavy feathers had soaked up too much moisture. She drifted downriver, and what she saw ahead caused her gut to twist. Just a short distance away, the Tail River dropped over a cliff—a waterfall!

Morningleaf dug her wings into the water, trying to stop herself, but the current had picked up speed. She shook the water out of her eyes and realized the waterfall was a steep one. She whipped her body around and kicked her legs, trying to swim upstream. She paddled hard, making no progress. Then she heard a voice.

"Over here." It was Shadepebble, waving her pale-pink feathers, trying to get her attention.

Morningleaf felt instant relief at the sight of her friend, and next to her stood Brackentail, prancing, his expression distraught. Morningleaf swam harder.

"You can't swim against the current," Brackentail whinnied. "You have to swim across it. It's just like flying."

Morningleaf paddled sideways as Brackentail galloped down the shore, following her. The river swept her along, and her hooves clunked on hard rocks, but she was gaining on the shore.

Brackentail leaned over an embankment, extending his flying limb to her. "Bite my wing," he neighed over the roar of falling water.

Morningleaf surged, swimming harder and faster, angling toward the shore and Brackentail's orange feathers. She was panting, and her neck ached from holding her head above water. *There!* She was in range of his wing.

Morningleaf craned her neck and bit into Brackentail's feathered limb. The big yearling colt dug in his hooves and pulled. Morningleaf scrabbled for the river bottom. When her hooves found purchase in the dirt and rocks, she was able to throw her body forward, and with the help of Brackentail, she landed on the shore, just a wing length from where the river collapsed over the edge.

Morningleaf lay on her side, gasping like a beached fish.

"You're safe," Brackentail said, also panting.

"What happened?" Shadepebble asked.

"I fell asleep in the water," Morningleaf wheezed. "I put the mission in jeopardy."

"Shh," Shadepebble whispered. "It's over, but where have you been all morning?"

"I woke up early, and I was hungry. I only went a short distance away to graze when two of Petalcloud's Ice Warriors spotted me. They chased me, and I led them away from you two, then I dived into the river to escape."

"Where are they now?" Shadepebble peered at the vast blue sky.

"Gone. I lost them." Morningleaf pricked her ears, examining her two friends, who still appeared worried. "Our plan is working," Morningleaf reassured them. "The two stallions think Star is close by."

Brackentail touched Morningleaf's shoulder with his wing, his eyes brimming with concern. "Please don't graze by yourself again."

Morningleaf flicked her ears at him and then shook herself dry, unsure how to answer. She hadn't asked Brackentail to come on this mission, but she hadn't stopped him either. And now he'd saved her from falling over the edge of the waterfall, proving his worth, but when she looked at him, she felt confused. She was beginning to trust him, but that felt like a betrayal of her friend Echofrost. The silver filly had not forgiven him for causing her capture by Mountain Herd steeds when they were weanlings. And Echofrost hadn't forgiven Star for letting Brackentail back into the herd. Morningleaf hadn't chosen sides, didn't believe in choosing sides, but she knew that any kindness toward Brackentail hurt Echofrost's feelings—and even though the filly was not here but far away in the Trap, Morningleaf felt guilty. "From now on we'll stick together," she agreed with a light shrug of her wings.

Brackentail nodded, satisfied.

"So where to next?" Shadepebble asked.

"To the southern nests of Jungle Herd," said Morning-leaf. "Echofrost said that Frostfire has scouts there, and we'll make sure they spot me too. The rumors will spread that Star is hiding in the south." She flexed her wings. "My feathers are dry now; let's fly so we don't leave hoof-prints."

The three friends kicked off and swooped over the edge of the waterfall.

Morningleaf gasped when she saw the drop she'd almost endured. It was a hundred wing lengths at least, straight down into a deep pool, but large, jagged rocks jut-ted from the cliff into the falling water. She might have survived the fall but not the rocks.

"It's beautiful," said Shadepebble, gazing at the spar-kling mist and the yellow desert flowers decorating the swimming hole.

Morningleaf snorted. "That's not what I was thinking."

10

AWAKE

DEEP IN THE TRAP, STAR SLEPT AND DREAMED OF waking up. He wondered if his heart would ever beat like it once had, with confident hard thumps, pushing blood through his wings and muscles?

As if reading his thoughts, his heart gave a violent shudder. Star's leg twitched, and then his heart thumped again, sending blood and pain through Star's limbs.

Star heard Sweetroot's voice. "Ack!" she whinnied. "He moved!"

And Star felt it too. His leg spasm had made contact with Sweetroot, kicking her in the shin. His heart beat again and again, slowly, but growing stronger with each compression. As his heart roared to life, blood rushed through his veins and into his brain, which helped him think clearer.

"He's waking up," Bumblewind neighed.

I am, Star thought gleefully. *I am.*

Star guessed that several hours had passed while his body slowly came to life, beginning with his legs. Excited voices gathered around him, and he heard Sweetroot shooing the pegasi back, to give him space to breathe. He tried to lift his head, and a blur of dim light pierced his dark world. It took Star a minute to understand that his eyes were open. He saw the muddy shapes of his friends surrounding him. He flailed his front legs, and then a wing pressed hard against his forehead.

"Don't try to stand," Sweetroot said. "You've been asleep a long time. You're weak."

Star blinked several times and cleared his vision. His trusted friends—Bumblewind, the battle mare Dewberry, Hazelwind, the new stallion, Clawfire, and his adopted dam, Silverlake, surrounded him. They appeared relieved and concerned at the same time.

Star looked down and was shocked at the sight of his body. His hipbones rose in sharp relief to his sunken, hollow muscles. His coat was dull and his hooves dry and cracked. Star scanned the gathered pegasi. "How long have I been like this?" he asked.

"Almost a moon," Sweetroot answered.

Star slid his wing aside so the medicine mare could listen to his heart. "Your pulse is gaining a rhythm." She lifted her head and turned toward the pegasi. "Star needs to rest and eat. Bumblewind and Dewberry, will you gather fresh lichen for him?"

Star's two friends nodded and trotted away.

"Lichen?" Star asked. "Where am I?" He peered at his surroundings. He was in a dark forest. A thick web of interlocking tree branches blocked his view of the sky. His breath blew out of his nostrils like smoke; it was cold, even though it had to be almost summer now. "Is this the Trap? Did you fly me here?"

"Yes," Silverlake said. "We moved you here . . . after the battle with Nightwing." The gray mare had aged several seasons since the battle, and her grief for her fallen mate was etched permanently into her expression. Star exhaled as he remembered what the Ancestors had told him about the Beyond, that any steed killed by the silver fire was trapped there, and the silver fire had killed Thundersky. His soul was stuck, but Star didn't tell Silverlake that. It was bad enough for her that Thundersky was dead, murdered by Nightwing.

Star pricked his ears, glancing around him, suddenly alarmed. "Where's Morningleaf?"

His friends hesitated to answer him, and in their silence, Star's delicate heartbeat fumbled. "Tell me," he rasped.

"She left on a mission," Silverlake said, clenching her jaw.

Star could tell the mare wasn't pleased. "Who sent her?"

Silverlake sighed. "She sent herself."

Star hurtled to his hooves and then promptly fell back on his side with a loud grunt. "My legs," he moaned.

Sweetroot rushed forward with a mixture of herbs he didn't recognize. "Chew these," she said. "They'll help with the pain." She dropped them by his nose.

"Is Morningleaf in danger?" he asked.

His friends shuffled their hooves, not wanting to upset him. He exhaled, watching his breath rise toward the treetops. Of course she was in danger; all missions were dangerous, and Star was in sorry shape to help her. He sniffed the herbs and chewed them, his empty gut protesting as he swallowed the foreign medicine. He couldn't remember much about his fight with the Destroyer—only the incredible pain, and the fact that he'd lost. "What about Nightwing; did I hurt him at all?"

Silverlake shook her head. "You don't remember?"

"A little."

"He has powers either you don't have or you don't yet know how to use," she explained. "He protected himself with a silver shell, like a shield. It blocked your starfire. You couldn't touch him."

The shield? A vague memory of it formed in Star's mind. It was translucent like a bubble, but solid to the touch.

Sweetroot smoothed his black mane along his neck. "Star, you should know that Nightwing broke three of your legs, and most of your ribs. Besides that, you've suffered massive bruising and burns. You've been healing, but slowly. You're not ready to walk or fly."

"I can take care of that right now." Star panted, readying his golden fire.

"No!" Sweetroot neighed. "Please wait, and listen."

Star closed his mouth.

Sweetroot continued. "The connection between your mind and Nightwing's was severed when he stopped your heart. Right now he can't sense you, or track you, but he might if you use your starfire."

"How do you know this?" Star asked.

"Echofrost followed him after he hurt you, and listened

to his plans. He doesn't know if you're dead or alive. Right now it's best if he thinks you're dead, to give us time to make a plan." She touched his injured legs. "You're mending fast on your own, faster than any of us would. Your starfire is part of you; it runs in your blood, but you must give it some more time. Soon you'll be as good as new. Better than new," she added.

"All right, I'll wait, but where is Nightwing now?"

"He's living in the Blue Mountains," Hazelwind answered. "We've hidden you here, and we have spies watching him. As long as you don't use your starfire, we believe he can't find you or direct his armies to you."

"His armies?"

Hazelwind nodded. "He's offered to make a pact with the first steed who kills your guardians and delivers your . . . your head to him."

"My head?" Star blinked, pricking his ears. "Just my head?"

Hazelwind nodded.

Star's gut roiled as he imagined warriors ransacking Anok to take his head. "No one agreed to this, did they?"

Hazelwind sighed, looking glum. "Frostfire and Petalcloud have formed opposing armies, and each is looking for you," he explained. "It's why Morningleaf left—she's drawing them away from the Trap."

"She's bait!" Star shuddered. He had to help her. He pressed his wings into the soil, trying to stand.

"She's not alone, Star," said Silverlake. "She has Shadepebble and Brackentail."

"They're yearlings," Star said, sputtering as his body collapsed. He needed food. He needed strength. And Brackentail? Why him of all colts?

"She refused the warriors I offered her," said Silverlake. "I guess she thought we needed them more than she did."

Star sighed and laid his head on the trampled soil, smelling bugs and rotting mulch. He suspected there was more to know about Nightwing and Morningleaf and the armies that hunted him, but he felt dizzy and sick. Sweetroot was right—he needed more rest.

Bumblewind and Dewberry returned and dropped fresh lichen by his muzzle, and Star forced himself to eat. It would take time to heal, and time to figure out how to defeat Nightwing.

11

SEA OF RAIN

MORNINGLEAF LED HER FRIENDS ALMOST TO THE end of the Tail River, where they spent the night tucked beneath the shade of a mesquite tree. "Tomorrow we'll cross the Sea of Rain," she said, "and then we'll be in Jungle Herd's territory."

"How do you know these territories so well?" Shadepebble asked. "Have you traveled them before?"

Morningleaf snorted. "I've been to Jungle Herd's territory, when Frostfire kidnapped me. But most of what I know I learned from listening to the stories of the elders and—"

"And she asks a lot of questions," Brackentail interrupted.

"I do not!"

"Do too." Brackentail faced Shadepebble. "When we were foals, one of our elder mares, Mossberry, could never finish a sentence without Morningleaf shoving her muzzle into the mare's flank to ask questions." Brackentail's eyes twinkled in the red sunset.

"But they were important questions," Morningleaf said, pricking her ears.

Brackentail huffed. "Not to us. We just wanted Mossberry to get to the battle scenes, but Morningleaf wanted to know how everyone was related and what the landscape looked like. Boring."

Morningleaf smacked Brackentail playfully with her wing. "Good thing I asked all those questions. Without me you'd be lost."

Brackentail lowered his eyelids. "I am lost," he whispered.

Morningleaf stared at him and then looked away. He often said things like that to her, cryptic comments that seemed to hold a deeper meaning, but she never asked him to explain. She wasn't sure she wanted to know what he meant.

The three yearlings rested in the sweltering shade in

awkward silence. Nearby, the river rushed past, flowing toward the ocean.

Shadepebble changed the subject. "So what's Jungle Herd's territory like? Not so hot, I hope."

Morningleaf exhaled. "No, but it's more dangerous." She flicked her ears, remembering her short time there after Frostfire had kidnapped her. "You can't swim in the lakes or rivers, drink the water, smell the flowers, or eat the plants. You have to stay on the animal paths. And it's best not to walk under any trees, but sometimes that's impossible."

"How will we survive there, then?"

Morningleaf softened. "The fruit is safe to eat, and we can drink rainwater off the leaves."

Brackentail squinted into the clear blue desert sky. "Rain? What rain?"

"It rains every afternoon in the jungle," Morningleaf explained. "Finding safe water to drink won't be a problem. At night we can sleep in the trees. Most of Jungle Herd is hiding in the Trap, and the rest have followed Nightwing to the Blue Mountains or joined one of the armies—so their nests will be empty. Once I've been spotted by Frostfire's scouts, we can fly back to Star."

"Making sure you're not captured will be the danger-ous part," Brackentail added.

Morningleaf ruffled her feathers. "We'll see."

The next morning the three yearlings landed on Turtle Beach, where the Tail River drained into the sea. They rolled on the hot white sand, digging their wings into the cleansing grains. They stood and shook themselves off, then faced the shore. The water was green and clear to the bottom. Shadepebble clapped her wings. "Look, turtles!"

Morningleaf watched the large creatures glide grace-fully underwater, then she narrowed her eyes and peered west, toward Jungle Herd's land. She couldn't see the dis-tant shore, only miles and miles of ocean. She swallowed, feeling nervous. The thing about flying over open water was that she and her friends couldn't eat or drink, and the only way to rest was to float on the surface. But after hearing Star's tale of the orca that ate Snakewing, the over-stallion who'd tried to kill Star when he was hiding on the coast, Morningleaf was afraid of the water.

Still, it was the fastest path to Jungle Herd's shore-line, and she wouldn't worry her friends. "Ready?" she asked them, forcing a cheerful expression.

"Ready," Brackentail answered. He reared and spread his wings, fanning his orange feathers before the flight. Morningleaf lowered her lashes and watched him, noticing he'd grown again in the last moon. His weedy muscles were thicker, his coat glossier, his wings wider. Morningleaf wondered if she was changing too. She didn't feel any different. She turned to Shadepebble. "Have you attended flight school yet?"

The spotted filly nodded. "I had two lessons before . . . you know."

Morningleaf nodded. She knew the rest of the story—Snow Herd raiders led by Clawfire had captured Shadepebble during flight school, hoping to add her to their herd, which had been decimated by the Blue Tongue plague. When Snow Herd realized Clawfire had stolen the filly of Mountain Herd's over-stallion, they'd exiled them, banishing them to wander the north alone. When an ice tiger attacked Shadepebble, she'd bolted and fallen through the ice of a northern pond. That's when Star had seen her and had saved her.

Brackentail nudged Shadepebble. "Don't feel bad; two lessons puts you ahead of us. We became yearlings right after Star's birthday, and there's been no time for flight school since then. River Herd hasn't even appointed an instructor yet."

"True," Morningleaf said, "but Star taught me how to fly over the ocean when we were living by the coast, before the Blue Tongue plague erupted and we had to move to the Ice Lands. Stay close to me, and I'll talk you both through it."

The three of them galloped down the beach where the sand was packed and firm, then leaped into the sky, their wings unfurling like flower petals in the sun. Morningleaf took a deep breath, filtering the warm air and the salty scents through her nostrils.

From the heights, the Sea of Rain was neither blue nor green. It was both. Morningleaf watched the massive turtles and the faster stingrays coasting offshore, flying underwater. Shadepebble squealed when a pod of dolphins zipped past, their backs rolling across the surface. Reefs appeared as black shadows far below, but if Morningleaf focused, she saw bright fish gathered around the coral, nipping at plant life and wagging their sleek bodies.

They glided for hours, enjoying the cool ocean breezes on their faces. Then, without warning, the three pegasi flew directly into a pocket of swirling crosswinds, and the waves below grew choppy. "Steady!" cried Morningleaf, drawing her wings closer to her body. Shadepebble was thrown sideways, and another current pushed Brackentail higher. Her friends flapped their wings madly, trying to regain control. Morningleaf struggled to fly straight. "Slow down," she neighed to them.

Brackentail, whose first instinct had been to outfly the turbulence, listened to her and slowed to a glide. But Shadepebble was tossed off course and had entered into a fierce battle with the winds, which she was losing. Her body rocketed away from them, and there was nothing Morningleaf or Brackentail could do to help her. "Don't fight the current," Morningleaf whinnied to Shadepebble. "It's pushing you out. Just let it carry you and then catch up to us."

Shadepebble relaxed, and the wind hurtled her toward the north. Morningleaf and Brackentail stayed close to each other, riding out the harsh swirls of air. Shadepebble shrank in the distance and then disappeared.

"I don't like this," Brackentail said.

"The wind will soon release her. It's best we stay on course and let her return to us."

The pair kept a slow pace, waiting for Shadepebble. The water was deep out here, darkening to blue, and it was devoid of reefs. Morningleaf kept one eye focused below and one trained on the horizon. After a while she grew concerned. "Shadepebble should have caught up to us by now."

"Let's go find her," Brackentail said.

The two veered north, scanning the sky for Shadepebble.

12

LOOSE FEATHER

"EAT THE TREE MOSS, STAR; IT'S GOOD," SAID
Bumblewind.

Star stepped toward his friend, his weak legs shaking
and his wings spread open for stabilization. It had been
three days since he'd awakened and walking was a struggle, but Star wanted to relieve his herd from the burden
of gathering ferns, grasses, and pine nuts for him to eat.

Bumblewind ripped at the moss and chewed while
waiting for Star. "You've got it," he encouraged.

Star reached the tree and halted with his legs wide.
"Newborns walk better," he complained, letting his wings
fall to his sides. They were as weak as his legs, and so flying was out of the question.

"The more you eat, the faster you'll regain your strength."

Bumblewind's words echoed Sweetroot's, and Star nodded his understanding. Nightwing's attack had decimated Star from the inside out, even crushing his starfire into a lesser version of what it was, but Star improved each day. He was healing on his own, as Sweetroot had predicted.

Star lipped at the tree moss and then shred it off the bark, grinding it between his teeth and swallowing. Bumblewind had lied; it wasn't good at all. For the past three days Star's friends had been bringing him the tastiest food they could find: sweet grasses, moist bark, and shucked nuts—they'd spoiled him.

"Do you remember the boundaries of River Herd's camp?" Bumblewind asked.

"Yes." He knew Silverlake had sectioned the Trap into camps for the members of each herd. Star had explored their camp before he left the north and traveled to Sun Herd's lands, where Nightwing had met him, and almost killed him.

"Good. We have a truce with the other camps, and our warriors are all training together, but we each stick to our own area unless invited."

"They won't turn me in to Nightwing?" Star asked.

"No. We've united our forces against Nightwing. Win or lose, we won't submit to him. We're outcasts now, rebels. Nightwing has control of the territories, but he doesn't have what he wants most—which is you."

Star's gut trilled. His guardians weren't just protecting him; they were protecting their freedom. A cruel over-stallion could be challenged and overthrown, but Nightwing was more powerful than any over-stallion, and he was immortal. If he gained control of all pegasi, his invincible authority would crush their spirits. Their foals would be born without hope. It would be the end of the pegasi as Star knew them, as proud and independent steeds.

The two friends grazed on the moss and the young spruce needles in silence. Then Star asked the question that had plagued him for the last three days. "If Morningleaf's mission is so dangerous, why didn't anyone stop her?"

"Stop Morningleaf?" Bumblewind snorted. "You're joking, right?"

"Right," Star huffed, unsurprised. His left hind leg buckled, and he began to tip sideways. Bumblewind rushed forward and pressed his shoulder into Star's, propping him upright. Star exhaled, ushering out the pain that shot through his injured legs. "I guess I thought she'd stay with me. It's strange that she's gone."

Bumblewind lowered his voice. "What she's doing is crazy, using herself as bait to distract our enemies away from the Trap, but it's also very brave."

The soft thud of hooves interrupted Bumblewind as Clawfire burst into view. He galloped between the trees with his wings tucked, and thin rays of sunshine highlighted his blue-gray feathers. He skidded across the fallen pine needles and stopped in front of them, panting. "Follow me quickly," he whispered.

His urgency left no time for questions, and Star felt hot energy rush through his weak muscles, lending him some strength.

"Help me with him," Bumblewind cried, nodding at Star. Clawfire took one side and Bumblewind the other, and Star wrapped his wings around their backs. They squeezed through the trees, keeping Star from falling over.

"What's happening?" Star asked.

"Intruders," the white stallion nickered quietly. Clawfire led them expertly through the dark maze of conifers, avoiding fallen twigs and pinecones that might shatter under their hooves. Star's broken bones were freshly knit, and searing pain ripped through his body as he trotted. He suppressed his groans.

"Hold still," Clawfire said when they arrived. This section of the Trap was the darkest. An upward slope in the land here had led to increased sun exposure on the highest branches, and that had created an extra-thick canopy of foliage. After Star's eyes adjusted to the dark, he saw thousands of eyes blinking at him. All the rebels had gathered here to hide.

Clawfire tucked Star and Bumblewind into the shadows and then found his own tree to hide beneath. Star lost his balance and staggered into a foreign stallion, bumping against his flank. "Sorry," he muttered.

"Shh," another pegasus rasped.

Star's heart thudded. He was still unsure what was happening, except that he knew it must be bad. Star stood as still as he could on his quaking legs.

Behind Star, a newborn bleated softly. Its dam quickly covered the colt's eyes with her wings, calming him. Next to Star, Bumblewind's breathing quickened. He stretched out his wing, eyes wide with fear, and pointed straight ahead.

Star squinted through the darkness, and then he saw them—six of Petalcloud's Ice Warriors. His pulse quickened. The patrol of pale-colored steeds crept forward in a line, making signals to one another with their wings. They were exceptionally graceful considering how huge and big hooved they were. The enemy scouts sniffed the wind and inspected the churned-up soil, gathering information.

Star tightened his gut and held his breath. Beside him, Bumblewind's eyes narrowed. The six Ice Warrior scouts were upwind of the hiding pegasi but so close that Star could see the leader's pulse thumping down his neck. Star unconsciously rattled his feathers, and the Ice Warriors froze, listening.

Star cringed. *I've done it now,* he thought. He was going to get his herd killed.

Around him it seemed that every steed held its breath. Star's right leg began to wobble from the strain of keeping still. He gritted his teeth and willed his knee joint to hold strong.

The scouts prowled forward, their ears swiveling for noises and their eyes searching for their enemy.

Sweat erupted on Star's brow, tickling his face as the droplets rolled down toward his muzzle. It took all his willpower not to shake them off.

Bumblewind suddenly stiffened, and Star saw why. A

single brown-tipped gold feather shed off his wing, caught an air current, and drifted toward the Ice Warrior patrol.

The steeds nearest Bumblewind tensed, all eyes glued to the errant feather.

One white stallion glanced their way but stared right through them because he was standing in a patch of light and they were tucked in darkness.

Star bit his lip, and his sweat dripped faster from his forelock and down the large white star on his forehead. He tilted his head sideways, watching as Bumblewind's brown-tipped feather swirled toward the stallion who was still looking their way. Star's gut flew with the feather, drifting and twisting with it, making him dizzy.

The stallion walked into a sharp ray of sunshine that blinded his eyes, but that telltale feather was also about to enter the light. If any of the scouts spied it, they would investigate, and then they would find Star. He bit his lip so hard he tasted blood.

Behind him, Star could feel the tension building as all eyes remained locked on Bumblewind's floating feather. The energy was palpable, like static before a storm. Some-one was going to spook, and soon; Star could feel it. If that happened, it would give them all away.

Star stared at the twirling feather, willing it to go

unnoticed. Then a small blast of wind shot through the trees and ruffled the white stallion's mane. He looked behind him just as the feather reached the sunlight and twirled into view. But the stallion was looking away. The wind snatched the feather and lifted it up to where it became entangled in the tight branches overhead.

Star dared a small, short breath. The white stallion had not seen the feather. He waved to his friends with his wing and resumed his search, leading the small patrol away from Star. The hiding steeds exhaled with relief, but then another steed trotted into view, and Star recognized her instantly.

It was Petalcloud.

13

CLOSE CALL

STAR HAD NOT SEEN PETALCLOUD SINCE HE'D offered to heal Snow Herd of the Blue Tongue plague. The illness had ravaged her steeds soon after Star received his power, but she'd refused his help, unwilling to owe him for the favor. Now here the mare was, following her patrol into the Trap and keeping company with the largest stallion Star had ever seen. He squeezed between the trees behind her like a giant moose, and he was dapple gray with no markings. His quick black eyes swept the surroundings, and his black mane flowed to the ground. Star watched his hooves pound the soil like boulders, their edges so sharp they glinted in the dark. Star flattened his ears, taking short, shallow breaths.

Petalcloud sniffed the trampled moss on the forest floor. "The rebels have been here," she whinnied to her massive companion. He halted next to her.

"And not long ago," he said, agreeing with her, "but there's no sign of Star or his body." The stallion's voice was deep but softer than Star expected from the size of him.

Petalcloud curled her lip. "We'll keep searching."

"It would be foolish to hide him here, with all the others," the gray stallion said.

Petalcloud coiled back her neck and made a hissing noise like a cobra.

The huge stallion tucked his tail and closed his mouth. Star saw the cold ferocity in Petalcloud's eyes. "You will leave no thicket unturned, Stormtail," she commanded, her voice as slick as winter ice.

A brown mare with white spots across her hind flanks loped through the forest and halted behind Petalcloud, who twirled around, her hooves slicing up the soil. "What do you want?" she snapped.

Star was stunned. Petalcloud had sharpened her hooves since he'd last seen her.

The new mare lowered her head and spoke quickly. "A spy has brought news," she said, out of breath. "Morning-leaf was spotted in Desert Herd's territory."

"When?"

"Just days ago."

Petalcloud's eyes softened. "She's with Star." Petalcloud whistled for her Ice Warrior patrol. The six steeds returned at a gallop and bowed their heads to her with expressions of sheer devotion, and Star wondered at it. This mare inspired them like no other. Was it her beauty or her ambition? Star guessed it was ambition that inflamed their hearts for her. If Petalcloud was anything, she was single-minded and pure in her quest for power, her dedication absolute. Any steed following her could expect results.

"We leave for the desert tonight," she whinnied.

Petalcloud reared and galloped away, toward the edge of the Trap, with her steeds trailing behind her.

When the echo of their hoofbeats had faded, the hiding pegasi exhaled in a long, collective breath. Several collapsed right where they stood, others paced nervously, and others rattled their feathers in triumph.

"That was close," Bumblewind said.

"Your feather!" Star gasped. "I thought they would see it."

Bumblewind shuddered. "I never liked that feather."

Star nickered, and then his knee finally buckled and he fell down.

"Are you okay?" Bumblewind asked.

Star nodded. "It feels good to lie down. Did you see the size of that stallion with Petalcloud?"

"The beast with rocks for hooves? Yeah, I saw him."

Sweetroot stumbled forward and lowered her head, sniffing Star. "I'm glad Clawfire found you." She gave Bumblewind a sharp glance. "You two should not wander so far on your own."

Hazelwind and Silverlake approached. "Morningleaf's plan is working," Silverlake said, her eyes glowing. "Sightings of her across Anok will confuse the armies."

"She's smart," Star said, his voice barely a whisper. But he wished she were here, with him.

Silverlake took a deep, shuddering breath. "I met with the United Council last night. Now that you're awake, we'll move you soon, and we'll keep moving you so you won't be found."

Star shook his head, wishing he had the strength to stand up. "No."

Silverlake paused, flicking her ears and staring at Star. "What do you mean, *no*?"

"Just what I said. I'm going to stay here and fight with all of you."

Bumblewind gaped at Star, and Star knew how he

looked—defying the United Council's decision from the ground because he was too weak to stand up—but he also understood it was time he made some decisions. This wasn't an issue between herds; this was an issue with a destroyer who threatened the future of Anok. "I know what you're thinking," Star continued. "That I'm injured, that I didn't defeat Nightwing like everyone thought I would, and that maybe I'm still a dud, a useless black foal."

"What?" Bumblewind whinnied. "No one is thinking any of that."

Star swiveled his head, assessing the dark forest and the pegasi he'd invited here to hide from Nightwing, feeling like he'd failed them. "Maybe not, but it's what *I'm* thinking."

Star lifted his head and forced himself to stand. He was taller than most pegasi, and he raised his neck so they would have to look up at him. "It's time I learned how to fight like a stallion—a *warrior* stallion. Petalcloud's Ice Warriors and Frostfire's Black Army aren't magical; we can defeat them. Nightwing will see that we can't be conquered by war. And he's afraid of the Ancestors who protected me on the battlefield—it's why he's offering the pact. Don't you see? He doesn't want to come after me himself." Star glanced at each of them. "From now on I'll battle by your side. I'm your largest steed and your best flyer." Star glanced at Hazelwind. "Train me. Train every steed in the Trap."

Hazelwind gasped.

The trees swirled around Star as a wave of dizziness overcame him. His body crumbled, and he rested his head on the moss. "But first, please let me sleep."

14

CONFESSION

AS MORNINGLEAF AND BRACKENTAIL CRUISED the currents over the Sea of Rain searching for Shadepebble, Morningleaf observed Brackentail out of the corner of her eye. Questions that had lingered in her for a long time surfaced now that they were alone. Brackentail had never spoken to her about his and Echofrost's captivity with Mountain Herd back when they were weanlings, and certainly no steed wanted to hear about it, but now that they'd befriended Rockwing's filly, Shadepebble, she was more curious than ever. "Did you meet Shadepebble when you were living with Mountain Herd?"

Brackentail's head shot up, and he faltered. His captivity was a sore subject, and Morningleaf knew that, so she waited, giving Brackentail time to think and then answer her. Finally he said, "Rockwing didn't allow me near his filly, but she spoke to me a few times he didn't know about."

"What did she say to you?"

"She asked if I missed home and if I was being treated well." He trailed off, and Morningleaf felt a stab of old anger. Brackentail *had* been treated well, everyone knew that, but Echofrost had not.

Morningleaf bit her lip, knowing her next question would upset Brackentail, but she'd never understood why Echofrost had been tortured. It was not customary to attack foreign youngsters for no reason. As they glided over the sea, she asked, "Why were the pegasi there so mean to Echofrost? She was just a weanling."

Brackentail curved his wings and braked, hovering over the sea, his eyes filling with tears. "I tried to help her," he said, his voice cracking. "She doesn't know it, but I tried."

Morningleaf hovered next to him, listening, shocked to see his tears.

Brackentail's gaze grew distant as he remembered. "Rockwing kept me guarded. He wanted information, about Star. I helped him; it's true. Everyone knows what

I did." Brackentail's chest heaved, and his lower lip trembled. Morningleaf felt her anger begin to melt as the colt confessed.

"But one day I saw Echofrost walking past me, and I noticed her tail." Brackentail blinked, and the tears rolled down his cheeks. "It was ripped out. And that—that was just the beginning." He paused for breath, and Morningleaf nickered to soothe him. "The yearlings made a game of harassing her. I told Rockwing about it, but he didn't care. So I tried to bargain with him. I said I wouldn't give him the information he wanted unless he let Echofrost go." Brackentail winced at the memory and then glanced at Morningleaf with haunted eyes. "But that made things worse for her."

Morningleaf's heart ached at the thought of her best friend being tortured by bigger, older steeds.

Brackentail continued. "Rockwing led me into a forest where we were concealed by trees. Two of the meanest yearling colts dragged Echofrost into view."

"No," Morningleaf cried, regretting her questions. "Don't tell me."

"You asked," Brackentail said with a bite to his voice she didn't expect.

Morningleaf's heart fluttered and she felt weak, but

she listened as he told his story, realizing he needed to tell it.

"They took turns kicking her with sharpened hooves, leaving trails of blood dripping down her beautiful coat." The warm winds took his words and cast them across the sea, but not before Morningleaf heard them, absorbed them, and they pricked her heart like thorns.

Brackentail continued with a shudder. "I galloped toward her, but Rockwing clubbed me and knocked me down. He said her beating was my punishment for thinking I could bargain with him. He said if I threatened to withhold information again, he would kill her." Brackentail looked at Morningleaf. "When the yearlings finished kicking her, they dropped Echofrost in the grass and left her by herself. Rockwing forced me away."

Brackentail choked on his words, blinking back a waterfall of tears. "But as Rockwing dragged me through the trees, Echofrost looked up and saw me. I wanted to whinny to her, but Rockwing had warned me not to speak. We just left her there, alone, and . . . and I will never forget the look she gave me." Brackentail groaned and his legs stabbed the sky, and Morningleaf saw he was tortured too.

After a moment he regained his voice. "Echofrost is right to hate me. All of it—all of it—was my fault."

Brackentail eyes widened, bearing the weight of his guilt. The information he'd given Rockwing had helped the over-stallion defeat Sun Herd in the battle that followed. It was only Silverlake's intervention that had saved them from a worse massacre.

Morningleaf had no idea of the depth of Brackentail's guilt and sorrow. She tried to soothe him. "Rockwing was coming for us either way."

"Maybe," Brackentail agreed, sniffling. "But I helped him—I will never forgive myself. And it's my fault Echofrost was hauled into it. No one hates me as much as I do." He said this last bit while peering at the horizon, his neck arched and his eyes softened. He took a deep breath, as though resigned to his burdens.

Brackentail's confession dissolved the last of Morningleaf's anger toward him. "You were a weanling too," she said.

Brackentail exhaled. "There's no excuse for what I did. But I was wrong about Star. I'm dedicated to him now. I believe he's the healer and that he'll unite the herds." He peered at Morningleaf, leaving the rest of his feelings unspoken.

Morningleaf glanced around them. "I still see no trace of Shadepebble."

They resumed flying and searching. "At least there's nothing out here that can hurt her," Brackentail said.

Just then Shadepebble's terrified screams carried to them across the sea.

15

STRENGTH

MORNINGLEAF AND BRACKENTAIL BANKED INTO the wind and dived toward the sound of Shadepebble's screams. Morningleaf racked her brain, ticking off the dangers that might have befallen her friend: foreign pegasi, wing cramps, or more turbulence. She flew as fast as she could, scanning the sky and the sea.

"There!" Brackentail whinnied. "In the water."

Morningleaf looked down and saw Shadepebble bobbing in the waves, a circle of blood expanding around her. Morningleaf sucked in her breath, and tears sprang to her eyes.

Brackentail dropped into a nose dive, and Morningleaf followed. Six large sharks with odd-shaped heads coasted around her, slow and lazy, until bursts of excitement caused them to dart spasmodically. Their jaws snapped in short, fast bites. They were tearing at pieces of white flesh floating on the surface, and Shadepebble was staring at the creatures, paralyzed with terror.

Morningleaf scanned the yearling filly and whinnied to Brackentail. "The blood's not hers."

Brackentail soared closer to Shadepebble and neighed in her ears. "Fly!"

Shadepebble snapped her head toward them, and her expression melted with relief. She fluttered her wings, and Morningleaf understood the problem. On land, Shadepebble needed a running start to fly. Taking off from a motionless position was impossible for her misshapen wings.

"I'll distract the sharks," Brackentail called out. He flew low and kicked at the water, splashing and drawing the sharks' attention toward him.

Morningleaf hovered over Shadepebble. The sharks had killed a large fish, and most of it had been eaten. "You have time; don't panic," Morningleaf encouraged. Her friend's eyes were blank with shock.

"I'm so tired," Shadepebble said. She grit her teeth and flapped her wings, but could not lift herself out of the water.

"Swim then," Morningleaf urged, keeping an eye on the feeding frenzy. "Let's get away from this blood."

Shadepebble nodded and paddled toward Morningleaf while Brackentail teased the sharks. "She can't fly," Morningleaf neighed to the brown colt.

"Let's pick her up," he whinnied, Morningleaf flew low and gripped the root of Shadepebble's left wing in her teeth. Brackentail took the right wing, and they heaved her out of the water and away from the sharks.

They flew like this through the night, using the stars to guide them, and Morningleaf struggled to keep Shadepebble out of the water. The pink-winged filly was small but so was Morningleaf. Shadepebble's hooves skimmed the waves, and she panicked several times when she saw large creatures cruising beneath the surface. Halfway through the night, Morningleaf's strength gave out. She and Brackentail lowered Shadepebble into the ocean, and Morningleaf floated beside her. "I have to rest."

Brackentail flew circles over them, watching for sharks, and the two fillies paddled west. After a while Brackentail whinnied a warning. "I see something under the water. It's big."

Morningleaf clutched her hooves tight to her belly.

"I've rested enough; come help me lift her."

Brackentail coasted toward Morningleaf, and they each took one of Shadepebble's wings. Soon they were flying again, but Morningleaf continued to struggle with Shadepebble's weight. The tension kept all of them silent, and Morningleaf became confident they would die in the sea and never be found. Hunger tugged at her gut, and incredible thirst burned her throat. She had not realized Jungle Herd's territory was so far away.

Finally the sun rose, coloring the water pink, and her friends were still alive and airborne.

"There's the shore," whinnied Brackentail.

Morningleaf wanted to cry with relief. She adjusted their course when she saw the strip of sand bordering the ocean and the thick foliage beyond: the jungle. The climate had changed dramatically. The air was warm and heavy with moisture. Morningleaf remembered this from her captivity in the lava tubes. The jungle was the exact opposite of the desert. Everything here was damp and green and wet.

It was several more hours before they reached the shore, and when they did, the three of them tumbled onto the sand and collapsed.

"Ahh, that feels good," cried Shadepebble, grinding her sore shoulders into the sand as she rolled. It was exactly how Star used to rub his back on the banks of Feather Lake when he was a foal.

Morningleaf rolled too, scratching between her wings, and then led her friends to the edge of the rain forest. She showed them the wide, curved leaves that captured and held rainwater. "This is safe to drink," she said. "But the lake and river water will make you sick." They slurped the fresh water out of the leaves, and it soothed Morningleaf's dry throat.

Shadepebble's chest shook with pent-up emotion. "I'm not as strong as you two."

Morningleaf tossed her mane. "You're plenty strong, Shadepebble." Morningleaf admired the spotted filly. She'd risked banishment when she refused to return home after Frostfire ordered her to, and she'd committed treason against her sire when she flew to Hazelwind in the Sun Herd lands and warned him of Rockwing's imminent attack. Morningleaf gasped as a thought struck her.

"What is it?" Brackentail nickered.

She reeled in the hot sun, thinking. Both Shadepebble and Brackentail had committed treason against their herds, so why did she admire one and not the other? Both steeds thought they were helping—and if Star had turned out to be a destroyer, Brackentail would have become a hero.

Morningleaf stared at her two friends, who were staring back at her, and she dashed forward and wrapped her wings around them both. To go against your own herd required more strength than Morningleaf could imagine. "You two are the strongest pegasi I know . . . next to Star," she quickly added.

Shadepebble and Brackentail relaxed and leaned into her.

"She's lost her mind," Shadepebble nickered.

Brackentail nuzzled Morningleaf, tucking his nose under her chin, and for the first time, his close presence didn't irritate her, and this startled Morningleaf. She pulled away from her friends and wiped her eyes. "Echofrost said Frostfire sent scouts from his Black Army to Jungle Herd, and they could be anywhere." She glanced at the clear sky overhead. "But I think we all need to rest before we tangle with them. Agreed?"

Her two friends nodded. They had flown all day and all night without much of a break.

"Come on; we can sleep in Jungle Herd's southern nesting grounds. Can you fly now?" she asked Shadepebble.

The little filly galloped forward, flapping her wings, and then she lifted off.

Morningleaf and Brackentail galloped down the beach after her, jumped off the sand, and cantered into the sky.

16

THE UNITED ARMY

SIX DAYS AFTER STAR'S SPEECH ABOUT FIGHTING
the Ice Warriors and the Black Army, which he'd delivered
from the ground because he was too weak to stand, the
River Herd Council met to enact Star's plan. Nightwing
had been spotted flying over the Wastelands in the south.
He was just cruising, and he'd returned to the Blue Mountains at dusk, but it was clear to Silverlake and the others
that it was time to increase the size of their army. The
River Herd pegasi gathered at the stream in their camp to
hear what the council had to say.

Hazelwind clapped his wings, drawing everyone's
attention to himself. "Morningleaf's plan is working.
She's luring our enemies away from us, but eventually

117

the armies will realize that Star isn't in the south. Petalcloud's and Frostfire's scouts will intensify their search for him, and they cannot find us vulnerable. Every ablebodied River Herd steed will train as a warrior."

There was excited nickering and whinnying, especially among the yearlings.

This was Star's idea, and he was grateful to Hazelwind for telling it to the herd. Star tucked his wings, relaxing, when a stealthy movement caught his eye. He threw up his head, swiveling his ears. "Quiet," he whispered.

His sudden alarm swept through the herd. The pegasi flared their wings and nostrils, and the warriors flattened their ears. Star knew to trust his eyes, and he focused on the shifting light between the dense foliage.

Then a Jungle Herd mare stepped out from between two trees, startling them all.

Hazelwind trotted forward, his feathers rattling.

The foreign mare lowered her head and pricked her ears, showing she meant no harm. With a sharp exhale, Hazelwind recognized her as one of the United Council and lowered his wings.

"Are you passing through?" Hazelwind asked.

The Jungle Herd mare, a dark bay steed with yellow and green feathers, answered him. "No. I'm Ashrain, and I've come to speak to your herd." Star noticed she'd brought six stallions and six mares with her.

Hazelwind's dark eyes glittered as he assessed the group for signs of violence. Star was struck again by how much Hazelwind resembled his sire, Thundersky.

The wiry Jungle Herd mare glanced from Hazelwind to Star. Her chest expanded, and her hooves shuffled as she searched for words. Because her wings were tucked and her ears relaxed, Star guessed she hadn't come to fight. So what did she want?

As if reading Star's mind, the mare answered, "I heard what you just said to your herd, and we've come to the same conclusion. We're also training our nonwarriors to fight, and I think we should train them together."

Hazelwind nodded but said nothing.

The dark bay mare cocked her ears forward. "River Herd steeds fight best in the open sky, but Jungle Herd understands tight spaces. We know how to fight in the trees." She looked directly at Hazelwind. "We're offering to show you our ways, and I've spoken to Redfire of Desert Herd and Birchcloud of Mountain Herd. They also want to share their knowledge. Desert Herd will teach us their ground-fighting techniques, and the Mountain Herd mares will teach us their aerial formations, in case we're lured into the sky. I propose we form a United Army now, before our enemy arrives. If we train together, we'll fight together better, and we'll hold out longer."

Hazelwind shifted from hoof to hoof, thinking.

Silverlake stepped forward. "Our council will discuss this, and we'll return our answer to you this evening." She dipped her head. "Thank you, Ashrain."

Ashrain dipped her head in return and then cantered away with her envoy.

The River Herd pegasi erupted after Ashrain disappeared into the woods.

Train with our enemy?

They'll learn our secrets?

But we'll learn theirs too.

Hazelwind trumpeted a sharp call over their heads, quieting them. A long discussion followed as pegasi vented their fears. Some drifted off to graze, leaving the decision to the River Herd council, others stayed and argued, but as the evening wore on, the objections diminished. The truth was, they had a common enemy, Nightwing, and a common goal, to survive. There was no denying that the four herds in the Trap would be stronger if they trained together. The decision to form the United Army ended up being unanimous. "We have nothing to lose," Silverlake said at the end of the vote.

Hazelwind left to inform Ashrain.

Bumblewind nudged Star. "Hazelwind acts like we're doing Ashrain a favor, but I think it's the other way around. She's doing us a favor. No one fights in the trees better than Jungle Herd, and look at all these trees."

"That's true," said Star, feeling grateful and hopeful. He would learn the warrior ways of River Herd, Jungle Herd, Mountain Herd, *and* Desert Herd. When in the history of Anok had there been an opportunity like that?

"Are you strong enough to begin training?" Bumblewind asked.

"I'm getting there," said Star. The two friends drank from the cool stream and then trotted back to River Herd's camp.

Star's thoughts drifted to Morningleaf. He imagined her flying for her life, getting captured, or injured, and he felt sick. Other times he imagined her playing and nickering with her companions, Shadepebble and Brackentail, and he felt something else—but he didn't know what it was—maybe envy that they were with her and he was not. He was sure of one thing; he missed her like he would miss his own wings if they were gone.

Star let Bumblewind take the lead as his tears formed and fell, leaving a trail of white flowers blooming behind him.

17

THE SOUTHERN NESTS

MORNINGLEAF CRUISED OVER THE CLOUD FOREST, her hooves brushing the uppermost leaves, looking for Jungle Herd's southern nesting ground so her friends could rest after their long flight across the Sea of Rain. "In the jungle, always assume a predator is right behind you, and you'll never be wrong," she advised.

"How do you know so much about this territory?" Shadepebble asked.

"Before Frostfire hid me in the lava tubes beneath the volcano, we traveled through Jungle Herd's territory a bit," she answered. "I remember all the strange noises and creatures, and Frostfire warned me not to touch colorful plants or animals because they're usually poisonous."

Shadepebble pricked her ears and ducked to dodge a tangle of glossy green banyan leaves. "Was Frostfire kind to you?"

Morningleaf exhaled. "He was neither kind nor cruel," she answered, feeling ill. In comparison to Rockwing's treatment of Echofrost, this was true, but Frostfire had been cruel by any other standard. He'd stolen Morningleaf from her family; murdered her protectors; attacked his own sire, Iceriver; and then he'd forced Morningleaf to hide in terrifying darkness. But he had not beaten her, and for that small mercy she was grateful.

"Look!" Morningleaf whinnied. "It's the Jungle Herd nesting ground." She veered sharply, and her friends followed close behind her.

Morningleaf slowed and hovered over the oldest portion of the cloud forest. Here the trees were close together and heavy with long branches and leaves. She lowered her voice. "There's a cluster of pegasi nests. Let's get closer." She darted into the foliage and stared at the woody brown platforms built almost a hundred wing lengths off the ground, exhaling with wonder.

"I imagined them like birds' nests," Shadepebble said. "But they're flatter." She flew under the nests, which were even in the center and gently curved at the edges, studying the construction. Morningleaf and Bumblewind dropped by her side.

Brackentail nudged the base with his muzzle. "How do they build them?"

Morningleaf shook her head. "I don't know." The nest was fixed to the tree with sinuous vines and roots, tightly intertwined to support the heavy, shifting weight of a pegasus. Each steed built and maintained its own nest.

"There are hundreds of them," Shadepebble nickered, gazing around her. "You're sure they'll hold us?"

Morningleaf nickered. "Sure. Why not?"

Shadepebble flew to the top of a nest and stepped into it. It swayed, and she squealed.

"It's fine," Morningleaf assured her. "I'm going to try this one." She glided to a bigger nest and settled into it like a bird. Brackentail chose one between the two fillies and did the same.

Morningleaf studied her nest. It was large, probably belonging to an adult stallion. He'd left behind some munched leaves and a few coconut shells that had been picked clean by insects. The floor of the nest was lined with gold feathers, broad leaves, and soft mulch. The frame of the nest consisted of supple branches held together by woven vines and an adhesive tree sap. The nest shifted with the winds, but Morningleaf felt secure. She glanced at her friends. "Let's try to sleep while we can."

They each tucked their legs and curled their wings over their bodies. In seconds Morningleaf was asleep.

Hours later she woke, stretched, and noticed her belly grumbling. Brackentail heard her movements and opened his eyes, yawning. Shadepebble spoke first. "I'm starving," she said.

"Me too; let's go." Morningleaf lifted smoothly out of her nest, followed by Brackentail. Shadepebble leaped out of hers, needing the momentum of falling to catch the wind.

Morningleaf cruised over a particularly large nest and noticed an odd arrangement of flowers and feathers decorating its rim. Her heart fluttered at the sight. "Look at this," she whinnied, and dived toward the tree.

Brackentail and Shadepebble glided after her, and all three hovered, staring at the special nest. It had been reinforced and repaired each season and so it was thick with layers of old and new vines and branches. The top edge of the nest was adorned with colorful feathers and bright flower petals all the way around. Red stones, shimmering lava rocks, and pretty seashells sprinkled the nest floor.

Morningleaf's gut tingled. "I think this is Spider-wing's nest," she said. "Mossberry told me that Jungle Herd maintains it and that the steeds leave gifts for him here." She hovered closer to the interior of the nest. "He used to sleep right there," she said with a gasp.

"I wish I had learned the legends," said Shadepebble.

"Your elders didn't teach you?" asked Morningleaf, baffled.

"No," answered Shadepebble, chewing her lip. "Rock-wing banned the teaching of most legends. I heard some things, whisperings in the grazing meadows, but I didn't ask questions. I obeyed my sire's wishes." She clenched her jaw, remembering. "He taught me that foreign steeds are evil, that the legends are lies, and that Mountain Herd steeds are superior to all others. Except for me of course." She glanced morosely at her stunted wing.

Morningleaf and Brackentail listened quietly, letting her speak.

Shadepebble peered at Morningleaf. "Since I met Clawfire and joined River Herd, I've learned that every-thing I thought was true is not."

Morningleaf's throat tightened with sadness. "Well, I can teach you about Spiderwing," she said. "He and

Nightwing were each born to Jungle Herd, but a year apart. They were friends, but also opposites. When Nightwing received his power, he fled Anok, but why he left and where he went is a mystery." Morningleaf swiveled her ears, listening always for danger. "What we do know is that when he came back, he turned on his guardian herd and attacked all the pegasi of Anok, setting their grasslands on fire and driving our ancestors to near extinction."

Brackentail joined in the telling of the ancient legend. "But Nightwing wouldn't, or couldn't, hurt Spiderwing, who was leading a small herd of his own. Eventually Nightwing vanished, and Spiderwing's foals split to form the five herds we have today. If it wasn't for Spiderwing, there would be no pegasi left in Anok."

"That's incredible," said Shadepebble. "And *this* is his nest?"

Brackentail nodded. "No one uses it anymore, but Jungle Herd maintains his northern nest and his southern nest in memory of him."

"I'm going to leave a gift," said Morningleaf. She yanked an aqua feather free with her teeth and placed it on the rim of the nest.

"I'm going to leave one too," said Shadepebble. She plucked a long pink feather and wove it between two branches. Brackentail rolled his eyes, but he also plucked a feather and dropped it into the nest.

Without warning, Brackentail whipped his head toward the clouds and then dived toward land. "Follow me. Hide!"

Morningleaf tucked her wings to speed her drop to the jungle floor. When they landed, Brackentail tugged her into a thicket of trees. Shadepebble followed, breathing heavily.

Brackentail sheltered the fillies' brighter feathers with his wings. Morningleaf pressed close to him, watching his pulse flicker down his long neck. He motioned to indicate he'd seen something in the sky. Morningleaf willed herself to be as silent and still as possible. Shadepebble folded her wings and flared her nostrils, scenting the wind.

Morningleaf peeked through Brackentail's feathers, trying to see the sky. Soon she saw what Brackentail had seen: an army of pegasi flying in tight formation. Her chest heaved when she caught sight of their leader. He had one blue eye and one brown—it was Frostfire!

Fear bubbled in her gut, and several aqua feathers shed off and floated to the ground. Brackentail closed his wing around her back to steady her. "I won't let him take you again," he whispered into her flattened ears.

His words helped quell the rapid slam of her heart, but in truth, Brackentail couldn't stop Frostfire if the white stallion spotted her, and she wasn't ready to show herself—not without a plan.

Frostfire and his warriors veered west, toward the Valley of Tears, an open grassy plain where Jungle Herd steeds liked to graze. Morningleaf watched them descend toward land, and then they disappeared from her view. She and her friends waited a long time, holding perfectly still. When they were sure all the pegasi had passed over, they emerged from the brush. Morningleaf shook the leaves out of her mane.

"That was close," Shadepebble said.

Brackentail folded his wings. "He's got his entire army with him."

Morningleaf pricked her ears, and Shadepebble read the determined expression on her face. "No!" Shadepebble neighed. "We're not going to follow them, are we?"

"We are," Morningleaf said. "I need them to spot me in this territory, to confuse them. I just—seeing Frostfire caught me off guard, but it's our mission that I'm spotted."

Brackentail stamped his hoof. "By scouts maybe, but the entire Black Army? It's too dangerous this time."

"Keeping Star safe is more important," argued

Morningleaf. "If Frostfire spots me here, he'll assume Star is hiding close by—maybe even in the lava tubes. He knows the black maze under the volcano is a perfect hiding place, and he knows that I know it too. It will take him a moon to search all those tunnels, which will give Star more time to wake up, to heal and get strong. I *have* to let Frostfire see me."

"But how will you avoid getting captured?" Shadepebble asked. "You can't ride a jet stream again. Star's not around to catch you this time."

Morningleaf exhaled, and tears leaked from the corners of her eyes. She hated thinking about Star's absence. She hated not knowing if he was alive or dead.

"I'm sorry," Shadepebble said, biting her lip. "But it's the truth. How will you escape that army?"

Morningleaf shuddered. "I don't know."

18

TRAINING

AFTER THE RIVER HERD COUNCIL MET AND MADE the unanimous decision to train with the other herds, Hazelwind divided up the pegasi, placing them into groups that would rotate between the stallions and mares who'd volunteered to teach different skills. Star and Bumblewind were sent first to hoof sharpening.

"Come with us," Bumblewind said to Dewberry.

The fierce little mare pranced in the dim light between the pine trees. She flicked her tail at Bumblewind, her eyes sparkling. "I think I want to be a sky herder," she nickered, "and sky herders don't sharpen their hooves. I'm going with Sunray's group; she's that tall Desert Herd mare over there. She's teaching herding skills, and she's ridden jet streams and flown to the heights where the blue sky turns black."

Star glanced at the Desert Herd mare waiting nearby. Sunray was a golden buckskin with light-purple feathers. Her deep chest curved into a tiny waist, and her long neck was thin and corded with muscle. Her wide-set eyes bulged a bit, and her broad forehead wedged into a small, curved muzzle.

"You're staring at her," Dewberry said with a snort.

Star looked quickly away. "I can't get used to them; they look so different from us."

"Even their feathers aren't like ours," Dewberry nickered. "They're moist and waxy. And their hooves don't melt when they fly up there, where the sun's rays burn the rest of us."

Star lowered his eyelashes and glanced again at Sunray. Her build was extraordinary: designed for extreme heights, extreme heat, and extreme speed. "I guess it makes sense why they guard their lineage."

Dewberry nodded. "Mixed foals can't keep up."

Sunray whinnied for her trainees, and Dewberry kicked off, buzzing over the bushes toward the golden buckskin mare. "Have fun grinding your hooves," she nickered over her shoulder.

Bumblewind watched Dewberry fly away, his eyes trailing her long after she disappeared.

Star nudged his friend's shoulder. "Come on; let's go."

They trotted to Clawfire, who was teaching hoof sharpening. Hundreds of steeds had gathered around him from the four herds, mostly yearlings and some older mares from Mountain Herd who were also eager for the sharp weapons of warriors.

Clawfire placed his hoof on a rock, letting the edge of it hang over the side. "Take a close look at my hoof," he said. "This is your desired result, but don't start grinding until I've shown you how."

Each pegasus took a turn examining Clawfire's hoof. When it was Star's turn, he lowered his head and peered at the hoof's edge from all angles. He noticed that the very front of the hoof slanted into a thin, crisp edge. The sidewall was thick and smooth to support Clawfire's weight. "Can I touch the edge?" Star asked.

Clawfire nodded, and Star felt the rim of Clawfire's sharpened nail with his wingtips. The severe edge sliced right through Star's end feathers. He jerked his wing away, and the watching pegasi nickered in amazement. "That's sharp," Star said, whistling.

"Yes. That's the point," replied Clawfire with humor in his eyes.

Star stepped back and showed his cut feathers to the younger steeds, and then all eyes returned to Clawfire. The pegasi were silent, ready to learn.

"Sorry I'm late," said a female voice.

Star and everyone else turned to see that Echofrost had joined them and was standing in the low mist that rolled across the forest floor. Clawfire nodded, inviting her closer. She trotted forward and touched his deadly hoof with her wingtips, also losing a few feathers in the process. "Thank you," she said to the captain. She backed away and stood next to her twin brother.

"You're going to be a warrior?" Bumblewind asked.

"A spy," she corrected, "but I think it's wise to be ready for anything." Her eyes flicked from her brother to Star and then back to her brother.

"I'm glad you're here," Bumblewind said.

"Me too," said Star, but he wasn't so sure. Echofrost had seemed to enjoy watching Nightwing incinerate Rockwing not so long ago. It had brought her out of the depression she'd lived in since her release from captivity in Mountain Herd, but Star didn't think Echofrost had let go of her anger. He feared that instead she'd found an unhealthy outlet for it in violence.

Clawfire continued his training. "The secret to sharpening a hoof is finding and using the right stone. Come close."

The trainees scrunched around him. Clawfire pointed out a flat, smooth rock. "This one is good for polishing," he said, "but not for grinding." He walked through the dense pines with his eyes down. Star and the others followed him, also scanning the terrain and looking for rocks.

"What about this one?" Echofrost asked.

"That rock is too small," Clawfire replied. "Soon you'll understand why." Clawfire proceeded until he found a stone he liked. "Here, this one will do."

Star and the others stood in a semicircle around a piece of granite that was rough but mostly flat, and large—almost reaching to Star's knee. The morning fog had lifted, and bits of sunlight pierced the canopy overhead.

"It's helpful to let your hooves grow long before you sharpen them," Clawfire said. "The more hoof you have to work with, the better. And since the land here is soft, our hooves aren't too worn down, so most of us won't have any problems."

Clawfire kicked at the soft layer of pine needles and moss that covered the soil, and then looked up. "If you're a Desert Herd steed, come see me. Your hooves are different from ours. If you try to sharpen them, you might split them. Your hooves are better for kicking than slicing anyway." Clawfire nickered softly and said, "If you've ever been kicked by a Desert Herd steed, then you know what I mean."

Star and Bumblewind traded a glance. "I don't want to get kicked by a Desert Herd steed," Bumblewind said.

"Well, Frostfire is commanding an army of them," Star whispered. "So we'd better learn to defend ourselves. And our friends."

Star sighed. He never thought he'd *want* to fight, but here he was, in warrior training; and even stranger, he was enjoying it. Talk of Frostfire's Black Army sent his stallion blood coursing hot and ready. He couldn't use his starfire to fight because it would alert Nightwing to his hiding place, but he could defend his guardian herd with his hooves and teeth.

And for the first time, Star was beginning to understand the pegasi of Anok. The fierceness that had terrified him as a foal now flowed through his own veins, almost as powerful as the starfire itself, and he'd never felt more natural than he did at this very moment, standing with Bumblewind and training for battle.

"Jungle Herd steeds may also have a hard time with this," Clawfire continued. "You have the softest hooves of all the herds because your territory is always moist. You may not be able to carve a sharp edge, but Ashrain will have a special training for you to add the lethal embellishments of your warriors."

Star pricked his ears. That sounded interesting.

Clawfire explained. "I've been in several battles against Jungle Herd steeds. They press sharp rocks into the soft edges of their hooves, making them extra deadly."

The trainees blinked at him, curious.

"But most of our hooves aren't pliable enough for that," Clawfire continued. "So let's begin with the sharpening."

Star leaned in and studied Clawfire's technique. Like most yearlings, Star had tried to sharpen his hooves in the past but had only succeeded in shortening them. Clawfire began by grinding the sides of his hooves until they were perfectly even. He left the toe longer. He lifted his hoof so the others could each examine phase one of hoof sharpening. Star glanced down at his own hooves and noticed they were overgrown and uneven.

Bumblewind followed Star's gaze and snorted. "No wonder you walk funny."

Star nosed him in the chest with his muzzle, almost

pushing him over. Bumblewind whinnied and shoved him back. Nickering, the two friends head-butted each other like goats, and each tried to make the other fall over. Star was stronger, and he pushed Bumblewind accidentally into Echofrost, who squealed.

Clawfire whinnied. "Pay attention."

Star, Bumblewind, and Echofrost lifted their heads and pretended they'd been doing just that all along. "I'll get you later," whispered Bumblewind.

"If I don't get you first," said Star, his heart buzzing with contentment. He knew he shouldn't be this happy. Two armies were hunting him down, Morningleaf was on a dangerous mission, and the herds of Anok were in danger of being enslaved by the Destroyer. But like the rays of sunshine that pierced the canopy of leaves overhead, joy had pierced the darkness around Star's heart. For once all eyes were not on him. For once he was equal to his friends. He was as new to warrior training as they, and just as excited to learn.

Clawfire finished his lesson by showing the steeds how to grind down the long toe at the front of their hoof into a thin, sharp edge. The process involved shaving the top layer, a fraction at a time, and leaving the bottom layer solid and flat. If they carved the toe too thin, the end of the hoof would break. Too thick and the edge would not be sharp enough to cut through a thick hide.

Star, Bumblewind, and Echofrost each took a turn practicing on the rock. Echofrost picked up on the technique right away, and Clawfire complimented her on her first attempt. Star and Bumblewind struggled with the technique, and Clawfire had to help them.

After several hours, Clawfire released them for the day with their hooves in varying states of deadliness. Star and the twins trod into the forest hunting for moist tree bark to eat. As soon as they were alone, Bumblewind tackled Star and knocked him down. "Got you!"

Star rolled back onto his hooves and charged his friend. They circled each other as Echofrost cheered on her brother. "He's bigger, but you're stronger, Bumblewind!"

Star and Bumblewind reared and crashed into each other, chest to chest, falling onto their backs with the impact. Star chased him around a tree, and Bumblewind kicked at the air. Echofrost joined in and they tried to ram her, but she lifted off, hovering just above them, and they smashed into each other and skidded across the soft moss. They stood and she landed, each panting, their manes entangled with pine needles, and they nickered at one another in delight.

"Come on," Echofrost said, "I'm hungry."

The three friends trotted through the dank forest. Star hadn't played like that since he'd been a foal in Dawn Meadow, and his heart beat hard with the joy of it, but there was a hole in the group, and it was Morningleaf. She was Star's best friend, and he'd never spent so much time apart from her. *Where are you?* he wondered. *Are you safe?* But no answer came to him from the empty space where she should be.

19

THE SWAMP

BRACKENTAIL, MORNINGLEAF, AND SHADEPEBBLE left the southern Jungle Herd nesting ground and trotted to the small mountain range west of the cloud forest. There, in the heights, they could spy on Frostfire's Black Army, which had landed in the grasslands called the Valley of Tears. Brackentail had devised a plan that involved revealing Morningleaf's presence to a small envoy of scouts at nighttime, and then luring them into a trap he called the Swallows. This would give Morningleaf and her friends time to get away. Brackentail peered at the dropping sun. "We'll wait until it's fully dark."

"Where will we trap them?" Morningleaf asked, looking down at the Valley of Tears, which was miles away from where she stood. From this distance it appeared as a large green circle surrounded by trees. It was in this valley that Spiderwing had outsmarted an entire army of Anok's strongest warriors hundreds of years ago, during the time of Nightwing. Morningleaf exhaled. She and her friends were about to attempt the same thing.

Brackentail pointed down the mountain toward a mangrove forest that grew out of a swamp on the western end of the valley, near the coast. "See where the mangrove trees are thickest?"

Morningleaf and Shadepebble squinted at the vast, wet swamp far in the distance. Sporadic trees, miniature islands, and flat expanses of shallow water were mixed with long reeds and jutting roots that spread out just north of the Wing River. "I see the swamp, but I'm not sure I see exactly where you're pointing," Morningleaf said.

Brackentail moved closer, pressing his cheek against hers and gently moving her head. "There," he whispered, also pointing with his wing. "On the inland side of the swamp, close to the Valley of Tears, just on the edge of the mangroves."

Morningleaf followed his gaze and then noticed a clump of trees so thick they looked black. "I think I have it now," she said. He remained close to her, and his nostrils flared, drinking in her scent. She held still, also catching his scent, and then she slid away.

"Frostfire has collected an impressive army," Shadepebble said.

Brackentail pinned his ears. "They're all traitors, and Frostfire is a fool to trust Nightwing. Why would the Destroyer make a pact with anyone? Pacts are made *before* the black foals receive their power, not after."

"It's because Nightwing's afraid of the Ancestors who came down and protected Star," Morningleaf replied. "He doesn't want to face the pegasi he murdered four hundred years ago."

Shadepebble twisted her neck and squinted at Morningleaf. Her pink feathers glistened, looking almost orange in the sunset. "I think it's more than that," she said. "I think he enjoys pitting us against one another."

"Why?" asked Brackentail.

Shimmering tears formed in her eyes. "My sire, Rockwing, played the same games. He'd set his captains against each other, forcing them to compete for his favor and making them hate each other. Don't you see?" she said, fluttering long lashes that trapped her tears. "Nightwing is already destroying Anok, and he doesn't have to lift a feather to do it. He only has to dangle a prize: power."

Brackentail exhaled. "You're right."

"He's toying with us," Shadepebble continued. "And he's enjoying it. Rockwing enjoyed it too. And worse, the two steeds that took the bait are both related to me: my sister, Petalcloud, and her colt, Frostfire." Shadepebble shook her head. "They are the last of my family, next to my dam, Birchcloud."

Morningleaf sighed. "We have to keep Frostfire and Petalcloud away from Star."

Shadepebble flicked her tail, swatting a mosquito that had landed on her flank. "We can't keep them away forever."

"I know that, but since Petalcloud's scouts saw me in Desert Herd's territory, she'll be moving her Ice Warriors there. And once Frostfire sees me here, he'll ransack Jungle Herd's territory in search of Star's body. All this will distract Star's enemies and give him time to wake up . . . if it's true that he's only sleeping."

"Maybe he's already awake," Brackentail suggested. "We've been gone for sixteen days."

Morningleaf nodded. "I've considered that, and if your plan works, we'll fly home tonight."

Just then the volcano Firemouth vented steam and lava with a loud boom. Morningleaf glanced at the flat-topped mountain, shuddering.

"Well it's dark now," Brackentail said, nodding toward the horizon. The orange rays had vanished, and the last thin line of dusk melted into blackness. The night sky was clear of clouds, and the moon was a half crescent surrounded by glittering stars. "This is good. They'll see us, but not well," Brackentail added.

"There's a patrol!" Morningleaf neighed softly.

A group of six warriors kicked out of the Valley of Tears. The captains had formed their battalions into a massive circle, facing outward, and the steeds inside took turns sleeping. Frostfire was well prepared for the dangers of the jungle.

Morningleaf understood how patrols operated, having watched her sire command them. The patrol would circle the herd in a widening pattern. If she and her friends were quick, they could beat the six warriors to the mangrove swamp and be waiting when the steeds flew overhead. "Let's move," she nickered.

Morningleaf trotted to a clearing, unfurled her wings, and lifted off into the sky. She gripped the current with her feathers and glided down the mountain, skimming the topmost leaves with her hooves. Behind her she heard the wingbeats of her friends, and she was grateful to have them with her.

They skirted the Valley of Tears, avoiding the path of the patrol, and then dropped over the Wing River, following it to the ocean. When they reached the coast, they banked north and traveled toward the mangrove swamp. When they reached it, Morningleaf looked down and saw the slimy backs of crocodiles floating in the water. Her belly twisted, and her breathing quickened. "See them?" she whispered over her shoulder.

"I do," Brackentail answered.

"Me too," Shadepebble said.

"Don't land in the water," Morningleaf warned.

"But where then?" Shadepebble asked, cruising faster and flying next to Morningleaf, her short wing flapping faster than the other. The islands were thick with trees and exposed roots, leaving no obvious landing spots.

"We're going to have to land on the tree roots that are above water," Morningleaf explained. "Use your wings for balance."

Morningleaf dropped through the sultry air toward land. She cruised between the mangrove trees until she found a layer of roots thick enough to stand on. Shadepebble and Brackentail landed beside her.

Brackentail glanced toward the sky. "They're coming!"

Morningleaf's heart pounded, thumping blood that

raced between her ears. The six warriors, a mix of stallions and mares, flew her way. Their wings pumped mightily, and their eyes squinted, leaving no area unsearched.

"Hold steady," Brackentail whispered.

The six steeds swept their necks in steady arcs from side to side, scanning the terrain. Next to her, Shadepebble whimpered.

Then Morningleaf recognized one of the stallions—it was Frostfire himself. He was leading the patrol and vivid memories assaulted her. Frostfire had promised to hide her from Nightwing and had escorted her away from Star and River Herd, but he'd lied. As soon as they were far enough away, he'd clubbed Brackentail, almost killing him, executed the handsome young stallion Summerwind, and then had his sire's flight feathers yanked out so the old stallion couldn't follow them. She blinked hard, seeing again Frostfire's white hide splattered in blood—as if the killings had just happened. The mangrove forest warped, and Morningleaf felt dizzy. Fear shot through her exhausted nerves.

"Keep it together," Brackentail rasped, staring into her eyes. "Morningleaf?"

She locked her gaze on Frostfire, her breath coming faster and faster. His one blue eye seemed to grow as she stared at it. Her vision blackened, and the mangrove forest spun. "I—I . . . help me." Morningleaf tumbled off the thick roots and splashed into the water. The sudden immersion into the warm swamp revived her enough to kick out her legs and swim, but her crash into the water had attracted Frostfire and his patrol.

They soared toward the noise, toward Morningleaf.

20

DANGERS BELOW

MORNINGLEAF PADDLED IN THE MURKY SWAMP, her chest heaving. She could not stop staring at Frostfire's one blue eye as he hurtled through the night sky—he was going to spot her, but it wasn't time. They weren't at the Swallows yet. She would ruin Brackentail's plan and get herself captured.

I won't let that happen, she thought, and she dived under the water, swimming toward the bottom. Her heart hammered her ribs, and her panicked lungs tightened, already running out of air. Something touched her, a vine, and she sputtered, swallowing water. She opened her eyes wide, searching for crocodiles, but the water swirled with mud.

A pegasus plopped into the water next to her, but it was too dark to know if it was her enemy or her friend. She twirled away from him, but he followed her and snatched her wing. She faced him; teeth bared, and then realized it was Brackentail.

He swam her through the water toward a clump of sunken roots. When they reached the roots, he spun her around so their tails were protected. Brackentail coiled back his front legs, prepared to attack anything that came their way. Morningleaf's lungs burned so badly she bucked and pointed toward the surface. Brackentail narrowed his eyes and shook his head, his mane floating around his face.

Morningleaf held still, holding her breath. She peered up through the shallow waters and could make out the shapes of pegasi swooping overhead. She strained toward the surface, but Brackentail snatched her down. Frostfire would see her if she emerged now, but she desperately needed air.

Then a slapping sound reached her ears, and from the corner of her eye, she saw a shape charge her. It was long, flat, and fast. She screamed, letting out the rest of her air, and was face-to-face with a crocodile. It snatched her wing in its mouth. Forgetting Frostfire, she surged out of the water, still screaming, but the crocodile quickly yanked her back under.

Brackentail followed and struck the reptile with his hooves as it carried Morningleaf into deeper water. She pushed her nostrils to the surface, taking a deep breath. Then the creature flipped her over and rolled her. Morningleaf twisted around and around, sinking deeper toward the swamp floor. She saw the crocodile's wide smile, but its eyes were cold and flat, even in the heat of the hunt.

Morningleaf pushed against the reptile, kicking its underbelly. It paused, and she lunged for the surface. When her ears and nose broke through, she took a breath and heard neighing—it was Shadepebble and Frostfire, arguing with each other. Then the crocodile dragged her back under and pushed her into the soft mud, resting all its weight on her.

Morningleaf struggled, terrified and about to drown. The crocodile let go of her wing, probably to get a better mouthful of her. Hooves appeared, beating the crocodile—it was Brackentail trying again to free her—but the monster ignored him. Then a huge splashing occurred around her, and she spied another crocodile. Her heart took flight. The second crocodile attacked the first, and it rolled off of her—leaving her suddenly free!

Morningleaf swam to the surface and erupted into the warm night sky, but her feathers were too wet and her wings were too tired to lift her. She bobbed in the water, gasping. Below her the crocodiles thrashed each other, fighting over which one would get to eat her. In seconds they would be after her again.

Something sharp clamped her tail, and her body rocketed backward, creating a small wake. She glanced behind her and saw that Brackentail had grabbed the base of her tail, and he was pulling her toward the shore. When her hooves reached the shallows, she galloped out of the water and onto a mangrove island. "Are you hurt?" Brackentail whinnied.

Morningleaf couldn't answer; she was busy coughing up water and mud. She couldn't feel a thing. Her muscles were numb.

Above her, Morningleaf heard Shadepebble neighing at Frostfire. "*You* are the destroyer!"

Morningleaf stared into the sky where Frostfire and his aunt, Shadepebble, hovered and argued.

"Why don't you help *us* instead of helping Nightwing?" Shadepebble asked.

Frostfire's patrol steeds surrounded the pair, and none of them were looking at Morningleaf.

"I *am* helping you," Frostfire whinnied. "Nightwing is going to destroy Star, if he hasn't already, and then he will rule Anok. Who would you rather have by Nightwing's side? Me or Petalcloud?"

"Neither," Shadepebble snapped.

"I'll make sure he's good to the herds," Frostfire argued.

Shadepebble snorted. "Oh right, *you'll* control *him*." She whipped her tail from side to side. "He'll use you to hurt us, Frostfire, just like Rockwing used you. You can't control Nightwing."

Frostfire pinned his ears.

"We have to go," Brackentail whispered into Morning-leaf's ear. "We have to get to the Swallows and follow our plan to trap Frostfire and his patrol. Shadepebble can try, but she won't convince him to let us go. Trapping Frostfire is our only hope of getting away."

Morningleaf panted, regaining her breath. Droplets of her blood leaked into the water, and she watched nervously as new crocodiles swam toward the island. "What about Shadepebble?" she whispered.

"Once Frostfire sees you, he'll forget about her. You're the target."

"Okay," Morningleaf agreed.

"I'll get his attention." Brackentail reared and leaped into the sky, flapping his big orange wings. "You should listen to Shadepebble," he whinnied to Frostfire.

Frostfire glared at Brackentail with his mismatched eyes and flicked his tail, enraged. "You again!" he rasped. Frostfire had kicked Brackentail nearly to death twice— once when he'd expelled Brackentail from Mountain Herd and once when he'd kidnapped Morningleaf in the north. It was clear from his ferocious expression that he meant to end the brown colt's life for good this time.

Morningleaf flew up beside Brackentail, showing herself. Her wing ached where the crocodile had bitten her, and she was terrified of Frostfire, but all she had to do was imagine Star's injured body and rage blazed through her like wildfire, giving her energy.

"It's the blue-winged filly," said one of Frostfire's mares, and Morningleaf recognized her. It was the buckskin sky herder named Larksong, the little mare who'd tracked Morningleaf through the lava tubes. "We can't lose her again," Larksong whinnied to Frostfire, beating her dark-blue wings.

"Now! To the Swallows," hissed Brackentail.

He and Morningleaf whirled around and bolted with the five steeds and Frostfire hot on their tails. Shadepebble

155

tore off in the other direction. Now Morningleaf's friends would execute the second half of Brackentail's plan, luring Frostfire into a trap. "This better work," Morningleaf panted, feeling doubtful.

"It will," Brackentail answered, and she followed him to the edge of the swamp where, in seconds, she would learn if that was true.

21

HERD SECRETS

THE MORNING AFTER HOOF SHARPENING, STAR, Bumblewind, Dewberry, and Clawfire trotted through the Trap looking for the mare Ashrain to learn the fighting methods of Jungle Herd.

"I thought you wanted to be a sky herder," Bumblewind said to Dewberry.

She shook her head, throwing her long mane in his face. "They don't fight. They just harass the enemy and squawk in some weird language. I didn't get it."

Bumblewind studied her, but Dewberry wouldn't meet his gaze. "They kicked you out, didn't they?" he asked.

Dewberry huffed. "They thought I was making fun of them."

"Were you?"

She narrowed her eyes.

Bumblewind nickered. "What did you expect?"

Dewberry shoved him with her wing. "You talk too much."

"*I* talk too much," he muttered. Bumblewind edged closer to her and flared his nostrils, drinking in the scent of her tousled mane.

Star trotted beside them, his eyes trained on the ground. The morning fog was thick and rolling through the forest floor like a hungry cloud, swallowing the brush. Star tripped over rocks and roots hidden in the mist. His hide was damp, and crystal beads of water dripped down his forelock. He wiped his face with his wing and halted when they reached the soft, sloping hills between River Herd's camp and Mountain Herd's camp. Star whistled for Ashrain, but there was no response.

Bumblewind trotted through the trees looking for her.

"Are you sure you heard Ashrain's instructions correctly?" Star asked Bumblewind. "She's not here."

Bumblewind halted and nickered for Ashrain, his breath turning to steam in the cold morning air. He flicked his ears, and they all paused to listen. "She said to meet her in the hills at dawn to learn how to fight from the trees." Bumblewind peered through the fog. "These are the hills, and it's dawn." He shrugged, perplexed.

"Then she's late," said Clawfire, staring at the trees.

"And we're supposed to meet her *today*?" Star asked.

Bumblewind groaned. "Yes."

Dewberry defended Bumblewind. "It's not his mistake; it's Ashrain's. She must have forgotten."

Bumblewind glanced at her, looking grateful, but Dewberry turned her back on him.

"Ouch!" Star spooked when something struck his flank, and he crashed into Clawfire. "What was that?"

Clawfire tensed. "What was *what*?" Then Clawfire whinnied when he was struck in the shoulder by a flying object.

"That," said Star, flaring his wings. Another object whipped through the trees and slammed Dewberry in the neck. She took flight, hovering over the soil, her teeth bared.

Star heard excited whispering deep in the forest and then another object, a pinecone, smacked him in the chest. "Over there," he whispered, pointing his wing.

Dewberry landed, and the four friends flattened their necks and crept through the fog, slow and steady, letting the mist veil their approach. Another pinecone shattered against Dewberry's leg, and she trembled with fury. "I will kill whoever is doing this."

"Steady," Clawfire whispered.

As Star inched forward, facing unknown danger, side by side with his herdmates—he felt again the unfamiliar sensation of contentment. He was just a regular pegasus facing a threat, and he had only his hooves, teeth, and strength to rely on—like everyone else. Why this was comforting to him, he didn't know, but he liked it. The truth was, his starfire confused him. Maybe he was better off without it.

Suddenly a flurry of pinecones rained from the heights, causing Star and his friends to scatter. "Come out where I can see you!" whinnied Dewberry, rattling her emerald feathers.

Star lifted his wings, but the trees were too tight here for him to fly. He turned in a slow circle, baring his teeth. Then he heard nickering. His friends heard it too, and the four of them galloped toward the sound, which was coming from the treetops.

Star burst through the fog and halted near the voices coming from above. He looked up and saw Ashrain. The warrior mare's eyes twinkled with mirth.

Dewberry, who was small enough to lift off in the

dense forest, darted toward the voices and hovered near Ashrain. "Very funny," she neighed, and Star knew Dewberry wanted to strike the mare, but Dewberry's curiosity distracted her. It appeared that Ashrain was standing in the tree. Behind her, several more trainees were also standing on the branches, many wing lengths above the ground.

"How are you doing that?" Clawfire asked Ashrain.

The Jungle Herd mare sobered. "If you hadn't been late to my training, you would know."

Dewberry whirled, staring down at Bumblewind. "So we *are* late," she whinnied.

Bumblewind chewed on his lip. "She said 'dawn.'"

Ashrain flicked her ears. "I said 'before dawn.'"

"Well, we're here now," Clawfire snapped. "How are you standing in those trees?"

"Come up," Ashrain said. "We broke some branches over there, making a path so you can fly." She pointed to her left.

Clawfire, Star, and Bumblewind found the path and flew up to Ashrain. They hovered, examining the four contraptions Ashrain had built in the trees.

"In Jungle Herd we call them *hoofholds*," Ashrain explained.

Clawfire flew closer. "Are they like your nests?"

"Not really," Ashrain said. "Our nests are much larger. You see these branches I've woven together? Each one holds a hoof, so I can stand in the trees and keep my balance." Ashrain flew off of them so Star and his friends could get a better look.

Star did not fully understand what he was seeing. The branches were stuck together in unnatural shapes that were strong and the perfect size to hold a hoof. "How did you make them?" Star asked.

"That part will remain a secret," Ashrain said. She glanced at her fellow Jungle Herd steeds, and they nickered to one another, thrilled to know things that River Herd did not, and Star felt heat rise in his chest.

Ashrain glanced at Dewberry. "I will say it wasn't easy," she huffed. "There are no vines here in this home you call the Trap."

"This isn't our home," Dewberry snapped, clenching her jaw. "It's not our fault there are no vines."

Clawfire interrupted. "So you won't teach us how to make a . . . hoofhold?"

Ashrain shut her mouth, thinking, and then she spoke. "No. I can't show you, but I've made you each a set so I can teach you something else."

Star peered around him and noticed dozens of empty hoofholds. He flew to a set and placed his hooves in each gathering of branches that formed four perfect hoof supports. The footings were solid, and he folded his wings, amazed. He was standing in a tree.

"Wait," Clawfire said. "Why can't you teach us how to make them?"

Dewberry interrupted. "Who cares? I'm not hiding in any stupid *hoofholds* during battle."

Star and Bumblewind gaped at her. Dewberry pinned her ears, staring at her set like it was a poisonous snake.

Ashrain nickered at her, unoffended. "You might change your mind after I show you how to use them." She glanced at Clawfire. "And it's not that I can't teach you. I won't teach you. Construction secrets belong to Jungle Herd, just like jet stream secrets belong to Desert Herd."

Clawfire considered Ashrain's words and decided not to argue. He flew to an open set of hoofholds and settled in. "Okay, so how do we use them?"

22

OUTBURST

ASHRAIN EXHALED, ANSWERING CLAWFIRE'S question about how to use the hoofholds. "I will show you."

The rest of her trainees had become antsy, shifting from hoof to hoof. Now they all settled and paid attention along with Star, Bumblewind, and Clawfire. Dewberry refused to take her place; instead she hovered, waiting, and Ashrain ignored her.

The Jungle Herd mare picked up a stone in her wing. "Our territory is similar to the Trap in one way: we have a lot of trees. We've learned to use them, like the animals do. They hide and they wait. We also hide and we wait. When the enemy comes, we kill them with rocks." She lifted the stone for all to see.

"You kill with *rocks*?" Dewberry sputtered, suddenly interested.

Ashrain nodded. "We set hoofholds all over the jungle. Our foliage is thicker there, and our feathers match the jungle leaves, so we're well camouflaged." Ashrain pointed to a nest of twigs near her front hooves, and Star saw that it was loaded with stones. "In Jungle Herd, we call this a *basket*."

"Basket," Star repeated, his tongue rolling over the strange word.

Ashrain continued. "We attack like this." Ashrain lifted a stone out of the basket and rolled it into the crook of her wing. "See that pinecone hanging?"

Star looked and saw a distant pinecone dangling from a branch. He nodded.

"Now watch me." In a blur of action, the mare cocked her wing and then hurled the rock with such force that it hit the pinecone and exploded it.

Dewberry gasped. "No way!"

Ashrain grabbed another rock and exploded another pinecone. "A well-aimed rock can kill an adult pegasus," she said. "We strike between the eyes. We can also break wings and bones with larger rocks."

"Show me how," Dewberry whinnied, her eyes bright.

Ashrain snorted. "You said it was stupid."

"Well that was before I knew I could explode stuff."

"Pick a set of hoofholds and grab a rock out of the basket," Ashrain said. "We call the big rocks *bone breakers*," she explained. "You can throw them at a warrior's legs or wings, breaking them and stopping the warrior. You don't have to have perfect aim, because the rocks are big. The little stones we call *zappers*. Zappers are for between the eyes. To kill a pegasus with one—you'll need perfect aim and maximum velocity."

"Nice," Dewberry said, and she flew to a set of hoofholds.

Ashrain flung her forelock to the side. "Notice I filled your baskets with bone breakers. There's no way you'll learn how to throw a zapper in a short time. It takes years of practice to develop the precision required."

"I doubt that," Dewberry said.

Star and Bumblewind rolled their eyes, and Clawfire jumped into the conversation. "Let's see you throw a bone breaker, Dewberry."

Dewberry selected a rock out of her basket, aimed at a dangling pinecone, and hurled it. "Ack!" The force of her throw tumbled her out of her hoofholds, and she somersaulted toward the forest floor. She spread her wings before she hit the ground, landed with a stumble, and glanced quickly toward her pinecone. It was still dangling. She'd missed it completely. "What?"

Ashrain and the other Jungle Herd steeds nickered at her. "Do you believe me now?" Ashrain asked.

Dewberry flew back up into the tree, more determined than ever. "That rock was too heavy for me. I want you to teach me how to throw the zappers."

Ashrain pinned her ears, her patience gone. "I'm not bargaining with you, Dewberry. I'm already giving up a Jungle Herd secret to protect him." She pointed at Star. "He's not even part of my herd. He's part of yours, and if Thunderwing had killed him like he was supposed to, we wouldn't be in this mess."

Absolute silence followed her words. Star's heart thrummed, and his breathing increased so quickly he felt light-headed.

Ashrain threw open her wings. "I didn't mean that," she said, distressed and looking at Star. "I don't know why I said it."

Star's sense of belonging wilted, and he felt his mood sinking. He closed his eyes, wishing he could disappear.

"I'm truly sorry," Ashrain said gently. "Look, I miss my home in the jungle. Here I'm always cold, and I'm always worried about Nightwing."

"You're scared," Clawfire stated.

"Yes," Ashrain admitted. "I guess I am."

Clawfire nodded. "We're all scared."

Ashrain flew to Star, hovering near the hoofholds where Star stood. "I didn't grow up with you. I don't really know you at all. I just know you woke Nightwing when you received your power. Sometimes it gets to me."

"You're one to complain," Dewberry snapped. "Nightwing was born to *your* herd, you know. If Star is our problem, then Nightwing is yours."

"That was four hundred years ago."

"So what!" Dewberry whinnied, narrowing her eyes. "The Destroyer is here because *your* guardian herd failed."

"Stop it," Clawfire neighed. "Neither herd can change the past." He peered at Dewberry. "Ashrain is helping us. She's offering us her herd secrets, and this rock throwing will be useful in the Trap. We can hide and snipe our enemies before they see us. It's brilliant."

"You're right about the past," Ashrain agreed. "We can't change it."

Dewberry huffed, and Star opened his eyes. Ashrain was staring at him, looking concerned and bashful at the same time. "Please accept my apology," she said.

Star glanced at Bumblewind. The pinto yearling nodded encouragement. Star exhaled. "I accept."

The steeds around Star relaxed.

"Can we get back to exploding stuff?" Dewberry asked.

Ashrain nodded and showed them how to cradle the stones in their wings, how to engage their shoulder muscles in the throw, and how to aim with one eye closed.

Star practiced with his friends and slowly began to feel better, but the truth was there and wouldn't go away: he would never completely fit in with the pegasi of Anok. He would always be different.

23

THE SWALLOWS

MORNINGLEAF SOARED BEHIND BRACKENTAIL. They dodged trees and skimmed the crocodile-infested water, luring Frostfire and his patrol toward the Swallows, where Brackentail planned to trap him. Her breathing filled her ears, and her heart raced away in her chest. The distant volcano Firemouth belched again, causing the water below her hooves to ripple. Morningleaf's wing throbbed where the crocodile had bitten her. In her peripheral vision she saw Frostfire gaining on them. Shadepebble had fled. "Hurry!" she whinnied to Brackentail.

He flapped his wings faster.

"I won't lose you two again," Frostfire neighed. He pinned his wings and shot forward, aiming for Morningleaf.

Morningleaf tucked her tail, imagining Frostfire's hot breath on her flank. She peeked over her shoulder and gasped. His eyes gleamed, and his lips curled back, exposing his big white teeth. He drew back his front hooves to strike, and the moonlight reflected off their sharp edges.

She tucked her wings and plummeted, dropping altitude to gain speed. Sweat erupted between her ears and dripped down her face. The pain from her injuries sapped her strength, and she leaked a trail of blood and sweat into the swamp.

Ahead of her, Brackentail swept under the thick layer of trees he'd pointed out to her from the cloud forest. A small island appeared in the middle of the swamp, and its center was clear of trees. "Here it is," Brackentail hissed. "The Swallows." He landed and motioned her toward him.

Morningleaf touched down with a hard stumble. Brackentail trotted forward and pointed at an expanse of flat, treeless mud. "We want Frostfire in there," he said, panting and pointing. "We're going to lure him and his patrol into the sucking sand."

Morningleaf nodded. Brackentail had explained to her that the dark mud called the Swallows would sink their enemies and trap them, but the flat ground looked harmless to her. She and Brackentail whipped around to face

Frostfire and his small patrol as they landed behind them.

"I'm surprised to see you back in the jungle," Frostfire said to Morningleaf, winking his one blue eye. "Did you miss me?"

Morningleaf pinned her ears, ready to charge him, her mind spinning with horrific memories of the lava tubes where he'd held her prisoner. Sometimes at night she dreamed about the tubes, and the dreams were so real she could feel the claws of the rats as they skittered over her body, and she could smell the putrid bat guano on her feathers.

Brackentail blocked her, holding her back with his wings and whispering into her ears. "No. Stick with the plan."

She trembled and her gut churned angrily, but Brackentail's words reached her, and she took a deep gulp of warm air, calming herself.

Frostfire stepped closer, followed by Larksong and his patrol. Larksong pricked her ears, ever curious and utterly fearless. "Where is Star?" she asked Morningleaf.

"I'll never tell you."

"If *she's* here, Star must be close," Larksong said to Frostfire.

Frostfire pawed the soil and advanced toward

Morningleaf. "I can make you tell me. Where is Star?"

Morningleaf fought the urge to strike him, but Frostfire was too powerful for her, and Brackentail had a plan, however crazy it sounded. She backed closer to the swallowing ground.

"Careful," Brackentail warned under his breath.

Morningleaf fluttered her wings, lifted a feather's length off the soil, and hovered. Brackentail also lifted off.

A hidden signal from Frostfire sent his patrol galloping forward.

"Retreat to the trees," Brackentail whinnied, keeping his voice loud enough for the patrol to hear him. He and Morningleaf flew low, just over the Swallows, their hooves skimming the sandy mud as they headed to the dense forest on the other side.

The warriors charged forward on hoof, not wasting time to lift off because Morningleaf and Brackentail were not racing for the sky. And this was Brackentail's plan, to keep Frostfire and his patrol on the ground.

Morningleaf thoughts spun. If this didn't work, they'd be captured.

Suddenly an angry squeal sounded behind Morningleaf, followed by the distraught thrashing and neighing of Frostfire and his companions.

"Land here," Brackentail said to her, excited. He dropped to the ground on the other side of the Swallows. Morningleaf touched down next to him and turned. Her breath hitched in her throat. Frostfire and the others were sinking. "H-how?" she stuttered.

Brackentail arched his neck, pleased. "The ground looks solid, but it's not. It's a mixture of sand and water. Heavy creatures sink fast, and that's why Jungle Herd calls it the Swallows."

"How did you know about this?" Morningleaf asked.

Brackentail shrugged. "The elders mentioned it once, referring to some battle many years ago. You see, I wasn't always fooling around during story time."

"Help us!" Frostfire whinnied to his one stallion who had not plunged into the Swallows. That stallion snatched Frostfire's wing and tried to pull him out but couldn't budge him. Frostfire had sunk in up to his belly. So had Larksong. Two stallions closer to the edge had not sunk in as deep, yet.

"Stop struggling," Larksong snapped. "You're making it worse."

"Time to go," Brackentail whispered to Morningleaf. He darted out of the swamp with Morningleaf close behind him. They hovered over the Swallows for a moment, watching the loose stallion toss a long branch to Frostfire. Frostfire snatched one end of it, and his warrior slowly began to pull him toward solid ground. "We don't have much time," Brackentail rasped. He looked up. "Where's Shadepebble?"

Morningleaf whistled, loud and clear, the signal of a lead mare to gather her herd. It was a call she'd learned from her dam, Silverlake. Relief followed when Morningleaf saw the unmistakable glint of Shadepebble's pink feathers in the moonlight.

"You're safe?" Shadepebble whinnied.

"Just barely," Morningleaf gasped.

The three joined, creating a small V formation with Brackentail taking the headwind, and they sailed northeast, toward home.

"I thought we were all goners," Shadepebble cried.

Brackentail nodded and glanced at Morningleaf. She noticed his heaving chest and the frothy sweat that had gathered between his back legs. His stress reminded her that he'd also been terrorized by Frostfire, not once but twice. She flew closer to him. "You did well," she said, praising him.

Brackentail blinked at her, looking stunned but proud.

"You saved my life," she added. He'd saved her several

times on this mission. Her jumbled thoughts about him began to clear. Everyone in River Herd said Brackentail would do anything to protect her, and maybe they were right. Could it be that he'd been guarding her since they were foals? That all his bullying of Star had been to keep *her* safe?

Morningleaf glanced at Brackentail flying beside her, noticing how golden his eyes appeared in the moonlight. He was growing into a powerful and smart young stallion. His dull brown coat had shed, revealing a glossy hide, and his weedy mane and tail were now thick and straight, and his tail would soon reach the ground. She sighed, feeling grateful, and a little bit confused. Star had a strong and dedicated supporter in Brackentail, and it seemed, so did she.

After several hours of flying, Morningleaf's heart calmed, and exhaustion made her wings feel heavy. "I need to rest," she whinnied.

Brackentail dropped, leading them into the rain forest. They were still in Jungle Herd's territory, but far from Frostfire. Brackentail landed them on the shores of a wide, deep river.

Morningleaf's friends rushed toward her as soon as her hooves touched the soil. "You're hurt," Shadepebble cried, noticing Morningleaf's torn feathers. She examined the crocodile bite, and Morningleaf winced. "We need to clean this wound," Shadepebble said to her. "Let's soak your wing in the river."

"No!" neighed Morningleaf and Brackentail at the same time.

Shadepebble glanced at the water. It was flat and calm on top, but below were crocodiles, flesh-eating fish, and poisonous water snakes. "Right, I forgot where we are."

Brackentail looked up. "It will rain soon; it always does. Then we can wash the wound and drink out of those cupped leaves over there." He pointed his wing toward a set of trees with broad foliage capable of catching and holding the raindrops.

The air was moist and hot as dark clouds rolled over the sky. Morningleaf pranced, her ears pricked for danger. "I need to lie down."

"I'll scout the area," Brackentail said, glancing around them and then trotting away.

A snake slithered out of the foliage, disturbed by his hooves. It was as long as Morningleaf and spotted like a leopard. "Watch out!" Morningleaf whinnied to Shade-pebble. The two fillies lifted off and hovered a wing length above the snake. It slid forward, flicking the air with its tongue. Morningleaf exhaled, relieved. It was just a con-strictor, and too small to harm them. She touched down, feeling weak. She noticed her muscles quivering outside of her control.

The snake twisted past them and slid into the river, then Shadepebble landed. "Are you all right?" she asked Morningleaf, gently touching her back. "You don't look so good."

Sudden dizziness threw Morningleaf off balance. Already weak, she staggered into Shadepebble. "Not again," Morningleaf whispered, and then she slammed onto her side and everything went black.

24

FRIENDS

THE SOUND OF RAIN PELTING THE LEAVES WOKE
Morningleaf. She was curled into a ball and lying in a
thicket of ferns. A warm body pressed against her back,
and an orange-feathered wing covered her, protecting
her from the rain. She lurched upright, confused. The
last thing she remembered was the world fading to black.
"What happened?"

"Don't get up," a deep voice murmured. It was Brackentail.

Morningleaf obeyed but not because she wanted to.
Her head was dizzy, and her thoughts were swimming in
circles.

"When was the last time you ate?" Brackentail asked.

Morningleaf shook her head. "I can't remember."

"I sent Shadepebble to gather pineapples for you."

Morningleaf shuddered. "No. She shouldn't be alone. What if Frostfire has gotten unstuck and spots her?"

"We're far, far from Frostfire," Brackentail soothed. "And we can't leave here until you're strong enough to fly."

Morningleaf stared into his golden eyes, noticing dark-brown flecks around their rims. "Why did she go and not you?"

Brackentail shook his head. "She insisted I stay to protect you."

"I don't need protecting." Morningleaf staggered to her hooves. "This is *my* mission."

Brackentail lowered his ears. "Are you angry at me?"

Morningleaf swayed and propped herself against a tree. Her belly grumbled. The pineapples could not come fast enough. Sweat dripped down her face, and she was shedding feathers all over the thick undergrowth of plants on the ground. Why was she angry? She bit her lip. She was bruised from the crocodile attack, and her muscles were exhausted. But she wasn't angry about that.

She faced Brackentail; her gaze raking across his large-boned brown frame and his golden eyes full of concern. She sidled away from him and blurted, "I'm not mad at you. I'm not mad at anyone. . . . I want Star."

Brackentail exhaled like she'd kicked him.

Just then Shadepebble trotted into the thicket. "Here's breakfast." She dumped a wingful of pineapples at their hooves.

Morningleaf and Brackentail ignored her, staring at each other. Morningleaf saw hurt lurking behind his lashes, but he blinked, erasing it. He spoke, his voice flat. "If you want Star, then let's hurry home, but please eat first."

"What's this about Star?" Shadepebble asked, looking from one friend to the other.

"I just miss him," Morningleaf grumbled. She dropped her head, crushed a pineapple with her hoof, and then bit into it, peeling back its spiny hide. The fruit inside was sweet and delicious. After she ate her fill, her thoughts cleared and she felt renewed. She stared at Brackentail, horrified that she'd snapped at him. He was only trying to help. "I'm sorry."

His eyes met her gaze. "I know. You just want Star." Again his words concealed deeper feelings.

Morningleaf exhaled and trotted close to him. She had almost no memories of Star that didn't also include bad memories of Brackentail. Her thoughts swam through her head. She didn't know what they all meant, but she realized she needed to make room in her heart for both of them. Brackentail was no longer Star's enemy, or hers; he'd proved it several times over, and she wasn't betraying Star to befriend him. No, of course she wasn't.

Morningleaf stepped forward with her head low, and Brackentail held his breath, watching her. Shadepebble dropped her pineapple, glancing from one friend to the other. Morningleaf lowered her muzzle to Brackentail's, her nostrils quivering. He stiffened, waiting to see what she would do. Morningleaf blew softly into his nose, exchanging breath with him, memorizing his scent, and bonding herself to him like she had with her other friends when they were foals.

Brackentail softened, then exhaled, bonding himself to her too.

Shadepebble cocked her head but looked pleased.

Morningleaf wrapped her aqua wings around Brackentail's neck and squeezed him tight, speaking no words.

Slowly each muscle relaxed, and he curled his neck around hers.

Morningleaf released him and looked at Shadepebble. "Let's go home."

The three friends finished eating the pineapples and

then lifted off, flying northeast, toward the Trap, and Star. Morningleaf's mission was successful; the Ice Warriors and the Black Army had spotted her, and she'd triggered rumors that Star's body was in the south. She set her gaze on the horizon and hoped that when she arrived, Star would be alive . . . and awake.

25

TO FALL IS TO DIE

STAR GRAZED WITH HIS FRIENDS IN RIVER HERD'S camp, feeling alert but self-conscious. Several days had passed since Ashrain's outburst about Star's guardian herd failing to kill him as a foal, and news of it had spread through the herds. The steeds appeared divided on how they felt about Star. Half encouraged him with kind words, and the other half avoided his gaze as though they shared Ashrain's sentiments—that the herds would be better off if Star had been executed as planned—but none were willing to join forces with Nightwing. They remained united against their common enemy, and they were determined to protect Star from the two armies that hunted him.

The sound of galloping hooves crashed through the

fallen pine needles. Star threw up his head, pricking his ears and flaring his nostrils. A pegasus was coming.

Seconds later, Echofrost burst into view. "Listen! Gather 'round," she whinnied.

Silverlake and Hazelwind and hundreds of River Herd pegasi snaked through the trees toward her voice. When most of the herd had appeared, Echofrost continued. "Two of our spies returned," she said. "The Ice Warriors are on the move, on their way to Desert Herd's territory, and the Black Army spotted Morningleaf in the swamps by the Valley of Tears."

Star's heart thudded with excitement. "Morningleaf's plan is working."

"Yes," said Echofrost.

"But is there news of *her*?" asked Star, his nerves twisting inside him. Two armies had spotted her, but where was she now?

Echofrost lowered her head. "No, there's no news of her." She took a breath; Morningleaf was her friend too. "But I think she's safe. Our spies would know if she'd been captured. She would have been taken prisoner and probably questioned by Nightwing. We're watching him as close as we dare, and he doesn't have her."

"What is Nightwing doing?" asked Silverlake.

"He keeps his distance from the pegasi who follow him," said Echofrost. "He orders them where to eat and where to sleep; he rarely flies. Mostly he stands and scents the winds. He's just waiting."

Star shuddered. Nightwing was waiting for news of him. With their starfire connection severed, Nightwing couldn't feel Star. He didn't know if Star was dead or healing from his injuries, which explained why Nightwing wanted his head—its removal from his body would disable Star's ability to heal, would render his immortality useless.

Star flattened his ears at the thought. If he was to beat Nightwing, he'd have to destroy him completely—turn him to ash. But Star didn't know how to do that. His silver fire had failed to defeat the ancient stallion, and then Nightwing had erected his shield against it. Star was missing something about his power; he knew that, but he didn't know what it was. There had to be a way to beat Nightwing. Good was supposed to be stronger than evil. His guardian herd believed it, had faith in it, but was it true? Or was Star not *good enough*?

Hazelwind interrupted his thoughts. "With Petalcloud and Frostfire in the south looking for you, we'll have more time to train the United Army," he said.

"I'll call a council meeting tonight," said Silverlake. "This is good news, but it will only delay the inevitable. When the armies don't find Star in the south, they'll resume their hunt, heading north I'm sure." She shook her head, looking *more* dejected, not less.

Bumblewind nuzzled Star. "Come on, that big red Desert Herd steed is teaching ground fighting. Let's go learn."

Star folded his wings, also feeling dejected. He'd hoped for better news, for a sighting of Morningleaf, something to ease his mind about her.

"She hasn't been captured," Bumblewind said as if reading Star's thoughts.

"You're right. We'd hear about it. Let's go to the training."

Star followed Bumblewind to the training grounds. When they arrived, Redfire was already teaching. Star settled, listening as the leader of the Desert Herd camp lifted his head. "All battles eventually end up on the ground," Redfire said.

Star studied Redfire as he spoke. The foreign stallion's coat shimmered like the veins of copper that streaked through river rocks. He had a large white star on his forehead and his feathers were dark gold. He sported the tiny waist and the deep chest of the Desert Herd pegasi, but he was exceptionally tall, like a long shadow at dusk. His voice projected loudly but with a soft vibration that Star had noticed with all the Desert Herd steeds. "Wings tire before legs," he said, "and if you don't know how to fight on land, you won't prevail. In Desert Herd we ground-train before we sky-train." Redfire's confident authority caused all the young steeds to stand a little taller.

"More herd secrets," Dewberry whispered.

Star's hide prickled. Desert Herd and Jungle Herd steeds were willing to give up their herd secrets to protect him, and Star's emotions about this bounced between embarrassment and awe.

Redfire continued, gazing at each one of them. "We learned our ground-fighting techniques by studying the land horses that live in our territory."

"Horses?" nickered a yearling.

Redfire pinned his ears. "Horses aren't the meek creatures you think they are. They avoid conflict whenever possible, but they will fight, and they do."

"I've never seen a horse up close," Dewberry whispered.

"I have," Star whispered back. "During my first migration, when I was a weanling and still a dud, a herd of horses joined us when we got trapped in a forest fire. They're lightning fast."

"That was the fire that killed the elder mare Mossberry, right?"

"Yes," Star said, his ears drooping. "She wasn't fast enough."

Redfire called Hazelwind over to him but kept his eyes on the trainees. "When you're standing on the ground, your kicks pack more power than they do when you're flying because you have leverage," he explained. "And your strength evolves naturally from your stance. If you're off balance, you'll fall—and to fall is to die."

Redfire murmured something to Hazelwind. The two walked a few paces apart and then faced each other. "Watch Hazelwind's legs," Redfire ordered the trainees. Then he galloped forward and rammed Hazelwind low, in the rib cage, knocking him over. "You see how his stance was narrow?"

Star and the others nodded, but Star was embarrassed because he hadn't noticed anything unusual about Hazelwind's stance. He glanced at Bumblewind with questioning eyes.

The pinto shrugged. "I didn't see it either," he muttered.

"Pay attention," Dewberry snapped. "Redfire is the top captain in the Desert Herd army. He's never lost a battle." Dewberry sighed, staring at Redfire.

Bumblewind pinned his ears at her. "How do you know all this?"

"Because I pay attention to things that matter," she rasped. "Now stop talking."

Bumblewind crossed his wings, sullen. Star focused on the lesson.

Redfire waited for Hazelwind to stand up, then he continued. "Because his stance was narrow, Hazelwind was easy to knock down. Let's try again."

This time Hazelwind widened his legs and lowered his haunches. Redfire rammed him again in the same place. Hazelwind remained standing. "See the difference?"

This time Star did see the difference.

"When on land, always be ready for a strike," Redfire neighed. "You're weakest when you're off guard. Most warriors will pause to survey a battle. When your enemy's head rises, his stance narrows, and this is the time to strike him. If you need to survey the battle yourself, do it from the air. Every moment on the ground, unless you're fighting, keep your necks low and legs wide. And don't forget—when you see a warrior with his head up, ram him.

As soon as he falls, break his neck or his skull quickly. To fall is to die, that goes for your enemy too. Clawfire will teach deathblows tomorrow."

Star's heart raced as he imagined himself on a battlefield, surrounded by his foes and friends.

Redfire continued. "We'll practice the stance in a minute, but first I want to show you how to kick." Redfire pranced, and his trainees circled him, their attention tight and focused. "I'm going to use this tree as my enemy." Redfire pointed to a medium-sized fir tree. "This kick I'm about to throw would kill Hazelwind, and I don't want to do that, at least not today." He said this with a flash of teeth, reminding everyone that this truce in the Trap was temporary.

"He is awesome," Dewberry simpered, and Bumblewind huffed.

Redfire faced the tree; it was old and dry and had few branches on its lower half. "Don't blink," he said to the trainees.

In a flurry of golden feathers, Redfire whirled, slammed the tree with both back hooves, and snapped the trunk in half. The tree tumbled over, almost crushing a young mare who scurried out of its way.

"Did that hurt your hooves?" Dewberry asked, trotting

boldly forward to inspect the damage.

"Nope, but I can't speak for the tree."

Star exhaled. He was larger than most steeds, and he wondered if he could break a tree in half. "I want to try," he said.

Redfire swiveled his head. "You will. You all will. This is a kick we rarely use in the sky, but on the ground it's quite effective. Done correctly, it can stop a heart, fracture legs, and snap ribs. Or you can use it to toss steeds out of your way or into other steeds. But it's dangerous too because it involves putting your back to your opponent. You can't miss. To miss is to die."

Star noticed the rounded eyes of the yearling students, especially the fillies. They seemed in awe of the glossy stallion with the brilliant gold feathers.

"Just don't try this kick in battle unless you know you won't miss," he reiterated. "Now let's practice it. Everyone find a tree."

Star turned in a circle, scanning the area looking for a suitable tree. A second later he was thrown off his hooves, and he toppled onto the ground with a grunt.

"Your neck was up," Hazelwind said with an amused nicker.

Star spit out dirt and mud and glared at the buckskin

stallion who trotted away and rammed another unsuspecting yearling. Star watched Redfire ram Bumblewind. Dewberry slammed into a Jungle Herd filly, sending her sprawling across the pine needles. "Hey," the filly snapped.

"To fall is to die," Dewberry jeered, and she tore off to knock down another steed.

"We're supposed to be practicing the kick," a young stallion complained.

Redfire whinnied over the confusion. "I told all of you to watch your stance when on the ground. Your attackers aren't going to warn you they're coming."

"But we're not in a battle," complained the Jungle Herd filly, spitting dirt.

Redfire narrowed his eyes. "That's the final lesson for today, warriors: you are *always* in battle."

The pegasi spread out and continued to practice ramming and kicking.

Star kicked the same tree over and over until his hooves were too sore to continue. He couldn't break it in half, not yet, but he left severe dents in the bark. As he practiced, he remained watchful of his stance on the ground because Bumblewind, Redfire, and Dewberry playfully rammed him several more times—but each time Star stayed upright.

Eventually Redfire announced a break. "Spread out and graze," he whinnied.

Star stretched his wings and considered taking a nap. He wasn't tired or hungry, but his hooves ached. He glanced down at them and noticed he'd chipped the sharp edge off his left hind hoof. "Blasted tree," he grumbled.

Suddenly, a gray figure trotted into his line of vision and halted in front of him. It was Silverlake, and she nickered for Star to follow her. Bumblewind and Dewberry were arguing nearby, paying no attention to him. Curious, Star followed the gray mare into the woods.

26

ADVICE

STAR FOLLOWED SILVERLAKE FOR SEVERAL MIN-
utes before she halted and turned around. He cantered to
her quickly, closing the distance between them and bury-
ing his muzzle in her mane.

Silverlake exhaled, exchanging breath with him
and drinking in his scent. They hadn't spent much time
together since he'd lost the battle with Nightwing a moon
ago. "I know you're practicing, but may I speak with you?"
she asked.

"Of course, we're taking a break anyway." He nodded
toward the training ground. "Let's walk and talk."

Silverlake led the way, and Star followed closely. Her
strong flanks rocked back and forth as she moved, and her

beautiful silver feathers, still shiny and bright in spite of her age, reflected the thin rays of sunshine that pierced the overhanging branches. Star felt like a foal again, following his mother, trusting her, and feeling safe with her. His grief for her lost mate, Thundersky, and his intense love for her crashed through him, and he was shocked when his eyes suddenly filled with tears.

Silverlake flicked her ears, listening to Star cry, letting him do this without comment, and she walked on, patiently waiting for him to finish.

When his sniffling subsided, Silverlake halted and wiped his face dry with her wing. She said nothing at first, and in her presence, Star's pent-up feelings overwhelmed him. "I miss Morningleaf," he said, his breath hitching. "And I'm scared," he admitted. "But not for me, for all of you."

"Don't be afraid for me," Silverlake said gently. "When I die, I'll be with Thundersky and my friends."

Star choked on his gasping breath, remembering what she didn't know, that Thundersky's soul was trapped in the Beyond along with the other steeds Nightwing had murdered.

"What is it?" Silverlake asked him.

"Nothing . . . everything," Star said, hating to withhold

the truth from her. Thousands of steeds were stuck in the Beyond and would remain there until Nightwing was vanquished. But Star could not tell her that. The golden meadow was the solace of every living pegasi. Knowing that they would reunite with their friends and live in peace was what made death bearable to them all.

Star took a deep breath. "What did you want to speak to me about?"

Silverlake resumed walking, but now she turned her head and looked at Star. Her eyes were also wet with tears. "You're growing up, Star, and your stallion blood is coursing through your veins. Can you feel it?"

Star nodded. He'd noticed new desires developing—his sudden interest in battle and a calling to return home, to his birthland. "The feelings are powerful," he admitted.

"It's normal, Star. It's all part of growing up." Silverlake swished at the mosquitos troubling her. They were nearing a shallow creek where the annoying bugs thrived in large colonies. "And I've been watching you train. I think you're well suited for battle."

Star pricked his ears, and his chest puffed with pride.

"But I don't think you should attempt it."

Star's ears drooped. "Why?"

"For three reasons. First, I don't think you'll like it.

It's not the thrilling thing the warriors pretend it is."

"Thrilling?" Star huffed. "No one pretends that." But the truth was, the yearlings were all excited and scared, which was kind of thrilling, and Star was one of them.

Silverlake ignored his comment. "Second, you might be tempted, or forced, to use your starfire—and then Nightwing will know exactly where you are."

Star tossed his long forelock out of his eyes. "No. I won't use it."

Silverlake narrowed her eyes. "You can't promise that. In the heat of battle, warriors react; they don't think."

Star grunted, but he couldn't argue, having never been in a battle.

"Third, if we lose, you'll be delivered to Nightwing, and the winning steed will make a pact with him."

"I won't let them turn me in," Star whinnied, thinking of his head and knowing what they planned to do with it. "I'll blast any steed who tries it."

Silverlake exhaled. "See, that just proves my point. If you use your starfire, then we're back to reason number two: Nightwing will be able to locate you, and you'll undo everything Morningleaf has done to keep you safe. You'll end up captured. But my point is, you can't be captured if you're gone."

"Gone? What do you mean?"

"I think you must leave Anok."

"What?" Star's taut wings collapsed at his sides. "Leave Anok?"

Silverlake nodded.

"No. I can't do that. I've been training. I know how to fight."

Silverlake walked close to him and pressed her forehead against his. Star leaned into her, smelling her long-familiar scent.

"Yes, but you'll grow even stronger in time," she said. "And then you can return, but for now I think you should go."

Star reared away from her, his heart thudding. His starfire flared deep inside him, and he spun in a circle, outrage searing his veins. She was suggesting he abandon the herds. His hide sparkled, and Silverlake's eyes rounded.

"Please calm down," she whispered, trying to soothe him. "This is only to protect you."

Star opened his mouth to speak and a spark fell to the soil, sizzling a dry pine needle.

"Please," Silverlake nickered, waving her wings and speaking to him as she would speak to a terrified foal, only *she* was the one who was terrified. Her eyes drifted to the flash of clear sky visible overhead, as if Nightwing were already on his way from the Blue Mountains.

Star closed his mouth and his eyes. His body trembled, and the starfire shot through his veins like liquid lightning. He wanted to explode the trees. He squeezed his eyes tighter and focused on his breathing. He had to quell the fire before it gave him away, but Silverlake had caught him off guard with her request. She meant well. He knew that. He took deep breaths and cajoled the starfire back into his gut, folding it into that ever-ready ember that burned day and night. He shook his mane, opened his eyes, and stared into Silverlake's. He folded his wings and said, "I won't go. Don't ask me again."

"Star," she gasped.

"I've heard you," he said. "But I won't abandon the herds to Nightwing."

"But—"

Star held up his wing. "I understand what you're saying. That I should stay away and grow up and practice with the starfire, maybe become stronger than Nightwing, and then return—but that would take, what, a hundred years or more? And by then you'll all be dead."

"It's about saving the *future* pegasi of Anok, not about saving us."

Star flattened his ears. "You *are* the future, Silverlake. Tell me this: What will I find if I return in a hundred years or more?"

She clenched her jaw, not answering.

"I'll tell you what. I'll find a herd of dull beasts, slaves of Nightwing, pegasi afraid of their own shadows. You'll be turned into a herd of horses—mindlessly following one stallion."

Silverlake ruffled her feathers, listening, saying nothing.

"I won't go."

"But how will you defeat him? You can't help us if you're dead."

Star reeled at the truth of her words and then narrowed his eyes. "I have the Ancestors on my side. He's afraid of them. I—" Star paused. "I can't promise you anything, Silverlake, but I won't leave. Your fate is my fate. I'll . . . I'll submit myself to him, if I have to. If he enslaves you, he enslaves me."

They stared at each other for a long time. Her dark eyes were sad and hollow. She'd risked her position as lead mare to hide him, her filly's life to nurse him, and she'd lost her mate when he woke the Destroyer. Star respected her and her advice, but she was wrong, and he was hurt that she'd suggested it to him, *as if he would consider abandoning his herd.*

Silverlake blinked slowly and then exhaled, her back sagging under her folded wings. "All right," she said. "I have to trust you."

He turned to leave.

"Star?"

"What?"

"Do you at least believe me about the starfire? You must learn to control it."

"I believe you," he said, and trotted through the forest, back toward Redfire and the others.

27

MISSING

TEN DAYS HAD PASSED SINCE ECHOFROST HAD
brought news from the spies that both armies—the Ice
Warriors and the Black Army—had left the north. The
short spring season had quickly erupted into summer.
Long hours of daylight were followed by short nights, and
the pegasi were exhausted. Star trained, rested, and worried about Morningleaf. One morning he returned from
the drinking creek and noticed his friends were not in
River Herd's camp. "Where are the other yearlings?" Star
asked Sweetroot, who was sorting herbs nearby.

The medicine mare swiveled her head, peering through
the trees. "Maybe they're at warrior training," she said
as she worked. Sweetroot spent hours gathering, tasting,

and testing foreign plants for their medicinal qualities—
assisting the United Army in her own way.

"No," Star said. "That's not until later."

"Umm," Sweetroot mumbled. She was gingerly chewing and spitting out a selection of leaves and making all
sorts of sour faces as she did so.

Star nickered. "Do you ever get sick from testing
plants?"

"Sick?" She rolled her eyes. "Twice I've almost died.
Sometimes the strongest medicines are the most toxic."

Star unfolded his wings and swiveled his ears, listening. The Trap was silent except for the chirping of the
birds and the quiet nickering of the nursing mares. Most
of the adults had gathered to search for new food sources.
The terrain around each herd's camp had been trampled
into mud. Most of the moss, lower leaves, and edible bark
had been stripped from the trees and all the pine nuts and
first birds' eggs consumed.

"That Redfire is a popular steed," Sweetroot said.
"Maybe your friends are in the Desert Herd camp listening to his stories again."

Last night Redfire had entertained the yearlings with
Desert Herd legends, mostly about Raincloud, the filly
who'd lived four hundred years ago. She'd been friends

with Nightwing before he received his power. Redfire had shared details of her lineage, her flying skills, and her fierce love for Spiderwing to a transfixed group of steeds, mostly fillies. Star was there but not listening, because thoughts of Morningleaf had besieged him. How she would have loved to hear Redfire's tales about the ancient mare Raincloud, one of Morningleaf's favorite heroes.

Then, when Redfire was finished, Echofrost had shared the story about Morningleaf riding the jet streams to escape Frostfire. The foreign steeds, especially the ones from Mountain Herd, had overwhelmed Echofrost with questions about Morningleaf, and it was as though she were a legend too, like Raincloud. Star left the gathering feeling depressed. He wanted Morningleaf back; she'd been gone too long.

"You're probably right," Star said to Sweetroot. "I'll check the Desert Herd camp." He tucked his wings onto his back and trotted into the depths of the trees. It was dank and foggy, and the spongy lichen squished beneath his hooves. He followed the beaten path from River Herd's camp to Desert Herd's. Along the way he passed Jungle Herd. Ashrain spotted him and waved her wing.

"Star!"

Star tucked his tail and halted, spinning slightly to

face the wiry bay mare. He pranced from hoof to hoof, hoping Ashrain wouldn't take up too much of his time. Star glanced up and saw that most of the Jungle Herd steeds were napping in their nests.

Ashrain joined Star on the path. "If you have some time, we could go to the hoofholds and practice rock throwing."

"Just us?" Star asked. He'd had many lessons since warrior training began, and he enjoyed throwing the rocks.

Ashrain nodded. "Hazelwind, Clawfire, and I have been watching you, and it's what you're best at."

Star's ears grew hot with the praise. He was thrilled, but also embarrassed. All the younger pegasi wanted battle positions, and Clawfire had already chosen Bumblewind to fight alongside him, but Star hadn't taken to ground fighting. It looked like he would be a sniper. Star sighed. "I understand."

As if reading his mind, Ashrain nickered. "You have the largest wings, incredible strength, and good aim, Star. The ground warriors need pegasi like you in the trees. You'll see."

Star nodded.

Ashrain continued. "Hazelwind asked me to spend

extra time with you, and you won't be training with any-one else from here forward. Once those armies realize you aren't in the south, they'll come here." She scented the air as if sniffing for them. "Come with me; I've been collecting the biggest stones for you to practice with."

Star was pleased that Ashrain had noticed him and wanted to use him in battle, unlike Silverlake, who wanted him to run away. "I would like that, but first I need to find my friends."

"Are they missing?"

"I'm not sure. I left for a drink, and when I came back they were gone."

"Well, they aren't here," said Ashrain, looking around. "But I'll help you look for them."

Star broke into a slow canter, with Ashrain follow-ing. He unfurled his wings and let them trail behind him, open but not dragging. Everything inside him itched to fly, to feel the dizzying thrill of lifting into the heights and cruising over the land, higher than the birds. The desire pulsed, aching like an open wound, but the only balm was to lift off, and he couldn't risk being spotted. The two armies had moved south, but they'd left scouts behind, circling the sky.

Star's wings twitched in response to his thoughts.

He knew his friends felt the same way, and so did all the pegasi who were hiding. They all wanted to fly, and the stress of living on the ground was building in the herds like a storm. "Maybe they're flying," he said to Ashrain.

The mare flexed her wings. "I wouldn't blame them if they were, but let's hope not. The sky isn't safe. I'm getting worried."

"So am I." Star flattened his neck and galloped faster, hoping his friends were near. He had no idea where to search, but he doubted the yearlings would abandon the protection of the forest, no matter how strong the urge to fly. Star chose a path that lead deeper into the Trap, where it was darker and denser.

He glanced above him at the interwoven canopy of branches that blocked out the sun, the rain, and his view of the sky. If a predator attacked him and Ashrain, their only hope would be to outrun it. Star shook off these thoughts and picked up his pace, dodging branches as he followed a thin deer trail. Ashrain's even breathing and the rhythmic cadence of her hooves soothed him.

After a while the two pegasi halted to drink from a puddle of rainfall. "I hear something," said Ashrain.

Star pricked his ears, and the sounds of excited nickering reached him. "I think it's my friends," he said. Star and Ashrain galloped toward the voices.

There was sunlight ahead, not much, but enough to indicate a small clearing. The noise was coming from there. Star and Ashrain cantered toward it, and Star saw his friends standing in a circle, fluttering their wings and speaking all at once.

"What's happening?" Star asked.

"Star? Is that you?" said a voice in the center of the circle.

Star pricked his ears, his heart suddenly pounding. He knew that voice.

"We're back," she said.

As if his thoughts had created her, Morningleaf stepped out of the circle.

28

REVELATIONS

STAR STARED AT MORNINGLEAF, BLINKING IN DIS-
belief. Brackentail and Shadepebble stood with her; all
three had safely returned from their mission. Star bleated
like a foal, the youthful noise erupting from the depths of
his throat before he could stop it. "Morningleaf!" He cantered toward her.

"Star!" She bolted his way.

The two loped across the clearing and slammed into
each other.

"You're alive; you're awake," she cried.

Star couldn't speak. He buried his muzzle in her neck
and drank in her scent. She was thin, and her muscles
had hardened from traveling. She smelled of dirt and

blood. "You're hurt?"

"I'm fine," she nickered. "You—how are you?"

"Never better," he whispered. Her amber eyes glowed, and he basked in her gaze, losing himself in the depths of her eyes.

Bumblewind and Echofrost trotted to Morningleaf and greeted her. Brackentail and Shadepebble stood near, looking tired. Star greeted them with soft nickers.

"Morningleaf's mission was successful," Brackentail said.

"Yes, we heard news of it from our scouts," said Bumblewind. "She lured the armies away."

Star took a deep breath, imagining the excitement and dangers Morningleaf, Shadepebble, and Brackentail must have encountered. "Tonight you can tell us all about it, at the gathering, but for now you should eat and rest."

"What gathering?" Shadepebble asked.

"The herds in the Trap are working together. We formed a United Army," Bumblewind answered. "We're training together, and the last few nights we've all gathered at the twin pines to share stories. Everyone will want to know about your mission. It will be a good time to tell your story, and tell it once."

Morningleaf leaned into Star's body with a sigh. "That's a good idea."

Star pressed his cheek against hers. "I can't believe you're here. I was so worried."

She snorted. "*You* were worried."

The yearlings, Ashrain, and Dewberry turned and began to walk back to River Herd's camp. They peppered Brackentail and Shadepebble with questions, unable to wait until the gathering, but Star and Morningleaf drifted apart from them, and Star was glad because it left them alone to talk.

Tears welled in Morningleaf's eyes, brimming over and splashing down her chestnut face. "When I left, I . . . I thought you were dead. Not dead like you'd flown to the golden meadow, but dead like you were asleep forever, like you were stuck in some place where you couldn't live or die." She shook her head, and her mane flew in a flaxen arc. "I can't explain it."

"I *was* stuck," Star said.

Morningleaf wiped dry her tears. "But you woke up. And you look good, healthy."

"The Ancestors came to me," he said. "They helped me."

She exhaled. "That doesn't surprise me."

He cocked his head. "What do you mean?"

She turned and faced him; her eyes brilliant even in the darkness of the Trap. "I saw them, an army of weanlings. They flew down from the golden meadow to shield you from Nightwing."

"Right, I heard about that."

"We all thought he'd killed you." She wiped her eyes, crying freely.

Star's wings sagged as he listened and imagined how powerless she must have felt. She was not like him. She couldn't heal her best friend or bring him back from the dead.

Morningleaf exhaled. "A spotted bay filly led the Ancestors' attack on Nightwing, and you probably know the rest. We lifted your body and flew you to the Trap."

Star also let out his breath, and the two picked up their pace. "That filly you mentioned is called Hollyblaze."

Morningleaf halted, her hooves rooted in place. "Yes, Hollyblaze. I heard Nightwing say her name." Morningleaf was quickly panting again, but with excitement. "She's Spiderwing's sister. What did she say when she visited you?"

Star bit his lip, wondering if he should tell her about the Beyond. He hadn't told anybody.

"Tell me, Star," she pressed. "Hollyblaze wouldn't have

visited you if it wasn't important."

Star exhaled, deciding to tell her. "She said that the steeds killed by Nightwing's silver starfire don't fly to the golden meadow."

Morningleaf pinned her ears, and her pulse quickened. "What do you mean? Where do they go?"

Star's throat tightened, making speaking difficult. "They go to a place called the Beyond. It's a realm that's not here and not the golden meadow. Their souls are stuck there. The only way to free them is to destroy Nightwing."

Morningleaf staggered toward a small pine tree and leaned against it, breathing hard. "My sire is in the Beyond?"

"Yes," said Star.

"Does my mother know?"

"I haven't told her," he said. "I haven't told anyone."

She covered her face for a long moment, then she lowered her wings and gazed at Star, her amber eyes ablaze. "You must destroy Nightwing, Star. You must."

Her words stabbed his heart, and he was overwhelmed by her sorrow. "I will, Morningleaf. I'll free your sire, or I'll die trying."

She dissolved into sobs, and Star held her tight in his wings. When she was ready, they resumed walking.

"Did you know that Hollyblaze and Nightwing were once best friends?" she asked him.

"Like you and me?"

"Yes."

"I didn't know that," he answered. "But I do know they aren't friends any longer. They're enemies." Star wondered what could have happened to change things between Nightwing and Hollyblaze.

Morningleaf peered at him, taking a deep breath. "We won't repeat the past, Star. We'll change the future."

"I hope you're right."

Morningleaf bumped him with her hip, and he bumped her back. "Let's go home," she said, referring to River Herd's section of the Trap.

They galloped the rest of the way back. Brackentail and Shadepebble had already arrived and so the herd knew that Morningleaf had returned from her mission, and they gathered to greet her.

As the herd rushed forward to wrap their wings around the chestnut filly, Star felt he was witnessing a glimpse into the future. Without doubt, he believed that one day Morningleaf would surpass her heroes and become one of Anok's greatest legends, though to him she already was.

29

CELEBRATION

FOR THE NEXT FEW DAYS NEWS OF MORNING-leaf's return traveled quickly from camp to camp in the Trap, and a feeling of hopefulness accompanied it. With the Ice Warriors and the Black Army heading away from them, the unrelenting tension that had besieged the united herds released.

Star, Morningleaf, and their friends were dozing in a small pocket of sunshine when Bumblewind stretched, waking up. "We should celebrate," he said.

"Good idea," whinnied Dewberry, yawning. "But how? We can't leave the Trap, and there's nothing fun to do here, nothing new to see."

Star twitched his tail, knocking a flurry of tiny gnats

away from his flanks. He closed his eyes and let his ears droop. It was enough for him that Morningleaf was safe.

Brackentail spoke. "We saw some amazing things while we were gone."

"Like what?" asked Dewberry.

Star pricked his ears, wondering what they had seen, but kept his eyes closed, pretending to be asleep. He heard Brackentail fluff his feathers. "Like Spiderwing's nest."

"It still exists?" asked Bumblewind, awe evident in his voice.

"Yes, Morningleaf found it. The Jungle Herd steeds put fresh flowers and feathers in his nest each season, like they're leaving him gifts."

"What else did you see?" asked Echofrost.

For the next hour, Morningleaf and Brackentail chatted excitedly about their adventures, often finishing each other's sentences and arguing amicably over details.

Star opened one eye and stared at Brackentail. He'd heard that the yearling colt had saved Morningleaf's life twice—once pulling her out of a raging river and once saving her from the jaws of a crocodile. And he was grateful, but also . . . irritated. He watched Brackentail and Morningleaf nicker together, their eyes glowing, like they were old friends. Brackentail glanced at Star and caught him staring. The brown yearling quickly looked away. Star tensed as heat rushed though his body, making him uncomfortable, and he wondered why he felt upset. He should be glad Brackentail had protected Morningleaf.

"I know what we can do to celebrate," Echofrost said, standing. "Follow me." She trotted onto an animal path, deep into the heart of the forest. Star and the others cantered after her.

It was late afternoon. The birds fluttered busily, flying from branch to branch on the hunt for food. Large hares hopped through the underbrush. Star sniffed the wind for predators but smelled nothing. "How much farther?" he asked.

Echofrost halted. "We're here!"

Star tucked his wings and glanced at Bumblewind, who shrugged. Star saw nothing interesting to do here. They were still in the Trap.

Echofrost nosed aside a dark-green bush that was about the height of her knee. "I found these yesterday—summer berries—but I wanted to share them." She plucked one off the bush and ate it.

"Don't swallow!" Morningleaf cried.

But Echofrost did swallow. "It's safe. I tested one first, the way Sweetroot taught us. They're sweet."

Morningleaf shook her head. "We were told not to eat berries."

"Bitter berries," Echofrost argued. "Sweet things aren't poisonous." She ate another.

Morningleaf fluttered her wings, shedding a few aqua feathers. "I don't think that's what Sweetroot told us." She sniffed the bush. "She said not to eat bitter plants and not to eat berries at all—*any* berries. We don't know what those are."

Echofrost shrugged her wings. "Maybe, but I saw rabbits eating these." Echofrost ate another and swept her wing at Bumblewind. "Come on, try them. If a little rabbit can eat them, so can we."

Bumblewind ignored Morningleaf's angry expression as he tried one, and then another. "Echofrost is right. They're good."

Star watched his friends, feeling wary, but then a brown hare dashed out of the brush with pink stains on his face.

"See, that's the bunny I saw," said Echofrost, pointing.

Star shrugged. "I guess they're safe."

The rest of the yearlings, and Dewberry, plunged their muzzles into the surrounding bushes and tasted the berries. "I'm so tired of eating bark and moss," Dewberry said, juice dribbling down her lips.

Brackentail sidled next to Morningleaf and whispered into her ear. Star saw her wings relax as the big colt soothed her, and she whispered something back to him. Star lifted his head, watching the exchange, noticing again how close the two had become, and he felt left out.

Brackentail saw Star watching and took a step away from her. "Want to try a berry?" he asked them both.

"Sure." Morningleaf took the berry from his wingtips and crunched down on it. Star saw she trusted him—completely. He tensed, feeling confused. His best friend had another best friend; why did he care?

"I'm not hungry," Star said. "I'm going to take a walk."

Dewberry jabbed him with her wing. "You don't eat them because you're hungry; you eat them because they're delicious."

Morningleaf pricked her ears. "Don't go, Star."

He touched her wing with his. "I want to."

Star trotted away from his friends, ignoring the devastated expression on Morningleaf's face. As he departed, he heard Bumblewind say to her, "Let him go."

Star's heart beat faster, and his spiraling thoughts gathered like rainclouds, then poured forth memories of Brackentail's past betrayals. Star tried to shake them out of his mind—Brackentail was different now. He'd saved Morningleaf's life, he'd joined River Herd, and Star had accepted him. But was Brackentail *his* friend, or *her* friend, or both? Right now all Star felt was anger, or betrayal, or some mix of the two. He also knew he should feel neither of these things. Morningleaf could be friends with whomever she wanted.

Star broke into a canter and folded his wings on his back. With all his heart, he wanted to kick off and fly, but his long wings barely fit between the snug tree branches. He glanced up and couldn't see the sky. Frustration nipped his heels, driving him deeper into the forest and farther from the noises of his friends as they squealed, enjoying the berries. He had to clear this emotion, whatever it was. It was dark and cold, like the silver starfire. It robbed him of joy, and it wasn't Brackentail's fault, or Morningleaf's. It was Star's problem.

When he could no longer hear his friends' voices, Star slowed to a walk, and then he stopped. The forest was silent. The busy chatter of birds and the crackling movement of the bunnies through the pine needles had vanished. He swiveled his ears, hearing nothing. He sniffed, and smelled nothing. The breeze blew his mane forward, and a chill raced up his spine. His mixed-up thoughts had thrown him off guard.

Star felt eyes on him.

Slowly, he turned, careful not to make a sudden move. His muscles flexed, ready to fight or to flee. He gulped, sensing the creature before he saw her, and then every sense jolted into high gear.

He was face-to-face with an ice tiger.

Her blue eyes blinked at him. Her small, round ears pricked forward. Her mouth dropped open as she panted, her breathes shallow. Star saw her canines, long and white, like tusks. Her paws spread, exposing her claws, and she growled so low and deep it rumbled Star's rib cage.

Sweat prickled his hide as he faced the white giant. His sharpened hooves seemed silly next to her massive head and quill-sharp claws.

His starfire bubbled in his gut, but Star couldn't deploy it without activating Nightwing's awareness and putting all the herds in danger. Star locked eyes with her.

She sprang, claws flared.

Through his peripheral vision he spotted a small boulder next to him. He gripped the stone in his wing and threw it. It slammed her shoulder. She snarled and bit the rock where it landed, yowling with pain when her teeth clacked against it. Star leaped into the air, hoping he could fit between the trees and fly higher than she could jump. He flapped hard, trying to pierce the overhang of branches, shoving his nose into the largest opening he could find, but he couldn't bust through.

The ice tiger leaped and swiped at his leg. Searing pain split his thoughts as her claws ripped open his flesh. He kicked at her, but she'd already fallen back to the ground. She paced beneath him, breathing through her mouth and sniffing his blood that had dripped onto her black-striped white fur.

Star surged higher and managed to stick his head deep into the branches, where he became stuck.

The tiger sprang and snagged Star's long, curly tail. She yanked him down. The branches scraped Star as he and the tiger fell. He slammed onto the pine needles, landing on his side and crushing his wing. The ice tiger pounced.

Star lunged, meeting her head-on. He sliced her chest with his sharpened hooves, tearing deep into her fur.

She backed away, shaking her head and assessing him, as if wondering if he was worth killing. She decided he was and sprang again.

Star guessed she had a hungry cub somewhere. His starfire raced through his veins, heating him and threatening to explode.

But he had to defeat her without it.

They faced each other, both breathing hard. She was determined. But so was he. Her white hide sparkled, and her eyes gleamed.

She blinked.

Her mistake.

In that split second Star spun in a half circle and let loose both back hooves, slamming her square in the forehead, just as Redfire had taught him.

The tiger grunted and crashed onto her side, her eyes closed.

Star sniffed her. She was unconscious but alive.

He galloped away. He had to warn his friends before she woke up and discovered them. Star's heavy breathing blocked out all sounds as he rushed back to where he'd left them. He flattened his neck, dodging trees and leaping over fallen branches and large rocks. Froth developed on his chest, and he left a long trail of shed feathers behind him.

Where were they? He couldn't hear a thing.

Star skidded into the clearing where he'd last seen them and stumbled into a pegasus body. He had to jump to avoid trampling her. It was Dewberry.

He tripped over another body—Bumblewind.

He stopped and turned in a slow circle. His friends' bodies littered the forest floor—their eyes closed, their bodies convulsing.

Then he saw Morningleaf's aqua wings flapping uselessly. She was lying on her side, struggling to lift her head. He rushed to her. "What happened?"

She opened her mouth, and a red berry slipped off her tongue and rolled onto the moss. "Help," she gasped.

30

DOOMED

STAR REARED, THREW UP HIS HEAD, AND TRUM-peted a distress call. His deep bray rumbled through the Trap, carrying for miles. River Herd would hear it and send help. Then he dropped to all four hooves and darted to each of his friends.

Echofrost was in the worst shape, with her hide drenched in sweat, her feathers crushed by her jerking body, and her eyes rolled back in her head. She wheezed, and her ribs shook hard. Star's heart galloped ferociously at the sight of her. "You're going to be all right." He lowered his head, listening to her heart. It was fluttering like a trapped bird.

Bumblewind groaned, and Star cantered to his side.

"Hold on," he said to his friend. "Sweetroot is coming."

Bumblewind's glazed eyes looked past Star, and when he opened his mouth to speak, he couldn't.

"Don't try to talk," Star said. Tears rushed down his cheeks and soaked Bumblewind's hide. White flowers erupted around the colt.

To Star's left, Brackentail crawled toward Morningleaf, dragging himself over stones and twigs, but he couldn't make it all the way to her. He stopped, gasping for air, and Star whinnied to him. "Don't move, Brackentail. Just hold still. Sweetroot is coming."

Star turned in a circle, speaking to all of them. "Sweetroot is coming." He repeated the words as though they could stop time until she arrived. Feathers and tears shed from Star as he waited in agony for the medicine mare. His starfire bubbled deep inside him, but he couldn't use it to heal the yearlings—not if he wanted to keep them safe from Nightwing.

Star heard hoofbeats approaching, and then he saw Sweetroot, Silverlake, Hazelwind, and others galloping toward him.

"What happened?" Silverlake asked, her voice croaking like a frog's. Sweetroot and the other steeds skidded to a halt, their eyes round and their wings drooping as they stared at the downed pegasi.

Sweetroot spotted the red berries immediately. She lifted one with her wing and sniffed it. "Did you eat any?" Her eyes scanned Star's body for signs of distress.

"No. I—I went for a walk." Star's throat tightened. *Why had he left his friends?*

"Do you know how many they ate?"

Sweetroot's calm questions soothed Star, but rattled him too. The medicine mare was taking charge, and that was good, but Star didn't know the answers to her questions. "Just help them. Please."

"I am helping them. Who ate first, can you tell me that?"

"Echofrost," Star said, relieved to know an answer.

Sweetroot nodded and kneeled beside Echofrost. Using her wings, she lifted the mare's eyelids, felt her heartbeat, and pulled open her mouth, revealing red-stained teeth.

Behind her, Silverlake gasped.

"It's juice, not blood," Sweetroot explained.

Silverlake dropped next to Morningleaf and stroked her back. "Shh," she said when her filly struggled. "We're here now. We'll help you."

Bumblewind groaned as a painful spasm gripped his gut, bending him in half. The healthy steeds each chose a fallen herdmate to soothe. Star stood in the center of them, swishing his tail, overwhelmed.

Sweetroot evaluated the other yearlings and Dewberry in the same manner she evaluated Echofrost. Then she gave instructions. "Gather water, as much as you can."

Clawfire and Shadepebble galloped off toward the shallow creek. They would carry the liquid back by overlapping their watertight wings in front of their chests, creating a pouch.

Sweetroot continued. "Straighten their necks so they have a clear airway to breathe."

The remaining pegasi gently straightened each steed's neck. Star noticed it did ease their breathing.

"Open their mouths and pull out any berries or leaves inside," the old mare neighed.

The pegasi pried open each mouth and swept out any debris. Sweetroot paused.

"Now what?" Silverlake whinnied.

Sweetroot dropped her head. "Now we wait."

"That's it?" Hazelwind asked. "There's no medicine for this?"

"I'm sorry, but no. When the water arrives, we'll offer it to them. Maybe it will dilute the poison. It's all we can do for them."

Echofrost shuddered, groaning, and Star looked from her to the others. Morningleaf lay on her side, panting like a fish out of water. Bumblewind twitched, and his body tensed into a ball, causing him to choke. Ashrain quickly uncurled his neck so he could breathe again. Dewberry cried silent tears and clenched her teeth, and Brackentail, the largest of them, quaked uncontrollably.

Sweetroot turned to Star, her eyes welling with tears. "Perhaps you should begin gathering stones," she whispered. "If they don't . . . survive, we'll need to bury them quickly, before the animals arrive."

"No!" Silverlake whinnied. "No, no. Don't say that." She sobbed into her filly's fluttering aqua feathers.

Agony squeezed Star's heart, causing his chest to burn. He would not gather burial stones. He stared from Silverlake to Sweetroot and then to his friends lying on the moss. His starfire flared, hot and ready. "I won't let them die," he said.

Silverlake's head snapped up, and she stared at him, her expression torn.

Ashrain nickered, alarmed. "You can't use your starfire. Morningleaf risked her life to lure the armies away from here. You'll undo everything she did for us, and for you."

Sweetroot trotted to Star's side. "You can't heal every injury or make us immortal, Star. We've talked about this before. Sometimes you have to let us die. It's natural. It's part of life." Her voice trembled. "I don't like it either."

Hazelwind stood, his thoughts racing wild behind his narrowed eyes. And Ashrain also stood, but Silverlake remained on the ground, crying into Morningleaf's feathers. Each steed stared at the other, and no one knew what to say.

"I won't let them die," Star repeated. He felt empty inside, like he was the one dying.

"No. You can't use your starfire," said Ashrain. "We're not ready for the Ice Warriors or the Black Army to find us. We need more time to practice, to build hoofholds, collect rocks, and sharpen hooves. Isn't that right, Hazelwind?"

"Yes," agreed the buckskin stallion.

"Will another moon or another season really make a difference?" Star asked.

"Yes!" Ashrain answered. "We have all the advantages in the Trap, and the ability to use the trees to divide their armies. We can defend ourselves against numerous foes. All we need is more time."

Star spoke to his adopted dam, his voice tight. "Silverlake? You can't agree with letting Morningleaf and the others . . . go."

Just then Bumblewind moaned, loud and low. It was eerie, like he was a foreign creature and not a pegasi.

Silverlake tossed her head, throwing her forelock out of her face. "Don't ask me what I think," she cried, her lips quivering. "Don't ask me if it's okay to do nothing."

Star turned away, unable to bear her ragged expression and grief-stricken eyes.

Echofrost's breath rattled and slowed.

"Sweetroot, please let me help them," Star said to the medicine mare.

She closed her eyes and said nothing.

A hard, painful lump formed in Star's throat.

"Listen to Ashrain," wheezed Brackentail from the ground. "She's right; we're not ready for war." Then the brown yearling turned his eyes on Silverlake. "Your filly won't be alone in the golden meadow," he whispered. "I'll be with her."

His words crushed Star to the core.

Silverlake shook her head, flinging tears.

Echofrost groaned and then relaxed. Her wings sagged, and the gleam of pain left her eyes. Star watched her chest flatten, her breathing slow.

He made up his mind. "I won't let them die." Star closed his eyes, seeking the dormant golden ember. He panted, fanning it into a flaming inferno of power, swirling it up through his chest and into his neck.

"No!" whinnied Sweetroot.

Star heard sudden hoofbeats, and he braced himself as a body slammed into his. A glimpse of yellow and green feathers told him it was Ashrain.

Star neighed at her, "Out of my way." Sparks flew from his throat and bounced off the moss, sizzling the driest ends. Star twirled, shedding more sparks. His hide crackled, and his hooves glowed gold.

Hazelwind rammed him next, but Star was bigger. He shoved the buckskin right back and knocked him over. "Move away," Star trumpeted.

Hazelwind rolled to his hooves and thrust his chest into Star's. The two stared at each other for a second that felt like an eternity. All Thundersky's fire burned in his adult son, and Star braced for a battle, because he would not back down from Hazelwind. His stallion blood raced, his muscles quivered, and his nostrils blew starfire.

Hazelwind's eyes widened, and he took a step backward. Star advanced on him, neck arched, ears pinned, threatening the older stallion with his taller stature and bared teeth. "I won't let them die," Star repeated.

Hazelwind tensed, debating battle, but when Star

flared his wide black wings, Hazelwind shuddered and lowered his head, submitting to Star. The other steeds followed Hazelwind's lead and dropped their heads. "Do what you must, Starwing," said Hazelwind.

Star pricked his ears, shocked that Hazelwind and Ashrain and the others had backed down. Star panted, bringing his starfire into his throat. He would save his friends, but he would also bring Nightwing's wrath upon them.

31

STARWING

CLAWFIRE AND SHADEPEBBLE RETURNED WITH their wings full of water, but they halted when they saw Star rearing, his eyes glowing. The air sizzled with static power, and Star's black hide shone bright, his eyes and hooves turned gold, and his sides heaved.

Star narrowed his eyes, and the gathered pegasi backed away from him. Shadepebble flared her wings, and the water she held splashed onto the ground. "What's happening?" she asked, but no one answered her. Clawfire dragged her out of Star's way.

Star eyed his dying friends, who were spread across the clearing. He sensed their heartbeats and heard their breaths—they were each still alive, even Echofrost, but barely, and not for long. He closed his eyes, circulating the power that he'd subdued since his battle with Nightwing. His thoughts calmed as his starfire awakened, and Star felt a connection to the land through his hooves and a connection to outer space through his heart—like a branch ran from the stars, straight through his body, and into the soil of Anok, staking him between two worlds.

As the heartbeats of his best friends faded, his starfire thumped through him, more powerful than he'd ever felt it before, as though not using it had made it stronger—or perhaps more eager. Star leaped off the ground and hovered over the strewn bodies. He opened his mouth and roared golden starfire over all of them at once.

The watching pegasi galloped out of the way, then turned, their eyes huge.

The power crackled forth from Star and engulfed Dewberry and the yearlings, standing their hair and feathers on end. Star's energy circulated through him and then out of him, renewing itself as he used it. He took a breath and deluged his friends again, dousing them in a second wave of starfire. The flames licked their hides and then lifted their bodies off the ground. His five friends floated a wing length above the moss and then slowly began to tumble around and around.

A flash of light blinded Star, and he stumbled.

"Star?" cried Silverlake.

"I'm fine." The light was followed by sharp pain behind his eyes. As he healed his friends, the image of Nightwing appeared in Star's mind. The Destroyer stood on a high ridge in the Blue Mountains, and he was looking northward. Star shook his head. "Go away."

Nightwing clacked his teeth. "I see you," he said, and then he reared and brayed for his two armies, his voice carrying for miles and miles, farther than any normal over-stallion was capable. The echo of it reached the Trap.

"This isn't good," Sweetroot whispered.

Star narrowed his eyes and stoked his power, keeping his blaze on high, soaking his friends in healing flames. Soon all five bodies glittered with health, their eyes bright, and they blinked at one another. Star was reluctant to put them down, unsure if he'd healed them completely. Morningleaf stretched her wings, and he noticed that the chewed ends where the crocodile had bitten her were healed.

Then he turned to Echofrost. Her ragged mane and torn tail, ripped out during her captivity, were restored. Her scars from Mountain Herd were erased.

Star lowered his friends, and they each twirled right

side up and landed gently on their hooves. Star roared the fire through his own body, healing his injuries from the ice tiger, and then he closed his mouth, and the starfire evaporated from the air, popping as it vanished.

In spite of Nightwing's abrupt appearance in Star's mind, good and hopeful feelings overwhelmed him. He'd saved all five of his friends from certain death. It struck him how incredible that was, that his power was fantastic. He was not a regular steed; he had a destiny, and hiding from it served no one.

Star watched Silverlake, Hazelwind, and the others rush to his friends' sides, sniffing them and nickering in joy. He wouldn't listen to Sweetroot any longer, or Silverlake. They were driven by fear. His power was a gift. Star would use it when he wanted. He would save his friends over and over again if he had to. What had Silverlake said to him in the north: *Focus on who you are, not who he is.* Star would do just that. Nightwing was a destroyer, but he was a healer.

Star considered the possibility that his power might be stronger than Nightwing's. Perhaps he should have been practicing with the gold fire, not the silver. Star's chest swelled as he followed his thoughts, feeling confident. How could he and the United Army lose a war, or lose to

Nightwing, when Star could bring them back to life?

Streaks of sunshine poked through the trees and landed on his friends. Their hides sparkled, and their eyes glowed. Their hooves were smooth and free of cracks, their hair glossy, and their muscles toned and relaxed. They were healthier than before Star healed them. Morning-leaf galloped to Star's side and buried her muzzle in his chest, and the others followed. They surrounded him and nuzzled him. Brackentail lowered his head and bowed. "Starwing," he said.

"Starwing," the others repeated, and they all dropped to their knees in gratitude.

"Please stand," Star whispered. Across their backs, he locked eyes with Silverlake. She arched her neck and nodded to him, pride evident in her soft eyes. He saw she finally believed in him with her whole heart.

Sweetroot shook her head and clucked, but she only pretended disappointment. Her eyes also glowed with pride and relief. "Starwing," she nickered, her words twirling and settling in Star's heart. His decision to save Dewberry and the yearlings was the right thing to do. He believed it, in spite of the inevitable consequences.

"Nightwing knows you're here," Silverlake stated.

"He does," Star said with a sigh. "He's already calling

for Petalcloud and Frostfire to return with their armies."
Star looked at Morningleaf. "I'm sorry; I ruined all your
efforts."

"Sorry?" Morningleaf sputtered. "You saved our lives.
I know you probably shouldn't have, but I'm not sorry
about it."

Hazelwind interrupted. "We must make our final
preparations before they arrive. Come, let's return to the
herd."

Echofrost raised her head. "Wait, everyone, please. I
have something to say."

The pegasi halted, facing her.

"This is all my fault." She looked at each of them, her
eyes glistening with tears. "It was my idea to eat the berries. It's my fault Star used his power."

"You didn't know the berries were poisonous," Bumblewind said, comforting her.

Echofrost rattled her purple feathers. "It doesn't matter that I didn't know. If it wasn't for Star, we'd all be
dead." She bit her lip and glanced at Brackentail. "I guess
we're each capable of making horrible mistakes." She trotted to his side, the colt she'd hated with such passion, and
placed her muzzle next to his.

Brackentail startled, but Echofrost soothed him with

a touch of her wing, and then they exchanged breath. After a few moments Brackentail relaxed and wrapped his neck over Echofrost's. They stood together until Echofrost spoke again. "I was so mean to you, but I won't be anymore."

Brackentail sighed. "I deserved it."

Deep pleasure erupted within Star as he watched Echofrost forgive Brackentail. Her hatred of the colt was poisonous, like the red berries, but she'd healed herself of it. As the tension melted out of her, her dull eyes shined. Brackentail's head lifted as the shame he felt when he was around Echofrost evaporated, and Star understood how Brackentail felt: accepted. There was nothing worse than living with rejection by your own kind.

"Let's return to our camp," Silverlake said.

"Last one back has to eat a bird's egg," Echofrost neighed. She turned and bolted, her sleek body fitting neatly between the trees.

Star whinnied and charged after her, followed by Brackentail.

"No way am I eating a bird's egg," Sweetroot neighed, and she galloped after them, followed by the rest of the steeds.

As they chased one another through the woods, Star's

heart bubbled with affection. His guardian herd had risked their lives over and over again to protect him, but today he'd saved them. He was no ordinary steed, and the time for hiding that fact was done. Star galloped with his ears forward, hopeful about the future, whatever it might bring.

32

FEAST

WHEN THEY RETURNED TO THE CAMPS, HAZEL-
wind called the herds to gather at the twin pines. "War is
imminent," he announced, the timbre of his voice vibrating through the trees. He explained to them that Star had
used his power, thus giving up his position. "The time
for training is over. Sharpen your edges and fortify your
hoofholds. Load your baskets with rocks, and appoint your
sentries." Hazelwind arched his neck, looking confident
and fearless. Ashrain, Clawfire, Redfire, and Birchcloud
stood at his side looking equally fierce. Star glanced at
Silverlake and guessed she saw in her son, Hazelwind,
what Star saw: a young Thundersky—tough, committed,
and protective.

Hazelwind continued. "Return here at dusk. Tonight, we feast."

The pegasi from the four hiding herds trumpeted their battle cries, their voices rising and crashing through the trees, silencing the birds. They dispersed to prepare for the feast that preceded war, the last chance to fill their bellies as a united herd and to enjoy one another's company before the coming battles.

A tickling sensation teased Star's gut. This would be his first battle as a trained warrior. Well, as a *somewhat* trained warrior anyway.

"It's happening," Bumblewind whinnied.

Dewberry trotted to them, her eyes on fire. "I'm throwing zappers. What are you two doing?"

"I'm fighting on the ground," said Bumblewind.

Dewberry sized him up and nodded, for once not laughing at him.

"I'm throwing bone breakers," said Star.

Morningleaf heard them and galloped to Star's side. "I'm a spy," she whinnied, her amber eyes shining. "I missed all the trainings, but Hazelwind knows I'm good with numbers. I'll be counting the enemy."

"Shadepebble and I are relaying Morningleaf's information to the captains," said Echofrost. The two fillies leaned into Morningleaf, and they whispered, making plans.

"What's your position?" Star asked Brackentail.

The tall yearling colt stood near Morningleaf. "I'm fighting on the ground with Bumblewind."

"I'll be on the ground too," neighed Clawfire, "and watching out for you two." He pointed at Brackentail and Bumblewind.

Star's young friends nickered excitedly, and he knew how foolish they all sounded—Frostfire and Petalcloud were not playing games—but the excitement was catching. Star felt a strange peace about the coming war. Since it couldn't be avoided, he accepted it. Besides, he could bring his friends back to life—so it *was* almost like a game—as long as nothing happened to him.

"Which army will get here first?" asked Dewberry. "The Ice Warriors or the Black Army?"

"Perhaps they'll arrive at the same time," Clawfire replied.

"No," said Morningleaf. "My mother told me that the Black Army has been spotted. They're closer and should arrive first."

Her words rolled over the pegasi like cold fog, making them shiver.

"But now that Star's awake and the herds are working together, neither army will have an easy time with us."

Hazelwind interjected. "Listen, we can only guess at what will happen, but I think Morningleaf is right. The Black Army will arrive first. Our plan is to dispatch of them quickly. They don't know we've united. We'll use the trees and the fog to disorient them, separate them, and attack them. Silverlake, Birchcloud, and the Mountain Herd mares are acting as bait. They'll lure the Black Army toward our snipers. Frostfire won't know what hit him."

Hazelwind nickered. "I'm off to prepare," he said to the gathered herds. "I'll see you at the feast." He rubbed muzzles with his sister and then cantered down the deer trail leading back to River Herd's camp.

"We're going to eat well tonight," Morningleaf whinnied. "Sweetroot is sending scouts out for miles to gather fresh reeds, nuts, bulbs, and forest grasses."

"And my mother, Birchcloud, is collecting fiddlehead ferns, willow bark, fireweed, and late-season eggs," Shadepebble added.

"Where was all this food yesterday?" Bumblewind grumbled.

Dewberry smacked him with her wing. "You're always hungry."

Bumblewind rammed her and galloped into the woods. Dewberry tore off after him, and the two disappeared, squealing and nickering as they chased each other.

"They should save their energy," Brackentail nickered.

The brown yearling was correct, but Star didn't agree. This war would change his friends forever, even if it turned out well. They should enjoy themselves, but Star had a better idea than a game of chase. "Who wants to fly?"

Morningleaf gasped. "Fly!"

"Sure. Why not? The armies and Nightwing already know I'm here."

"I want to fly," Echofrost said.

"Me too," said Shadepebble.

"Let's go." Star threw an encouraging nod to Brackentail, turned, and galloped toward the edge of the Trap. His friends thundered down the path behind him.

They ran for a long time and then settled into a lope. Finally Star saw bright sunshine ahead. "There's the end of it," he whinnied. A few minutes later he burst out of the trees into daylight. He skidded to a halt, blinded by the sun. His friends did the same, squinting in the harsh light.

Star blinked, and his eyes adjusted. He gulped deep mouthfuls of fresh air that was untainted by the musty mulch of the forest. "Ready?"

"Ready," his friends nickered.

Star trotted forward, flared his wings, and leaped into the sky. He ascended so fast it seemed he left his belly behind, floating below his hooves. He flapped harder, soaring faster, flying straight up toward the drifting white clouds. He plunged into the mist, reveling in its cold chill, and his hide soaked up the cloud sweat, dampening his lips and eyelashes. He trumpeted his joy to his friends and then burst from the cloud and glided, letting his long wings stretch out and grip the current.

Morningleaf coasted to his side. "Great idea!" she whinnied.

"Watch this," Star neighed. He dropped his nose and plummeted toward the ground. As he was falling, he opened one wing and threw himself into a violent spiral. He whinnied happily as his body whipped in tight circles and the ground swirled faster and faster below him. He held the spin as long as he could and then he threw out the other wing, raised his nose, and pulled out of the dive. He rocketed across the tundra and then lifted back into the cloud layer.

"Nice!" whinnied Shadepebble. "Watch me!" The little filly flew parallel to the land and picked up speed until her pink feathers blurred. When she reached her top speed, she flipped over sideways and rolled across the sky, tumbling with her hooves flashing in a circle. As she lost speed, she righted herself and flew back to Star. "The advantage of one short wing is that I'm good at rolling," she nickered. "It's flying straight that's hard."

The six of them formed a V, with Clawfire at the head. They cruised high over the tundra, which was now green and dotted with bright flowers. The last time Star flew here it was still covered in snow. "Look there," said Brackentail, nodding to his right.

Star turned his head and saw thousands of elk moving toward a large lake. They had newborns with them, and they were cantering unsteadily between the legs of their parents. Two eagles coasted below the pegasi, but they returned to the trees when they noticed the larger shadows flying above them. Hordes of bugs swarmed near the banks of the rivers, and just seeing them made Star flick his tail in annoyance. Far away, a pack of wolves loped with efficient grace, heading toward the elk to hunt their calves.

Star drank in the scents of the north. The land that had been so harsh in the dead of winter was bursting with life and warmth. His heart soared, thrumming with pleasure, and his starfire coursed through him, feeding him strength and hope. Gratitude that he had not been executed as a weanling overwhelmed Star, lifting him, flooding his thoughts, and leaving him feeling small and humble, but in the best way, like he was part of something larger than himself.

"You were right all along," Star whinnied to Morningleaf. "Anok is to be enjoyed, not endured!"

"Yes," cried Morningleaf. "We needed to fly, to remember what we're fighting for."

"Not what we're fighting for—what we're living for!" Star whooped.

His friends celebrated with him as the sun began to set, casting orange and pink rays across the land and setting their feathers aglow, like they were on fire.

"Let's head back," said Echofrost. "It's almost time to eat."

The six friends banked and turned, flying back toward the Trap and to the feast, which would strengthen their bodies for the coming battle.

33

PROMISE

FOUR QUIET DAYS PASSED AFTER THE FEAST AT the twin pines, and the pegasi in the Trap were about to explode from the tension. Each twig that snapped, each rush of wind, and each deer that leaped past their camp caused a flurry of excitement—but every time that it wasn't Frostfire or Petalcloud, the steeds grew more anxious.

"Maybe they won't come," Echofrost nickered. She and Star and Bumblewind were standing head to tail swatting mosquitos off one another.

"No. They will," Bumblewind said. "Hazelwind's scouts spotted Frostfire and his Black Army in Mountain Herd's Canyon Meadow two days ago. Petalcloud's Ice Warriors are flying north along the Tail River."

Echofrost shook the bugs out of her mane, still blaming herself for causing Star to use his power. "I shouldn't have eaten those berries. If Star hadn't healed us, Nightwing would not have called the armies back, and we'd be training right now instead of preparing for battle."

"No," said Star. "It would have happened sooner or later. I didn't inherit this power to hide it, and I'll use it in the coming battles. I won't let anyone die."

"We can't lose," said Bumblewind.

"As long as nothing happens to me," agreed Star with a nod.

Bumblewind tensed, looking around him. "Has anyone seen Morningleaf?"

"She and Shadepebble are spying at the outer rim of the forest," said Star.

Just then the wind carried a truncated sound toward them, and Star flicked his ears. "Did you hear that?"

Bumblewind and Echofrost tensed, listening. The sound came again—louder this time. It was the screeching whistle of a hawk. "Is that Redfire, or a real hawk?"

Star closed his eyes. The whistle came a third time. "It's Redfire," he said. The copper-colored stallion had explained this unique Desert Herd trick to the other herds. They imitated the sounds of animals so they could communicate with one another without their enemies understanding them. Redfire had taught them the code, and three hawk screeches meant a foreign army was flying their way.

"It's beginning," Echofrost whinnied, her voice cracking.

Star's brave heart tumbled. This was real. The killing would be real, but Star's power glowed inside him, fueling his muscles, sizzling and ready, calming him. Star was finished with the silver fire—the dark power that caused only death, and had almost caused his own. He would use the golden fire and save his guardian herd if they fell. This war would be like no other. Star's friends couldn't die. He would bring them back to life, heal their wounds, and their enemies would be defeated. But that didn't mean it would be easy, or free from pain.

Bumblewind faced Star and Echofrost. "We have to get to our positions," he said, his eyes eager and wide. "We might not see each other again . . . until after."

Star's throat tightened. Bumblewind rushed forward and threw his wings around Star and Echofrost. The three huddled and didn't speak, couldn't speak. Star closed his eyes. A single tear fell to the ground, and one of Star's white flowers sprang up between their hooves.

Bumblewind broke the embrace and backed away.

"Let's meet at the twin pines, when it's over."

"Yes," said Star, his voice tight.

"Promise?" asked Echofrost. Star saw she was shaking.

"Promise," Bumblewind said to his sister. He lifted off the ground, hovering in front of them like a hummingbird, his brown-tipped gold feathers vibrating so fast they blurred, and then he darted into the trees, landed, and galloped away to find Clawfire.

Star exhaled, wishing Morningleaf were with them. As if reading his mind, Echofrost said, "Morningleaf, Shadepebble, and I are not fighting, Star, we're just spying. And Ashrain is going to slather us in mud to camouflage us and hide our scents. We'll be fine."

Star didn't answer. They both knew that every job was dangerous in a war, and Star didn't want his friends to get hurt.

Echofrost nuzzled him. "I'll keep an eye on her."

He nodded, his heart aching.

"The coming battles are not for land or food," she reminded him. "They're for power. Whatever happens, we're doing the right thing to fight against Nightwing's armies. Even if we lose."

Star pressed his forehead to hers, overwhelmed by the pegasi who were willing to die for him and who resisted the authority of Nightwing to follow him. He was just a yearling stallion, still learning about his power, and he wasn't mighty like Thundersky, or decisive like Hazelwind, or fierce like Dewberry. But he had the golden fire. He could heal his protectors, and he would. "We won't lose," he said.

Echofrost nodded and lifted off, paddling her purple feathers, and she cruised toward the outer rim where Morningleaf was spying. Star galloped to the hoofholds, where he knew Ashrain would be waiting for him, and Bumblewind followed, his ears pinned, his jaw clenched, looking every bit a warrior.

34

BONE BREAKER

STAR MET ASHRAIN AT THE SET OF HOOFHOLDS
that had been designed for him. They were extra sturdy
to accommodate Star's large size, and his basket was
stocked with bone breakers. "This is Springtail," Ashrain
said, indicating a light bay skewbald mare with dark-blue
feathers. "She'll gather fresh stones for you when you run
out, and she'll scout for you, warning you when the enemy
is near."

"Hello, Starwing," she nickered, dipping her head.

He greeted her. "But please call me Star," he said.

She nodded. "I'll attend to your every need. Besides
fresh stones and scouting, please let me know if you
become hungry or thirsty. There is water close, and I've

stashed a supply of nuts to give you energy."

Star's eyes widened, and he stared at Ashrain.

"It's her job," explained Ashrain. "She's a battle aide. She supports warriors and battle mares. Her job is to keep you fighting."

Star had never heard of such a thing, and he hadn't realized Jungle Herd was so organized. As a foal, he and his friends had believed they were weak and afraid because they attacked from the trees—but they'd been wrong. Jungle Herd and Desert Herd used their unique terrain in their favor, and their bodies had adapted to their kind of battle, from Jungle Herd's camouflage feathers to Desert Herd's high-altitude flight specializations.

Star huffed. He couldn't wait to tell Morningleaf he had a "battle aide." "Thank you, Springtail," he said, deciding not to inform her that he didn't need food or water or nuts for energy—not with the starfire crackling through him. It was her job to be helpful and so he would let her help.

Star leaped toward his hoofholds, flapping his wings to lift himself above them. He placed each hoof into its stand, folded his wings, and settled into the tree. In front of him was the tightly woven basket full of bone breakers, the huge rocks he'd be throwing to disable enemy warriors. His gut clenched at the sight of them.

Ashrain hovered in front of Star, pumping her wings. "I built another set of hoofholds in the tallest tree at the center of the Trap," she said. "The Desert Herd mare Sunray is there, watching. She spotted Frostfire's Black Army; they've landed on the tundra and are marching toward us. Our flying scouts reported seeing Petalcloud's Ice Warriors approaching the Wastelands. She'll arrive here by nightfall. There may not be much of a break between battles."

Star nodded, and sweat prickled his hide. A heavy, low fog had rolled into the Trap, masking his view of the ground.

"Look there," said Ashrain, pointing. "Dewberry is close."

Star squinted and saw Dewberry fluttering her emerald feathers at him from a distant tree.

Ashrain continued. "Silverlake's team will lead the Black Army here. You and the others will take out as many as you can with the stones."

"But I can hardly see," Star said.

"Their movement will disperse the fog," Ashrain explained. "Take out as many steeds as you can and then Hazelwind's team will engage them on the ground. You can join us then, when ground combat reaches its peak. We'll need your large size. And Hazelwind told me what you did to the ice tiger—your kicks have become quite accurate."

"I didn't kill her," said Star, thinking of the unconscious cat.

"But you could have if you'd wanted to," said Ashrain. "You're gentle, Star, I see that, and I won't lie. This battle is going to seem horrible to you . . . at first."

Star blinked at her.

Ashrain stared toward the sky, which was blocked by the thick overhead foliage. "But you will get over that, and then the blood of your warrior ancestors will begin to flow. You'll see that you are built for war, Star. You'll thrive on it, and you'll grow to love it."

Star gasped, not believing Ashrain. The mare nickered. "You don't believe me now, but you will later. Throw straight and don't think too much. I'll be close."

Star nodded and watched Ashrain fly away, and her absence left Star feeling cold. This war is worth fighting, he reminded himself. The Ice Warriors and the Black Army weren't attacking his friends for their own survival; they were attacking for power. They'd chosen to help Nightwing, and it was up to the United Army to show them that they had made the wrong choice. Star steeled himself for battle.

And he didn't have long to wait.

The twice-repeated call of a cardinal echoed through the Trap. It was Redfire's signal that the enemy had made landfall near the forest. "They're here," Dewberry whinnied.

"Shh," Star whispered.

He settled into his hoofholds and lifted a large stone out of the basket, feeling the devastating weight of it. He swiveled his ears, but the forest was unnaturally silent. A deer bounded past, looking terrified. *The animals know what's coming,* Star thought.

He waited, motionless, and then his ears pricked forward. Dewberry also tensed; she heard it too— hoofbeats, probably Silverlake's. It was her team's job to lure the enemy into Star's line of fire. He crouched, readying himself. A steed burst into view—it was Shade-pebble's dam, Birchcloud. The light bay mare dodged trees and leaped over branches, scattering the fog in her wake. She was gasping for air, and bleeding from a deep gash in her chest.

Star sprang into action. He drew back his wing,

clenching the boulder in its center. The tree swayed as he moved, but the hoofholds were well constructed, and they supported his shifting weight.

Three stallions galloped on Birchcloud's tail. Without thinking, Star hurled his first rock, slamming the closest stallion in the leg and snapping it. The stallion screamed and tumbled to the ground.

His companions jumped over him, their eyes wide and startled.

Star already had a new stone in his wing. He threw it, and then another, in rapid succession. He nailed one stallion in the head, knocking him out, and the other he hit in the back leg as he was running away. Both stallions dropped, and Birchcloud disappeared safely into the trees.

Star gasped for air. His blood rushed, and he felt sick. He watched the fog roll over the stallion's bodies, covering them. Springtail quickly loaded his basket with more rocks. "Good work," she nickered, and then she dropped back to her hiding spot in the brush.

Dark shadows emerged from the trees, stealthy and creeping, like jungle cats. It was Clawfire, Hazelwind, Brackentail, and Bumblewind. They slithered through the fog, making no noise—and Star's breath caught in his throat. He turned away as the sound of hoof against bone rang through the forest. His four friends killed the enemy stallions and dragged them away.

Star's body trembled, and he feared he would fall out of the tree. He stared up toward the sky as tears streamed from his eyes. War was horrible. He shook his head. *Keep it together,* he told himself.

Star's battle aide flew to his side. "Focus," she whispered. "More are coming." And then she darted away, leaving him alone.

Star had no more time to think, or cry. A slew of warriors charged toward him, chasing Silverlake and her team—the bait.

Star hurled rock after rock, breaking bones and downing pegasi, saving his friends from death. Blood splattered the trees. Feathers exploded and drifted through the air, floating toward the sky and then falling back to land. The fog grew thicker, hiding the fallen steeds from view, shrouding them in mist so their last breaths tasted of clouds.

Star dripped sweat and shed feathers, but he tirelessly threw the rocks. Somewhere, deep in his mind, he waited for the blood lust to take over. It was supposed to make him feel good and powerful, but it didn't come. The warrior blood flowed strong, he sensed it—it guided him—but it was cold, like the silver fire.

Springtail darted like a hummingbird from the ground, up to Star, and then back to the ground again. She refilled his basket and fed him nuts. He ate them because she insisted, but they made him feel ill, especially when he crunched into one that was crawling with worms. Springtail encouraged him and praised him, calling him Starwing even though he'd asked her not to call him that.

When he could, Star checked on Dewberry. She flung her zappers with enthusiasm, slamming steeds right between the eyes and dropping them in their tracks. She rattled her feathers in victory with each success, and she waved at Star, silently cheering.

When enemy warriors spotted Star, they flew up to attack him, but Clawfire met them in midair and dragged them back to the soil. They would disappear into the fog, but Star would see Bumblewind's brown-tipped gold wings fluttering as he and Clawfire, Brackentail, and Hazelwind swiftly ended their lives.

It appeared to Star that they were winning this battle.

But in reality it was just the beginning. For every steed they killed, two seemed to escape. The ground battle was in full force behind Star, and soon he would have to join it and kill his enemies muzzle to muzzle.

Star shuddered and threw his rocks, waiting and dreading the moment when Springtail would notify him that it was time to fight with the warriors.

35

COUNTING THE ENEMY

MORNINGLEAF DUCKED BEHIND A THICKLY FOLI-
aged pine tree. Ashrain had coated her bright aqua
feathers in mud, causing her to blend into the dark forest.
She hunkered in the fog, her breath mingling with the
mist and swirling around her muzzle. Her heart fluttered
in her chest like it wanted to fly away, far from here, and
she wanted to go with it, but she braced herself instead,
holding firm and clenching her belly.

She felt the vibrations of the hooves before she saw
the pegasi. She held her breath. A battalion of steeds
from Frostfire's Black Army trotted toward her led by
their captain. Her heart steadied as she counted them.
Fifty-two pegasi crept past her.

A branch cracked, and the captain halted not far from Morningleaf. He raised his wing, signaling his warriors to halt also. They were panting and listening, their ears flicking back and forth.

A mare from the United Army bolted out of the brush— it was Shadepebble's dam, Birchcloud.

"There!" whinnied the captain. The warriors charged after Birchcloud, and Morningleaf's heart thudded, matching the rhythm of the mare's retreating hooves, but this was Hazelwind's plan, to lure the enemy steeds toward the snipers.

When they were gone, Morningleaf exhaled and then cantered east to the twin pines. She met Echofrost there. "Fifty-two steeds, stallions and battle mares, heading to the hoofholds."

Echofrost nodded, whirled around, and flew a wing length off the ground to give the news to Sunray, the Desert Herd mare spying in the tallest tree at the center of the Trap. Through her whistles, Sunray told Redfire how many enemy steeds were racing his way.

Frostfire had split his army into dozens of smaller units because the trees were too tight for a unified attack. Morningleaf blew the fog out of her nose and galloped back to the edge of the forest. She'd counted six battalions so far, all about the same size, but she knew there had to be many more. If they survived Frostfire's assault, Morningleaf worried the United Army would not have the energy to battle Petalcloud's Ice Warriors when they arrived tonight.

Morningleaf tossed her mane. *Stop it,* she chided herself.

She flattened her ears and cantered to the edge of the forest where she peeked out of the trees at the vast green tundra. It was quiet out there. The smaller wildlife had gone to their dens and nests, spooked by the arrival of the pegasus army. The larger wildlife had vanished. The north was empty and mute, as though it were the dead of winter. Morningleaf glanced at the horizon, watching the sun slowly drop. She hoped Petalcloud would wait for tomorrow's daylight to attack so her friends could rest in between battles.

Morningleaf shook her head again and made a face. *One army at a time,* she thought, feeling frustrated. *Focus.*

She skirted the edge of the Trap, slinking like a shadow. She froze. Ahead of her, another battalion was sneaking into the woods. The fog rolled in thicker, and Morningleaf couldn't see well enough to count them. She crept closer, letting the web of branches hide her dark body. The mud Ashrain had applied to her feathers served to camouflage her scent as well as her color. She lowered her neck and slunk closer still.

Morningleaf halted when she heard two steeds talking, their voices echoing through the forest, amplified by the silence.

"What are our orders if we encounter Star?" asked a female pegasus.

"If you see him, run."

"But to complete the pact we need his head."

"I'll worry about the pact."

Morningleaf recognized the voices. It was Frostfire and his companion, Larksong, the sky-herding mare who traveled with him. Morningleaf gulped down her fear of Frostfire and the memories of her kidnapping. She swished her tail, struggling with the part of herself that wanted to gallop away from him.

Frostfire continued. "This is about pressure, Larksong. We annihilate everyone Star loves until he's broken and begging for death, or until he leaves Anok for good. The Destroyer just wants Star gone; he doesn't care how."

"But now that he's awake, what's keeping Star from killing us all? You know what he's capable of. He's a destroyer too."

"He could kill us, but he won't. Star is weak up here." Frostfire pointed to his head. "I've led warriors like him. They're duds; they don't like to fight, don't like to hurt anyone."

Larksong seemed unsure. "Maybe, but his herd and the Ancestors are protecting him." She glanced toward the sky that was shielded by leaves. "He won't be easy to subdue."

"The blasted Ancestors!" neighed Frostfire. "That didn't happen, Larksong. It couldn't have. Terrified pegasi make up stories."

"But they drove Nightwing away from Star."

"Do you doubt me?" he rasped.

She flailed. "No, of course not."

"This is what matters—Nightwing has killed every over-stallion and taken over the herds, Larksong. We're either with him or with Star; there's no other choice, and I won't choose the losing side."

"You're right," she said.

Morningleaf peered around the tree trunk just as a gust of wind blew a hole into the fog. She saw Frostfire and Larksong speaking alone, facing each other, their muzzles close together. She pricked her ears. Something had changed between them. Frostfire's frustration with

Larksong did not reach his eyes the way it had when she'd traveled with them to the volcano Firemouth.

Frostfire continued. "Nightwing is not afraid of Star, but Star's guardian herd is a problem. They'll never submit to Nightwing, but once we rid Anok of them, Star will have no one left to protect. He'll surrender to Nightwing or he'll leave Anok on his own accord. And then my army will destroy my mother's army." Frostfire struck his hoof against the forest floor. "Petalcloud will lose, and I will win the pact with Nightwing."

Morningleaf gasped and slapped her wing over her mouth.

Frostfire softened and wrapped his wings around Larksong. "Do you trust me?"

"I do," she answered.

Frostfire lifted his head and motioned to his battalion that waited nearby. "Move out," he ordered. Morningleaf counted ninety-six steeds in his group. She lifted off and flew to find Echofrost. When she spotted the silver filly, she gave her the information she'd learned.

Echofrost cantered off to tell Sunray.

Morningleaf slumped against a spruce tree. She'd thought everything would be all right once Star received his power, but everything was worse. Nightwing had returned to Anok, her sire was dead—trapped in the Beyond—and Star's enemies had made a powerful ally in Nightwing. Morningleaf glanced at a patch of empty sky, which had once held the Hundred Year Star. What would it take for the enemy armies to accept Star and quit fighting him?

She cantered back to the southern rim of the Trap, feeling weary and frustrated. Another battalion from the Black Army was coming, dropping from the clouds. She counted them, letting her work erase her thoughts. The herds in the Trap needed to defeat the Black Army as quickly as possible, before Petalcloud and her Ice Warriors arrived. Morningleaf braced herself for the long afternoon and night ahead.

36

WARRIOR BLOOD

THE MOMENT TO FIGHT ON THE GROUND CAME sooner than Star had expected.

"It's time," said Springtail. "Come with me."

Star swallowed hard and flew out of the hoofholds, dropping into the fog and landing beside the efficient mare.

She trotted forward, her black-and-white tail swishing through the mist. She led him first to the shallow creek bed. "Drink." Star obeyed her, though he wasn't thirsty. "Let me see your hooves," she ordered, her black eyes peering at him.

Star lifted each hoof so she could inspect their sharp edges.

"Not bad." She whistled a signal into the trees and waited.

Star shifted from leg to leg. His belly ached, probably due to the worm-infested nuts she'd fed him, and his head hurt. His wings were exhausted from hurling rocks, and they sagged to the ground. Star was about to ask who they were waiting for when two figures cantered into his view, dispersing the fog. It was Bumblewind and Clawfire. They were splattered with blood. Star gasped.

"It's okay," nickered Bumblewind. "We're not hurt."

But that wasn't exactly true. Bite marks and scratches crisscrossed their hides, and the hot stench of battle stung Star's nostrils, causing his pulse to quicken. Star pranced in place, his nerves humming, wondering what would happen next. In the distance he heard shrill squeals, crushing blows, and panting breaths.

"These two will take you the rest of the way," Springtail explained.

Star suddenly didn't want to leave his battle aide. He locked eyes with her.

She flicked her ears forward. "It's time to go, Star. You're bigger and stronger than most pegasi—they need you on the ground. Stay with your friends."

Star nodded.

"And Star," she added, gently touching his shoulder. "Don't count the dead. Count the living."

Star's eyes widened, and his hooves felt heavy, like the bone breakers he'd been throwing. Bumblewind nuzzled him. "Come on. I'll be by your side."

The three stallions left Springtail and galloped toward the battle. Star's heart thudded, his pulse rushed between his ears, and his nostrils flared, inhaling deep cold breaths. The thick fog closed around him, choking him and blinding him. Sweat or droplets of mist, he couldn't be sure, dripped down his forelock. He lifted his wings and flared them, making himself look larger than he was. Next to him Bumblewind clenched his jaw, and Clawfire arched his neck.

Star closed his eyes and imagined his old friend and mentor, Grasswing. The crippled palomino warrior had been the leader of the walkers when Thundersky was over-stallion of Sun Herd, and he'd accepted Star like a beloved colt. Grasswing had reminded Star over and over again that he was not the root of his herd's troubles. Now Star heard Grasswing's voice in his ears as if the old stallion were standing right next to him. "You're not alone, son," he said. Star opened his eyes, feeling reassured.

"There!" Clawfire neighed. He lowered his neck.

Star saw the clash of bodies ahead, and recognized Redfire and Brackentail and Ashrain. He lowered his neck too, remembering his training and bracing himself so he wouldn't fall if a stallion slammed him. Bumblewind narrowed his eyes, and Star thought his friend looked much older than a yearling should.

"Attack before you're attacked," Clawfire whinnied. "Don't wait." He charged into a Mountain Herd stallion and threw him off his hooves. Bumblewind surprised a muscular gray steed and knocked his head against a tree, propelling him into unconsciousness. Brackentail battled a yearling warrior. The two circled each other, trading kicks and bites.

Star panted, struggling to breathe, overwhelmed by the sights and sounds of battle.

A white stallion rammed Bumblewind from behind, and Star's friend staggered toward Clawfire. When the enemy pegasus reared to deliver a deathblow to Bumblewind, Star whirled and walloped the white stallion in the chest with both hind hooves. The foreign steed rocketed across the battlefield, slid under the fog, and did not get back up.

Star's sides heaved, but there was no time to think. Three battle mares approached. They were tall and lean, and their narrowed eyes gleamed with intelligence and violence. They surrounded him.

Bumblewind and Clawfire attacked their flanks as the mares lunged with teeth bared. Star reared and struck the closest one, slicing her from jaw to shoulder. She snorted, ignoring the pain. Star dropped and lowered his neck, meeting her head-on. When she rushed for his throat, Star dropped lower still and snatched her leg in his jaws. He flipped her over, and she squealed for help. Clawfire charged, quickly ending her life, and then he galloped away to help Brackentail, who was now fighting a full-grown stallion. The brown yearling was large, but his opponent was an experienced warrior.

Star reeled, backing away. Something had yanked his tail. He pivoted and came face-to-face with a gold dun stallion. The warrior taunted Star, making him spin circles trying to catch him. While Star was focused on the gold dun, another enemy appeared and hovered over him, kicking Star in the head. Two more galloped out of the mist and harassed Star, biting at him and landing blows to his body.

"Use your power," urged Clawfire. "Nightwing already knows you're here."

Star shook his head, snapping and kicking at the

steeds trying to kill him. His power was for healing. His hooves and teeth were for fighting.

He feigned an attack, and then spread his wings and jumped off the ground, hovering over his attackers. They hadn't expected that. He dived onto the first and knocked him onto his back. Star landed and rammed the second, flipping him over and toward Bumblewind, who finished him. The other two attacked Star from the rear, striking his flanks with crippling blows. Star collapsed, rolled onto his back, and kicked at them from the ground. Clawfire killed one, and Star broke the front legs of the other. That stallion dropped, shrieking with pain. Clawfire reared, ready to deliver the deathblow. "Leave him," Star said, panting.

Clawfire nodded and landed. The three friends stood in a circle, facing outward, as a throng of fresh warriors charged toward them.

Star's muscles fired at the sight, and hot blood shot through his veins. He saw the warriors in sharp focus: their yellow-stained teeth, each bristled feather, the striations on their hooves, and the bulging veins criss-crossing their chests. He tasted the tang of sweat and noticed small things like the breeze blowing from the south and the distant howl of a wolf. Behind the charging warriors he saw each individual pine needle standing on its branch.

Excitement lifted his feathers and charged his lungs. His hooves dug into the soil, and his body hummed with the warrior blood of his kind. In the tree he'd been alone, but here on the battleground the excited steeds around him multiplied his energy. Ashrain was right; Star liked the feeling of unity that battle brought, but he regretted its circumstances.

And, against all odds, his herd was winning the battle.

37

THE WOUNDED

AS THE SUN SIZZLED LOWER, THE FOREST DARK-
ened, and the fog lifted. The battle was over. Frostfire's
Black Army, what was left of it, had surrendered. Hazelwind trotted into Star's view, breathing hard and dripping
sweat. Frostfire had vanished into the woods, but his
defeated army lay wounded on the forest floor. Their
grunts, shallow breaths, and loud moans rose into the air.
Hazelwind spotted Star and exhaled. "Good. You're alive."

Bumblewind snorted. "You thought he wouldn't be?"

Hazelwind narrowed his eyes. "Of course not. He's
injured though."

Star glanced down and saw torn flesh across his
lower neck and chest where his hide had been sliced open.

Bumblewind, Clawfire, Hazelwind, and Brackentail—they were injured too. A deep wound, crusted in dirt, adorned Bumblewind's head; Hazelwind limped on a swollen leg; Clawfire's left wing hung crookedly from his shoulder, probably sprained; and Brackentail's body quaked from the agony of numerous cuts and bruises.

Sweetroot's whinny rang through the trees, calling for Star. It was time for him to heal the United Army. Star arched his neck, proud of his power. "Follow me," he said, "and I'll erase the day."

Star turned and galloped toward Sweetroot's voice, and the injured warriors followed him. The old medicine mare had a team of nursing mares who'd helped her care for warriors throughout the battle. They'd dragged injured steeds out of the fray and treated them as best they could while they waited for Star.

Now he was here.

Strewn throughout the trees were hundreds of pegasi, moaning and grunting. Star looked back the way he had come, thinking about Frostfire's wounded warriors.

"They're in pain, Star," said Sweetroot, indicating the steeds at his hooves and seeming to wonder at his hesitation.

"Right!" Star sought the seed of power in his belly and

panted, fanning it into a flame. He was getting quicker at drawing the power out and through his body. He spread his wings as heat rushed from his core to his extremities, and his hide sparkled with static as his hooves turned gold.

The pegasi near him backed away.

Star huffed faster and harder, swirling his power up into his neck, feeling it warm his throat. He gnashed his teeth, and sparks popped and sprayed onto the ground. The injured warriors of the United Army became silent, watching Star. Some struggled to stand, ready to bolt— unused to Star's power.

"Don't run," Sweetroot commanded them. "He won't hurt you."

Star narrowed his eyes as light beamed out of them. He stepped toward the nearest stallion, a captain, and blew golden starfire across his body, lifting him off the ground.

The captain whinnied, but not in fear.

Star realized that if he healed them one by one, it would take too long. Petalcloud and her Ice Warriors were expected by nightfall. So he reared and roared his golden fire in a wider arc, pushing the heat from his gut through his body and directing it farther. The injured steeds around him floated off the ground, and then they tumbled in the light, stabbing at the air with their uncertain hooves.

"Good, Star!" Sweetroot said. Her apprentices pranced beneath the wounded pegasi, their mouths gaping as they watched skin abrasions evaporate, cuts close, swelling disappear, and broken bones straighten. One apprentice touched the golden light with her muzzle, and it swept her off her hooves. She floated into the starfire, nickering with pleasure, and she stretched her wings. Her coat, which was dull from eating nothing besides lichen, turned glossy.

"Get out of there," Sweetroot scolded her. But the mare was trapped in Star's healing light, and she seemed thrilled about it.

Star walked forward, lifting up more injured battle steeds, including his closest friends, until all of them were floating around him. Droplets of sweat erupted on his neck and chest, and dripped down his hide. He concentrated heavily on two things: encouraging the fire in his gut, and expelling it far and wide. He briefly thought, *This isn't possible,* but when he did that, the steeds began to fall. He quickly vacated his mind and directed his attention to his starfire only.

Sweetroot cantered below the floating warriors, inspecting them. When she was satisfied that they were all healed, she nickered. "You can put them down now."

Star reduced the force of the golden fire, and the pegasi drifted toward the soil, landing on their hooves. When they were safe, he closed his mouth. The wounded pegasi were better than healed—they were vibrant.

No one spoke.

Star closed his wings and staggered, falling to the ground.

"Star!" Sweetroot whinnied. She galloped to his side.

"I'm okay," he said. "Just tired."

"Rest now," Sweetroot commanded.

Star heard the pounding of hoofbeats. He flicked his ears, sensing trouble. The steeds near him tensed. Then Morningleaf, Echofrost, and Shadepebble skidded to a halt in front of Star.

When Morningleaf saw Star lying on the ground, she choked on her words. "Wh-what happened?" She pushed through his protectors and dropped next to him.

Star tried to stand.

"He saved them," Sweetroot explained, indicating the once-injured army that was now healed.

Morningleaf gasped. "All of them?"

"Yes." Sweetroot was beaming.

Morningleaf flipped her head toward Star and leaned into him, sniffing his mane and inspecting his injuries. She glowered at Sweetroot. "He should have healed *himself* first, *them* second."

Sweetroot's jaw dropped. "I—I . . . didn't think of that."

"Star, please lie down," Morningleaf urged. "You need the starfire too."

Star dropped back into the moss, grateful to rest. He stretched out and closed his eyes. The starfire, far from being exhausted, was roaring inside of him, waiting. He released it through his body and healed his injuries.

Meanwhile, Morningleaf gave her report, her sides heaving. "The Ice Warriors have landed at Antler Lake," she said.

"What are they doing?" asked Hazelwind.

"Drinking and resting right now."

"Frostfire abandoned his army. Do the spies have news of him?"

Morningleaf shook her head. "I don't know. I saw him and Larksong before the battle but not since."

"Everyone rest," Hazelwind ordered. "Petalcloud is close. She'll either march on the Trap tonight, using the cover of darkness, or she'll let her warriors rest until morning. Either way, we don't have much time." He gazed at Star. "Thank you for healing my army, Starwing."

Star nodded to him, accepting the honor of the title. Hazelwind looked more like his sire Thundersky than ever, but he was changing. He was fueled less by anger and more by responsibility. He was a protector, like his sire, and he was growing wiser.

Star stood, his body still crackling with sparks. "I need to walk, to stretch my legs." He felt agitated, and he didn't know why. He stepped away from his friends and into the fog. On his way, he bumped into a white mare. "Hello?" he whinnied, surprised. She hadn't been there a moment ago.

The mare tossed her head, flicking her shiny white mane. Her hide glowed bright even in the blur of the mist, and Star closed his mouth. This was his mother.

Lightfeather moved closer and lowered her head, pressing her brow against Star's, but she was translucent like the mist. The scent of warm grass and milk wafted into his nostrils. He bleated softly.

She gazed into his eyes, and he saw that hers were as deep and as endless as space. He wanted to fly into them, to see what she saw. She placed her wing over his heart. "Remember what I told you the day you were born," she said. Then the image of his mother evaporated and twirled around him before drifting into the sky, but her last words lingered like the tail end of a dream. *"Heal them."*

Star exhaled, his legs shaking.

Morningleaf trotted to his side and pushed her muzzle into his thick mane. "You saw something, didn't you?" she asked. "Was it a vision? Was it Nightwing?"

Tears rolled from Star's eyes and dropped onto the soil, where white flowers sprang to life. "It was my mother."

Morningleaf inhaled and then breathed out with a soft exclamation of wonder. "Did she speak to you?"

"Yes." *"Heal them,"* she'd said, and his spine tingled as he realized instantly what it all meant.

Behind him, Hazelwind spoke to his warriors, and his voice interrupted Star's thoughts. "Come on, let's finish off the survivors."

"No!" Star neighed. It was pegasi custom to execute the survivors of a fallen army that refused to surrender. And with Frostfire gone, the Black Army was confused. They didn't have a leader to tell them what to do, and Hazelwind couldn't afford to wait, not with the Ice Warriors fast approaching. "Please," Star said, "I have a better idea."

Star reared and cantered away from his herd toward his enemy. His mind and heart brimmed with an unexpected emotion, a feeling stronger and better than the starfire or the unity he'd experienced in battle. It was his desire to fulfill his mother's last command.

When she'd given birth to him, her herd had become her enemy. They'd promised to kill Star before he turned one year old, and Lightfeather had been heartbroken, but she'd responded by whispering secrets into Star's ears, most of which he didn't remember, but one had stood out on the night of his birth, and again on the night he received his power, and now again on this day. "Heal them," she'd said. And she'd meant this not just for Star's friends, but also for his *enemies*.

Star's heart filled up with the love his mother had poured into him that night—her love for her colt and her love for the pegasi of Anok. She'd died, but she'd left Star behind as her gift to them, instructing her son to heal them. Star would not disappoint her.

38

HEALER

STAR GALLOPED TO THE BATTLEFIELD AND SLID to a halt. Frostfire's fallen army lay groaning and dying, or were already dead. The setting sun was so low its rays crept between the trees and turned the fog orange. Star cajoled his power into an inferno and blasted the warriors with starfire.

Screams erupted from them as they hid their faces in their wings.

"It's the Destroyer," they cried.

This amused Star. It was just like the pegasi to fight their own salvation. His starfire lifted the warriors off the ground. The gold light mixed with the orange sunset, and Star felt grateful, like he had when he'd saved his friends from the poisonous berries. His starfire was a gift, not a curse.

"Star! Stop!" neighed Hazelwind, who had followed him along with some others. "You're healing our enemy."

"Please," Redfire whinnied. "Listen to Hazelwind."

Bumblewind and Dewberry stared at the floating army with dropped jaws.

Bumblewind edged closer to Star, his voice shaky. "What are you doing?" he asked, prodding Star's shoulder.

Star ignored them all. They were afraid. He was not.

Ashrain brayed and called forth the United Army. They appeared between the trees and surrounded the enemy pegasi, who were tumbling head over tail, drenched in starfire, but none moved to stop Star from what he was doing.

After several long minutes Star guided the Black Army back down to the forest floor. The warriors blinked at him like newborn foals. Slowly, they stretched their wings and glanced at their bodies; the injuries that had plagued them moments before had vanished.

The United Army tensed at the sight of their foes upright and healthy. Hazelwind lifted his wing, commanding his warriors to hold steady, but no one was in the mood to fight again.

Star gazed at his enemies. "You're free to stay or to leave," he neighed at them, his strong voice vibrating his chest.

The Black Army peered at Hazelwind's army. Many of the steeds knew one another and had once lived in the same herds. In the warm glow of the sunset, they were not anonymous warriors. They were family and friends reunited.

A captain, a blue roan with dark-green feathers, approached Star. He was short and thick, a Mountain Herd steed. When he reached Star, he halted. Bumblewind tensed, ready to protect Star even though Star could protect himself.

The stallion's expression was baffled and yet hopeful. He kept a short distance between himself and Star's body, which was humming with the leftover current of his power. The captain's eyes narrowed. "Is this a pact?"

Star understood why the stallion was suspicious of his army's sudden good fortune in being healed. Star would have to allay the captain's doubts. He glanced at Morningleaf, who had followed him to the battlefield, and she nodded her head, encouraging him as though she could read his thoughts.

Star exhaled. He would look foolish if this didn't work. He dropped his head before the captain in the pose of surrender.

The blue roan scooted backward, alarmed. The steeds around him gasped.

Star spoke to the Black Army. "I don't expect you to follow me, and I won't lead your herd," he said. "I don't want a pact. I just want you to accept me, to stop fighting me."

The captain gaped at him.

Four battle mares galloped to Star, and they bowed to him. "We accept you," they whinnied. Star exchanged breath with them.

Then, in a rush, more warriors cantered to Star and bowed to him, including the blue roan. They repeated the mares' words individually. "I accept you." Others shook their heads in denial, backing away from Star.

"You're free to go," he repeated, and the suspicious warriors turned tail and galloped away, too wary to accept him.

When all of the steeds had either accepted Star or fled, the tension evaporated. The United Army rushed forward and welcomed back their past herdmates. The two armies swirled around each other, nuzzling and nickering excitedly.

Star watched them, feeling pleased.

Silverlake sobbed into her wings. "It's beginning," she said. "One by one, you're uniting the pegasi of Anok. I knew you could do it."

Everyone nickered at that because, even though Silverlake had risked more than any other steed to protect Star, they knew she'd doubted him all along.

"But the fight isn't over," Hazelwind said.

Star agreed. "He's right. Petalcloud and the Ice Warriors have arrived at Antler Lake, southwest of the Trap."

"Our army has just doubled in size," said Hazelwind, nodding to the blue roan captain. "Let's strike first. Attack her before she attacks us."

"It's a good idea," agreed the captain from the Black Army.

"We'll keep watch," neighed Shadepebble, sidling close to Morningleaf. Hazelwind nodded, and the two small fillies lifted off and darted through the woods, angling sideways when the trees were too tight. *There were advantages to being little,* Star thought.

"Assemble your battalions," Hazelwind commanded. "Ashrain, will you return to the hoofholds?"

The mare shook her head. "No, the sun has set. After

nightfall it's too dark to throw accurately. We'll fight on the ground."

Hazelwind trumpeted for the warriors to collect, and his words carried the regal bearing of his sire. The two armies merged and advanced as one toward Petalcloud.

39

NIGHTFALL

STAR PRANCED AT THE FRONT OF THE LINE, RAT-
tling his feathers with the warriors. He would fight to
defend his herd, and then he would heal the Ice Warriors—
that was his plan. Maybe Petalcloud's army would make
the same choice as Frostfire's Black Army had, and they'd
join him. Hazelwind, Clawfire, Ashrain, and Redfire trotted at his sides, and then they each peeled away, splitting
their large army into smaller, more agile divisions.

Bumblewind, Clawfire, and Brackentail stayed with
Star. Dewberry joined the sky herders, in spite of their
objections, and Echofrost followed Hazelwind. Morningleaf and Shadepebble had already galloped off to spy on
Petalcloud's approaching army, and it was their duty to

update Sunray, who was lodged high in a tree where she could whistle information to the captains.

The last breath of daylight had withdrawn from the forest, leaving it dim and colorless. Star could not see the night sky overhead, but hints of silver glinted through the thick foliage, telling him the moon was bright. His breath showed in twin puffs of steam, his hooves clunked against small stones and branches, and his ears swiveled round, searching for sounds of Petalcloud's army.

Clawfire tensed, raising his wing. The pegasi halted. Star peered into the darkness, seeing shadows. Clawfire crept forward with delicate precision. He motioned with his wings, splitting his group into two and sending them forward.

With one eye on Clawfire, Star slipped through the woods in the same fashion, lifting each hoof high and placing it slowly down, reducing his noise. He glanced at Brackentail. The brown yearling's eyes were round and alert, and he kept close to Star, always looking and listening. The forest was silent.

Bumblewind tripped and crashed onto his knees with a loud grunt.

The sudden noise caused the warriors to surge forward, thinking they were under attack.

Star spread his wings. "No. Shh!"

Clawfire galloped toward Star.

"It's okay," explained Star, "Bumblewind just tripped."

"Look behind you!" Clawfire neighed.

Star and Clawfire's small battalion of two hundred warriors whirled around, and Star's heart fluttered at what he saw. Glistening in the pale rays of moonlight behind them stood over two thousand Ice Warriors. They must have been there all the while, waiting, and by chance Clawfire had led his platoon right to them. The front line of white and gray steeds was steadfast, like a mountain range. They clenched their jaws and narrowed their eyes. Clawfire halted, placing himself between the heavy northern stallions and his much smaller squad. "You're fighting for the wrong side," he spat at them.

Their leader's gaze flitted to Star and then back to Clawfire. "We've come for just one thing," he said. "Give it to us and we'll go." He eyed Star's head, his dark eyes seething with desire for it. The stallion was Stormtail, the giant dapple-gray pegasus with the thunderous hooves who traveled with Petalcloud.

Star whipped his tail back and forth, frustrated. It didn't look like Petalcloud had split her army to move through the Trap. They were all here: her healthiest, most powerful steeds. Most of her Ice Warriors hailed from the north. They had survived the Blue Tongue plague and countless frozen winters. They were thick furred and big boned, afraid of nothing, and Star's small band of warriors couldn't beat them alone. Star lifted his neck, ready to try.

Clawfire's second captain trumpeted for reinforcements.

A sleek mare trotted forward. Star flared his nostrils, catching her scent. It was Petalcloud. Her gray hide was so dark it looked black. Her stallions parted, letting her through. She reached the frontline and stood facing him, her neck curved in a high arch.

Silence dropped on them all.

She pranced with her tail lifted, considering Star and his friends with narrowed eyes. Her violet feathers reflected the silver moonlight, and her white blaze was shocking against her granite face. Star watched her liquid movements as she trotted toward them, her tail hairs fanning like silken spiderwebs. She turned her gaze on her ex-captain, Clawfire. "I'm disappointed in you," she nickered to him with the lilting purr of a young filly.

Clawfire pinned his ears. "You betrayed me," he said. "I accomplished my mission, and you banished me for it."

"I sent you on a raid for yearlings, and you brought

back one short-winged runt. The fact that she was my sister was only half your mistake."

Star peered into the woods, hoping Shadepebble was too far away to hear her sister's words.

Petalcloud flicked her silky tail at Clawfire. "Don't blame me for your failure."

Star tensed. Petalcloud was baiting Clawfire, trying to lure him into a reckless charge, knowing his two-hundred-steed battalion was outnumbered by her two thousand. Clawfire's muscles quivered, but he resisted the bait. Star watched Petalcloud trotting back and forth—this mare who'd rejected her birth herd, cast off her sister, banished her loyal captain, and abandoned her colt, Frostfire—and he wondered how she could lead a herd when she cared for no one but herself.

Petalcloud huffed and changed tactics. "Star," she said, pricking her ears forward and widening her eyes. "You look well."

Star took a step toward her, and her moose of a guard took a step toward Star. Stormtail was thick and burly, but Star was taller. He lifted his neck, and this forced the dapple gray stallion to look up at him. Malice glittered deep in the captain's black eyes, and Star snorted, ignoring him and speaking to Petalcloud. "You refused my help when I offered to heal your herd of the Blue Tongue plague. You accused me of trying to make a pact with you. If you're so against pacts, then why are you trying to make one with Nightwing?"

She snorted. "You offered to heal sickly steeds whom I have no use for. He's offering the power to rule Anok by his side. I wouldn't have made a pact with you if you'd asked me on your knees."

Star flicked his ears, stunned. "But I didn't ask anything from you. I just wanted to help."

Petalcloud reared and stamped the soil. "Snow Herd is smaller for our losses, but stronger." She spread her wings to indicate the two thousand vibrant warriors standing behind her. "Your power is useless, Star. It does nothing for the strong. We don't need you. Anok doesn't need you."

Petalcloud pranced closer, breaking pinecones under her hooves, tired of talking. She raised her wing and whinnied to the Ice Warriors, "Bring me his head."

Her army obeyed instantly, and they surged past her.

"Retreat," Clawfire neighed.

Star reared and whirled around. There were too many Ice Warriors to fight.

Clawfire galloped next to Star as their battalion streaked through the woods. "We need to collect our separate units into one," he neighed. "You're the fastest. Go. Find Sunray. She can send a signal to the rest."

Star lowered his neck, pumping it as he ran. He surged ahead, remembering how much faster he was than other pegasi.

Star glanced over his shoulder. Petalcloud's heavy, muscle-bound warriors slowed, already tiring after their first huge burst of speed.

Star flattened his ears and sprinted through the Trap, dodging trees and leaping over bushes, searching for the tallest tree in the center. Sunray was there, standing in her hoofholds, waiting to relay information.

Star squinted in the intermittent light from the moon. When he reached the center of the Trap, he scanned the tree trunks for the largest one. *There.* Redfire had cleared the brush from around its base and stained the bark with the juice of crushed red roots, making it easy to find. Star flew straight up to the top of the tree.

Sunray was there, her body shaking.

"What is it?" Star asked, hovering.

She panted. "Nothing, I just wish I knew what's happening. Where is everyone?"

"I don't know, but we need to gather them. Petalcloud didn't split her army."

"That's not what we expected."

"It's not," Star agreed. "Call the battalions to unite and send them west."

Sunray lengthened her neck and whistled a series of varied sounds. Each meant something different, and Redfire had trained the captains to decode the signals.

Sunray inhaled. "Okay, I'm finished."

Star jerked his head toward her. "Don't worry. Whatever happens next, I can fix it."

"But—"

"When you hear Hazelwind's signal, join us at the River Herd camp. We're not going to lose this battle."

Sunray calmed herself and nodded.

Star hovered a moment longer, watching the forest below. He couldn't see through the trees, but he heard the instant galloping of hooves. The captains had understood the message. The small platoons were uniting and heading west, toward what Star hoped was their final battle. He curled his wings and glided to the soil, and then he cantered back the way he had come.

40

UNITED

STAR MERGED PATHS WITH SILVERLAKE, BIRCH-
cloud, and Sweetroot as he galloped east. He nickered to
them and they halted. "What's happening?" neighed Silverlake.

"Petalcloud is here, and she didn't divide her army," he
answered.

The mares nodded with quick understanding and
pinned their ears. "We'll follow you," Birchcloud said.

Star led them east. "Stay close to the battle and drag
our wounded to the twin pines so I can heal them when this
is over. And grab our enemies too; take *all* the wounded."

Sweetroot blinked her large black eyes. "If you say so,
Star."

"You were once opposed to me healing pegasi," he reminded her.

Sweetroot tossed her mane, glowering south toward the Blue Mountains where Nightwing lived. "I've changed my mind."

Star heard the snapping of twigs, turned, and squinted. There in the dark was the handsome stallion Redfire and his warriors. Star whirled around to join them. "I'll see you at the twin pines later," he called over his shoulder to the mares.

"May the Ancestors be with you, Star," whinnied Silverlake.

Star cantered to Redfire's side. "The Ice Warriors have formed a solid front line," he reported. "They're big but slow."

Redfire grimaced, his neck pumping as he galloped in the dark. "We'll divide them."

"How?"

"The sky herders can do it." Redfire slid to a halt and lifted his head. Piercing whistles rose from his throat and echoed through the forest as he called the swift little mares to the battle. Within minutes, dozens of them appeared, flashing between the trees, and among them was Dewberry. They rushed past Star in a blur, and he thrilled at their agility and speed.

Redfire charged after them with Star and the warriors galloping behind.

Two more battalions from the United Army surged from the trees and joined them, then three more found them as they advanced on the Ice Warriors.

"There!" trumpeted a Jungle Herd captain.

Ahead, a cloud of dust became visible in the moonlight, and the thud of hooves slamming against flesh carried to Star's pricked ears. The battle was near and already under way. His heart thumped fast and hard, his muscles loosened and then tensed with anticipation, and his tail clamped against his rear. The steeds around him traded excited glances and rattled their feathers. Star lowered his neck as they burst through the trees and into the thick of the battle.

The sound of Star's breathing filled his ears, and it seemed the pegasi around him fought in slow motion. He dodged a kick to his head, whirled around and just missed a blow to his flank. Ice-sharp hooves flew in close quarters, and Star could not get his bearings. He ducked when Dewberry soared overhead. She'd been kicked out of sky herder training, but like everything Dewberry attempted, she excelled at it. Star was stunned but not surprised to hear her already clicking and whistling to the other sky herders in their ancient language.

Dewberry's team swarmed like bats, diving at the bulky Ice Warriors and driving them apart. But the stallions seemed ready for this strategy. They *allowed* the mares to cut out members of their herd and drive them away. Star gaped but realized the problem. The Ice Warriors had not bonded to one another like an army should, so the sky herders could not drive them off as a group. They had bonded only to Petalcloud. This meant that the only way for the sky herders to gain control of her army was to first gain control of Petalcloud.

Star reared, exposing his neck, chest, and belly; but he caught the attention of Dewberry. "They're like bees," he whinnied. "Get the queen. Get Petalcloud!"

Dewberry nodded and tore off to tell her friends the new strategy, but few were still flying. The stallions were snatching them out of the sky and hurling them into trees.

Chaos surrounded Star, and he staggered in the midst of it, afraid to let loose his mighty kicks for fear of striking one of his allies. He darted to the side as a pinto stallion charged him. Without thinking, Star whirled and clubbed him between the eyes, knocking him to the ground unconscious.

Star's breathing slowed as he focused on the battle, and the sounds around him became clearer. Grunts, moans, sharp whinnies, and shattering bones rocked his ears. Loose feathers erupted and drifted on the currents, sticking to the trees and soil. Star reminded himself that he would heal these steeds later, but there was nothing he could do to prevent the pain and terror of battle.

"Help!" neighed a yearling colt.

Star raced to the voice. It was Brackentail. A stallion had him by the wing and was twisting it, throwing Brackentail off balance. Star reared and bit the crest of the stallion's neck. He leaned all his weight onto the stallion and drove his teeth in deeper until the stallion let go. Brackentail kicked the stallion's front legs out from under him, and he collapsed like a mighty tree. "Thanks," wheezed the brown yearling.

Star noticed Brackentail's wing was torn—the same wing Star had healed once before. He panted, drawing starfire, and healed the orange feathers and bones in a short burst of golden light.

The fighting around Star paused as every steed turned to stare at him.

"Seize him!" whinnied Petalcloud.

Dozens of sky herders regrouped and dropped on

Petalcloud from above, striking her so many times that her black eyes swirled in her head. Her warriors leaped to her defense and drove the sky herders off. Meanwhile seven Ice Warriors joined together and charged Star as one. He backed away from them and bumped into the flank of another, and then three more surrounded him.

"Fly!" Hazelwind whinnied to Star.

But the stallions were so close to Star that he couldn't spread his wings, and he couldn't run. They blocked him on all sides. Star gulped down the foal-like urge to bleat for help. All around him thick-necked Ice Warriors threw off their attackers and advanced on Star, their eyes murderous in the moonlight. His muscles seized, and his blood ran cold. Star had two choices: use the silver fire of a destroyer and win the battle, or fight his enemy with tooth and hoof, and lose.

41

DEATHBLOW

STAR SPUN IN A CIRCLE, KICKING AT THE CLOSEST
stallions, trying to think. Hazelwind, Clawfire, Ashrain,
and others attempted to lure the stallions away from him.
Bumblewind was kicked so hard he flew into a tree and
slid to the forest floor. Dewberry charged across the battlefield and landed by his side, fanning his face with her
wings.

Panic flooded Star's thoughts. He had to stop this. If
Petalcloud seized him, her stallions would detach his head,
and the pact would be sealed. Star's guardians would be
destroyed or enslaved. He glared at Petalcloud, feeling
angry and desperate, and the crackling hum of destructive starfire erupted from his gut, and silver sparks flew

from his eyes like tears. She blinked at him, terror and awe in her eyes.

The Ice Warriors startled and jostled one another. "Hold," Stormtail cried.

Darkness flooded Star's mind and crushed his desire to heal his enemies. A terrible but intoxicating thought raced through his brain—he could kill them all. . . .

Star reared, shaking his head. *No!* He'd promised himself never to use the silver fire again, and he wouldn't, but he had to do something.

The Ice Warriors took a step back, fearful of the sparks. They glanced at Petalcloud, and Star followed their gaze. She tossed her mane, and he saw that she'd squashed her fear of him.

Petalcloud flew free of her attackers and landed in front of Star. More of her warriors surrounded her and him, cutting off his friends. Petalcloud kept her black eyes trained on his, taunting him. "It's not too late to save yourself." Her voice tumbled from the depths of her throat like a bubbling creek. She lowered her long lashes and swished her tail, blowing her scent his way.

Star's nostrils flared, catching the musk of her, and he arched his neck in angry response.

"Leave Anok," Petalcloud nickered. "And never come

back. You were born dead. Did you know that? You don't belong here."

Loathing for Petalcloud struck his heart. Yes, he knew he'd been born dead. His mother had forced life into him by shoving on his chest, cleaning his nose, and then biting his ear—hard. She'd died right after, and Silverlake had sworn to protect him. Maybe Star wasn't supposed to survive, but he had, and it was because of his guardians. He would not abandon them.

"Go," she said.

"Never," Star answered.

Her soft eyes hardened, and her flirtatious expression cooled. "Break him into a thousand pieces," she nickered.

"But the starfire?" whispered one of her captains.

She lifted her neck, and disgust curled her lips. "He won't use it."

Star glared at her, angry because she was right. He would not dive into the blackness of the silver fire that ate his soul. The plain truth was that he couldn't stop her stallions from tearing him apart if they wished. It would be up to his friends to save him.

Hazelwind trumpeted, calling his army to resume

their attack, and chaos erupted as they battled Petalcloud's warriors for Star's life.

Her stallions surged on Star, biting and kicking him. He spun in circles, shielding himself as best he could, but he was soon overwhelmed with pain. In seconds they felled him, and Star smacked onto the pine needles that covered the ground. Redfire's words blared through his mind. *To fall is to die.* A pale-gray stallion seized Star's wing and bent it until Star screamed. The Ice Warriors surrounded him.

The United Army slammed into the circle of Ice Warriors over and over, but the enemy steeds mounted an incredible defense—gathering like oxen with the largest steeds on the exterior of the circle and then rows and rows of lesser steeds behind them, and Star lay in the center, suffering kicks and blows from seasoned warriors.

Through the throng of legs, Star watched his friends battle with every ounce of their strength, sweat flowing down their chests and froth foaming from their mouths.

He covered his head with his wings as his enemies attacked him, their eyes full of hatred. His body was one massive inferno of pain.

The circle parted to allow Stormtail, Petalcloud's

gigantic guard, to enter. He pranced, alarmingly light on his hooves, with his long black mane sweeping the ground, and Star cringed. This was the stallion who would execute him. And this time there was no one to save him. The stallion reared over Star's head, his hooves black and sharp and curling through the air as they descended toward him. A hush fell over the Trap.

Star's heart raced forward, pushing blood and starfire through his muscles. Instinct gripped him, and Star panted hard and fast, drawing on his healing power. Golden tendrils of starfire crackled across his hide.

The enemy stallion's hooves dropped like rocks. Star couldn't dodge the coming blow, and so he faced it, watching the sharpened hooves descend toward him. Time slowed, and his golden fire sizzled through him.

The gray beast clenched his jaw and struck.

42

SURVIVAL

FEAR ERASED STAR'S THOUGHTS. HE OPENED HIS mouth and roared, projecting his golden starfire in every direction. It sprung from his core and formed a perfect sphere around him, like a bubble. The big stallion's hooves collided with the shimmering orb and bounced off it, leaving Star unharmed.

He gasped. He'd sprung a shield! Nightwing had a shield, and he'd used it to protect himself from Star in the Sun Herd lands. Now Star had a shield too.

The Ice Warriors surged forward, pummeling the golden sphere, but they couldn't penetrate it. Star watched them as though they were a million winglengths away, or in a dream.

Inside the orb he had plenty of air. When he moved, the sphere moved with him. He spread his wings, and the sphere stretched to accommodate him.

Petalcloud flew over her army. "Stop," she bellowed. "Get away from him."

Her cold eyes burned hot as she landed in front of Star. "You're going to regret this," she hissed.

Star snorted. "I don't think so."

Petalcloud extended a violet wingtip and touched the sphere, then jerked away as though it had burned her. She flattened her ears, furious. "This isn't over, Star. It's just beginning." She pointed at him through the shield. "*You* woke the Destroyer when you took your power. You should have let your over-stallion kill you as he planned. You disobeyed your guardian herd, and you brought a darkness to Anok that will never leave."

Star gasped and glanced at Hazelwind. The buckskin stallion was breathing hard. He shook his head, letting Star know that he didn't agree with Petalcloud.

Petalcloud leaned toward Star, pressing her face against the golden orb. "You think you're different, black foal, but you're not. You've been fighting to survive since the day you were born—just like us." She scanned the pegasi surrounding them. The Trap was silent as everyone listened, hooked on her every word. Petalcloud lashed her tail and stared into his eyes. "When Anok is in flames and the pegasi are enslaved by Nightwing, it will be your fault and yours alone. Don't forget that, and don't blame me for choosing him over you." She lifted her head, facing the United Army but pointing at Star. "Nightwing is strong, and Star is weak. You've all made a huge mistake."

Star pinned his ears and spoke so everyone could hear him, but he kept his gaze on Petalcloud. "We should be fighting Nightwing together. *You* chose the wrong side." He stepped closer to her, keeping his shield intact.

Petalcloud ruffled her sparkling violet feathers and raised her voice. "I'll give the United Army one chance, and one chance only, to join me and follow Nightwing." She leaned into Star and whispered. "You offered to help my herd once, now I'm offering to help yours." She looked around her. "If any of you accept, follow me now."

Her invitation drifted through the Trap, over the heads of Star's friends, and their ears swiveled as they understood her words.

Petalcloud whirled around and trotted back toward Antler Lake. Stormtail took his position at her right flank, and the rest of her army retreated with her, throwing angry glares at Star.

Star waited.

The United Army held strong. None of the warriors followed her.

He sucked in his starfire and extinguished his shield.

"Petalcloud is wrong," said Hazelwind. "Maybe you did awaken Nightwing, but he'd never truly left Anok. Fear of his return has lived in the hearts of pegasi for four hundred years. It's kept us suspicious and angry—not just of him, but of one another. It's been like a poison, slowly destroying us."

Star dropped his head, suddenly tired.

"I'm with you, Starwing," Hazelwind said.

"As am I," said Clawfire.

"And I," said Morningleaf, emerging from the evergreens with Shadepebble.

"We all are," Brackentail agreed.

Star swayed. He wasn't tired—he was badly injured. His head throbbed, and pain shot through his muscles like fire. Morningleaf darted to his side. "Give him some space," she whinnied.

Star closed his eyes, resting for a long moment. His friends settled, also resting. Sweetroot, Silverlake, and Birchcloud took stock of the wounded pegasi.

Star wanted to sleep, but around him steeds were

dying. He opened his eyes and swirled his starfire through his body, healing his cuts, bruises, and broken bones. When he was finished, he stood and healed the fallen warriors on the battlefield, starting with Bumblewind, who'd been knocked out.

His pinto friend opened his eyes. "What happened?" Bumblewind asked, shaking his head as if bothered by flies. Amused nickering rose from the steeds, and a river of tension flowed out of the United Army.

Morningleaf nuzzled Star. "I leave you for one second," she said, teasing him and wiping his forelock out of his eyes.

"I learned how to use my shield."

"That's good, because this isn't over. The armies failed, but I doubt Nightwing will give up."

"He might," said Star. "He can't hurt me now that I have a shield too."

"Do you think it'll be that easy?"

Star stared at the blood that muddied the soil. "I wouldn't call any of this easy."

After resting a bit longer, the United Army traveled back to the twin pines, where Star healed the remaining warriors who'd been pulled to safety earlier. The forest was cold and dark, but oddly cheerful. The pegasi had survived Frostfire's attack, befriended the Black Army, and survived Petalcloud's Ice Warriors.

Sweetroot wrung her feathers together, looking lost but pleased. She'd prepared wingloads of chewed herbs, calming roots, and sticky poultices, and they were stacked against the trees, unused. Star had healed everyone.

"Is there any food left over from the feast?" Bumblewind asked her. "I'm starving."

"Yes, back at the River Herd camp," she neighed.

Dewberry nuzzled him. "Everything makes you hungry."

Hazelwind trumpeted the call of victory, summoning Sunray, the scouts, and any stray warriors still in the Trap. They trotted back to River Herd's camp.

Sweetroot and the nursing mares passed out tree nuts, soft bark, and fireweed. Some of the smaller steeds raided birds' nests for late-season eggs. The United Army rested and ate, speaking about everything except war.

Morningleaf cracked nuts, and Star inspected them for worms. "What are we going to do now?" she asked.

Star exhaled, feeling serene. "I don't know, but I feel better, safer. I'm going to practice with the golden fire. Maybe I can do more than project a shield."

Morningleaf paused, swiveling her ears. "Did you hear that?"

Star dropped his wingful of nuts and listened. From deep in the woods came a strangled sound, and then a loud moan.

Hazelwind and his warriors leaped to their hooves.

The moaning came again, louder. It sounded like an injured pegasus.

Star flicked his ears forward. "Someone is still out there," he whinnied.

"Who?" brayed Hazelwind.

The groaning quieted.

"I must have missed a warrior," said Star. "I'll go get him."

Morningleaf flinched. "I'll go with you."

"No, eat and rest; I'll be right back. I have the shield, remember. No one can hurt me now."

Morningleaf relaxed her wings, and Hazelwind called off his warriors.

Star left camp and trotted into the woods.

43

CRY OF THE WOLF

THE CRUNCHING OF PINE NEEDLES WAS THE ONLY sound Star heard as he trotted toward the soft groans in the forest. "Hello?" he neighed.

The groaning ceased.

Star pricked his ears, approaching the area where he'd last heard the sound. He halted. "Hello?" he repeated.

There was no answer. To be safe, Star projected the golden shield. It blew out of him like a bubble and then closed around him, flexing as he moved. He trotted farther away from the River Herd camp where the entire United Army had gathered, feeling curious but safe inside his golden shell.

In the brush he glimpsed pairs of eyes glowing in the

dim light, watching him, but they were too small to be pegasi. They were attached to shapes that dashed behind the bushes—wolves. Star's hide prickled, but he wasn't afraid of wolves, not with his shield around him. They shadowed him, keeping their distance.

Star remembered the time he and Silverlake had searched the Ice Lands during a storm. He'd created light with his starfire to pierce the whiteout; he could use it now to illuminate the darkness. He opened his mouth and projected his starfire in a wide beam. The light glowed past the shield and lit his way. The wolves startled, one yelping with surprise, and they bolted away from him. Star was pleased at that, and then he heard it again, the moaning of a pegasus in great pain.

Star trotted forward and soon discovered the source of the groaning—it was the buckskin mare Larksong, the sky herder who traveled with Frostfire. He'd met her in the north, and he remembered her as a feisty mare, always asking questions. Now here she was, crumpled in the ferns, bleeding heavily from her nose. Her breaths were shallow, and Star could see that her ribs were broken, but he guessed most of the damage to her body was internal. It appeared she'd been beaten and left to die. She lifted her head, gazed at him, and then dropped it back onto the foliage.

Larksong was his enemy, but Star wanted to help her. "I can heal you," he said, lowering his head.

Her eyes, mere slits, glinted with suspicion.

"I won't hurt you," Star added.

Her wings twitched as though she wanted to fly away.

"You're dying," Star told her.

"I know," she said, gasping. "I don't care about me. . . ."

Star was confused until he saw that her wings were holding tight to her belly. He'd seen pregnant mares do the same thing, but Larksong's belly was small.

"You're with foal?"

She nodded.

"I can save both your lives, but I won't do it unless you ask me to." Star thought it would be wrong to force his power on her.

Larksong grunted and tried to stand, but her eyelids fluttered, and she fell back onto her side.

"You don't have to join my herd," Star promised. "I'll let you go as soon as I'm finished healing you."

Her eyes snapped to his. Star nodded to reassure her. "But if you want to join my herd, I'll accept you. It's your choice, Larksong."

She blinked rapidly, looking confused.

Star waited, watching the mare's labored breath rise

from her nostrils in twin bursts of mist. Finally Larksong nodded. "Yes. Help me," she said.

Not wanting to scare her further, Star exhaled gently, warming her first with the golden light, comforting her. She tensed but soon relaxed. Star stepped closer to her and blew starfire all around her, steadily increasing it until she was floating at the height of his shoulders. She scrambled a bit, but then stopped fighting and let the light suspend her.

Star watched her broken ribs straighten and her battle wounds close. When he felt the strong heartbeat of the foal in her belly, he let Larksong down and then extinguished the starfire.

Larksong swayed on her hooves and blinked her eyes. Her mouth opened and closed, but no words came out. She wrapped her wings around herself and sobbed in a sudden spurt of tears and choking breaths. She looked up into Star's eyes; hers were soft and glowing. "I—I . . ."

Star nickered. "You don't have to say anything."

Larksong wiped her eyes. "No. You don't understand." She glanced around her, as though someone were near. "I'm sorry," she rasped.

Star flared his wings. "For what?"

"Run," she urged. "Run back to your herd before it's

too late." She tossed her mane, anguished. "Petalcloud did this to me. She beat me and left me here, to lure you away from your friends."

Star inhaled so sharply he choked on his breath.

"Run!" she whinnied.

He turned and fled; galloping through the woods back to where he'd left his herd. Ahead he saw a flash of silver light, and he heard the sound of an explosion, like lightning striking a thousand trees at once.

No, no, no!

Star charged, blinded by fear, fueled by terror. What had he done? He'd left his friends alone.

Star blasted through the trees and into the River Herd camp. It was empty—no one was there. The air swirled with feathers and dust. Star's heart pounded, and his breaths came in rapid bursts. He trumpeted the call of an over-stallion to his missing herd, his voice reverberating for miles. When the echoes died away, he froze and listened.

There was no response.

A gust of wind shot through the trees, kicking up the thick dust that drifted through the air. It choked Star. He drew on his golden fire, ejecting it in a wide bright beam, and he illuminated the area where his friends had been standing not long ago. The light filtered through the particles that irritated Star's eyes and throat. Where had all this black dust come from?

He trumpeted for his herd again, his cry ringing through the trees. He dropped his head, sniffing for his friends. He picked up a familiar scent, and it reminded him of the forest fire he'd experienced as a weanling. Star's mouth filled with the small flakes, and he halted to spit them out. They tasted like dirt. He froze and threw up his head. This wasn't dust—it was ashes!

Star reared, trumpeting again, but the sound came out more like the cry of a bleating foal than that of a stallion. He dropped and snuffled through the dirt, searching for clues. He caught whiffs of acrid blood, the clean dry fragrance of feathers, and the charred scent of wood . . . and flesh. Star's back legs gave out, and he sat on his haunches, realizing what had happened. The ash was the burned bodies of pegasi.

Petalcloud had tricked him! She'd injured Larksong so that he'd abandon his friends, leaving them unprotected from Nightwing. The Destroyer's armies had failed to kill Star's guardian herd, had failed to retrieve Star's head—and so Nightwing had changed his plan. He'd attacked what Star loved most: his friends and protectors. But where were they?

Star's head dropped low, and he sobbed. White flowers sprang up all around him, pushing through the ashes of his murdered herdmates and reaching toward the sky. He stood and stomped them out. This was *his* fault. Petalcloud was right. He was to blame for waking Nightwing, which meant he was to blame for *this*. Star spread his wings in the glittering black dust—he couldn't heal ashes! How many of his friends had died? Where were the rest? Surely Nightwing hadn't killed them *all*; there wasn't enough ash here for that.

Star returned to investigating. If Nightwing had taken the rest of his herd captive, how had they left the area so quickly? Star tossed his mane, perplexed. As he continued searching for clues, he spotted a large, round pool of moonlight brightening the forest floor. He approached it warily, snorting and huffing at it. In all his time living in the Trap, he'd never encountered such a huge patch of light.

He glanced up and saw that a massive hole had been blasted into the leafy ceiling. It was allowing in the moonlight that filtered between the thick clouds. "This is how they got out," Star whispered to himself. And suddenly he could imagine what had happened in his mind's eye, as if he'd witnessed it: while Star was healing Larksong, the

Destroyer had surprised his herd. He'd killed the steeds who stood up to him and blasted a hole in the top of the Trap—that was the awful explosion Star had heard—and then Nightwing had flown away with the survivors.

Star unfurled his wings and flew up and out of the forest. A heavy but intermittent cloud layer blocked any chance of spotting Nightwing or his friends in the sky. Star glided in a wide arc. Which direction had they gone? Where was Nightwing taking them? Star swiveled his ears, listening for wingbeats. Anok felt absolutely empty.

Far away, a she-wolf howled, a plaintive wail that carried for miles. She was seeking her pack mates. Star answered the lone wolf with a cry of his own, the desperate plea of a pegasus abandoned. It floated over Anok like the songs of the huge, harmless whales that migrated off the coast—a yearning moan that shook Star's chest and begged for answering.

The wolf raised her voice, joining it with Star's. Then another wolf, miles away, joined them, then two more wolves. All around the Trap their voices rose and resonated in the cool atmosphere between the ground and the clouds. Star felt their song vibrate against his ribs.

As the howling died, loneliness flourished. Star had

lost his guardian herd, and not since his mother died had he felt so alone.

He pinned his ears and curled his neck as fury ignited his heart. He would find Nightwing and free his friends. He vowed it under the moon and stars, in a breath of golden starfire that burst from his lips like steam and then drifted toward the blackness of space.

A NOTE FROM THE AUTHOR

I'm thrilled you're reading the Guardian Herd series! Since you've just finished book three, I thought it'd be a good time to share with you the story about how these novels came to be published.

I grew up crazy for horses, but I was born to a family that couldn't afford them. To satisfy my cravings, I read horse books, volunteered at stables, bought horse toys, took lessons, and played "horses" at recess with my friends. I wrote in my diary that one day I would be a published author, I would write about wild horses, and I would own a horse that lived outside my window.

In pursuit of my goal, I worked hard at school and earned a scholarship to UC Berkeley, where I studied English literature. I wrote in my college essay that my ambition was to write animal stories for children. After I graduated from college, I proudly purchased my first horse, a failed Thoroughbred racer named Splash. She reared every time I rode her, kicked me twice, and trampled me once—of course I loved her dearly. Meanwhile I wrote middle grade novels about animals, but I was intimidated and clueless about how to get them published.

Time proceeded and then unexpected events derailed my writing for fifteen years: I fell in love and got married! A few years later, we started a family. My writing and my horseback riding took a backseat as I focused on raising our three children.

Once my youngest child began school, I resurrected my publishing dreams. I still wanted to write that special book about horses, but I felt like every horse story had already been told. Then, in June of 2012, I was driving down the freeway and I was struck by an intense visualization. I saw a herd of flying horses and they were migrating. A white mare was struggling to keep up and I noticed she was heavily pregnant.

A burning curiosity to know more about the pegasi and the special unborn foal overcame me. As soon as I got home I began *Starfire*. My daughter, then eleven years old, began reading the chapters and became equally intrigued, asking for a new one to be ready for her each morning when she woke up. So I set my alarm for 5 a.m., and I wrote like mad to accommodate her. When the draft of *Starfire* was finished, I sent it to a literary agent who had previously rejected me. Everything happened quickly after that because as it turns out . . . not every horse story has been told!

I am now living the dream I wrote about in my diary. I'm a published author, I write about flying horses (a more exciting version of a regular horse, don't you think?), and my real-life horses live in a pasture outside my window. The Guardian Herd series represents the sum of me—my passions, my favorite animals, the interesting places I've visited, and the hopes and fears that shape me. I believe these are the books I was born to write.

As the reader, I want to thank you for sharing this world with me. These characters and their stories belong to you now as much as they do to me, and I hope they find a special place in your heart, as they have in mine.

Jennifer

For more information about the series,
please visit www.theguardianherd.com.

ACKNOWLEDGMENTS

I'm grateful for the vision and enthusiasm of each member of the Guardian Herd team.

Karen Chaplin, senior editor at HarperCollins Children's Books, is my first point of contact for all things Guardian Herd. She looks out for me, but she also looks out for you, the reader. If it weren't for Karen, my guess is that you'd all be terribly confused because sometimes I leave important plot details in my head. Karen's good at digging them out and getting them into the book where they belong. We can all appreciate Karen for that!

I'd like to thank the following people at HarperCollins Children's Books for their support and talent:

Kimberly VandeWater for her creative marketing ideas (and a shout-out to her mother, who I hear is cheering for Star!).

Heather Daugherty for designing the beautiful jacket and interior layout.

Andrea Pappenheimer and the entire sales team for reading the books and then sharing their enthusiasm with booksellers.

Patty Rosati and Molly Motch from the library outreach team. Because of their efforts, the Guardian Herd books are available for children to borrow. How awesome is that? It's pretty awesome.

Kathy Faber for meeting me at several conferences and letting me ransack her brain regarding all things books!

Extra thanks from me to Olivia Russo (previously Olivia DeLeon) for arranging outstanding and seamless school tours. Because of Olivia, I've visited thousands of children across the country and had a blast doing it.

Now if you follow me on social media or you've visited my website— you probably know that David McClellan is the Guardian Herd illustrator. I'm a huge fan of David's artwork. He draws the covers, the maps, and the interior character sketches. He's given the pegasi physical bodies through his art, and I'm forever grateful for that.

Another talented man behind the book series is actor Andrew Eiden. Andrew is the Guardian Herd audiobook narrator. His sincere performances have given the pegasi their voices, and I love hearing him read the books. Deyan Audio produces the audio editions and the attention to detail is fantastic. Thank you, Andrew and Deyan Audio, for your mad skills! (Please visit www.theguardianherd.com to read behind-the-scenes interviews with both David McClellan and Andrew Eiden as they discuss their fascinating professions.)

Overseeing this grand adventure is editorial director Rosemary Brosnan. I'm absolutely thrilled she saw something in the first draft of *Starfire* that made her want to read more. We all need someone to believe in us and take a chance on us, and she did that for me. Thank you, Rosemary.

To my agent, Jacqueline Flynn—I couldn't ask for a better advocate, not just for my career, but also for me as a person. Thank you.

Huge thanks to booksellers and readers everywhere—you truly complete me.

Much love to my family, my friends, my church, and my animals. You inspire me.

Lastly, I'd like to acknowledge my father, Charles Lynn Jewett. He passed away eight days after the release of book one, *Starfire*. I'm grateful that he lived to see my dream come true because he also was a dreamer. As I went through his belongings, I found a to-do list. My dad was famous for making lists, especially when we traveled. At the end of each list, he wrote, "Bring list!" (He loved exclamation points, and as you've probably noticed, he passed that on to me.)

So on this particular day, as I was cleaning out his apartment, I found one of his famous lists, which he wrote at the age of eighty-two. I'll never forget the second item on it for two reasons: One, because I know he believed he could accomplish the objective; and two, because I thought it should top the list, that it should rate higher than buying vitamins—but that was my dad: his priorities were never ordered by urgency, but by some logic only he understood.

So this is what he wrote: "#1, Buy vitamins. #2, Build empire!"

Yes, my father planned to rule the world, but he would buy vitamins first.

Charles Lynn Jewett (1932–2014)
I love you, Dad. Fly straight and find your rest. —Jennifer

TALES FROM

THE
⇒ GUARDIAN HERD ⇐

Shadepebble's Capture

BY JENNIFER LYNN ALVAREZ

After Star received his power and formed River Herd, life returned to normal for the yearlings in Mountain Herd. But for one yearling filly, life had never been normal. Born a runt, a dud, and the daughter of Rockwing, Mountain Herd's over-stallion, Shadepebble lived under strict rules meant to keep her safe. Her sire didn't allow her to play rough games or fly by herself. He explained to her that foreign pegasi were evil and that she would only be safe at home with him. But after Shadepebble taught herself to fly, she convinced Rockwing to let her join the yearlings in flight school. Then, when a foreign patrol raids them, Shadepebble learns that her sire has been shielding her not only from danger, but also from the truth. This is her story.

SHADEPEBBLE CURLED UP IN THE SHADE, WATCH-
ing the Mountain Herd yearlings play tackle-tail in Canyon

Meadow. It was early morning; the sun had just peeked over the highest ridge and lit up the glittering frost that beaded the grass. Shadepebble nickered when a big roan yearling tossed her friend Ashwillow onto the grass. "You're out," he whinnied, and flew off after another yearling.

Two teams played in the valley. The object of the game was to snatch the tail of an opponent and slam the steed to the ground. If the targeted pegasus landed with all four legs in the air, the tackle was considered a pin. Once pinned, the target was out of the game. The last yearling still flying was the winner.

Each yearling in Mountain Herd played except for Shadepebble. Rockwing, her sire and the over-stallion, forbade her to play rough games because she was his last foal. With eighteen brothers born dead and her only sister, Petalcloud, gone, abandoning them to join Snow Herd, Shadepebble carried the full weight of her sire's love, and his disappointment.

She was not impressive or robust like her sister, and she was not powerful like the colts Rockwing dreamed of siring. Shadepebble was a runt and a dud, born with one wing shorter than the other. When Rockwing first saw her, he'd stomped the ground and made her mother cry. But upon realizing Shadepebble was *alive*, he'd rushed to her side and accepted her, licking her ears and look-ing grateful. Now, his mission was to keep her safe, so he wouldn't allow her to do anything dangerous—and play-ing with young pegasi was dangerous.

"Oof." A pinto yearling thumped onto the grass in front of Shadepebble, and she heard the soft crack of a bone. She looked up as the pinto limped off the playing field, holding back tears, to see the medicine mare—and he was the sec-ond yearling to visit her today. Shadepebble hated to admit it, but her sire was right. Tackle-tail was a dangerous game.

Ashwillow trotted across the meadow with her head turned skyward. "Greenblade is cheating," she huffed, speaking of the red roan yearling who'd tossed her out of the game.

Shadepebble followed her eyes and saw Greenblade charging after a filly, his muscles rippling, his sage-colored wings gripping the wind, and she swallowed, imagining the warrior he'd one day become. "No, I think he's winning fair enough."

Ashwillow dropped her head and butted Shadepebble in the rear like a mountain goat. "Get up and play with us."

"You know I'm not allowed."

"But your sire's not here. He won't know, and we won't tell him."

Shadepebble stood and folded her mismatched wings, hiding the smaller one under the larger one. "This isn't a game I'd win."

Ashwillow snorted. "I never win either, but it's still fun."

Shadepebble nodded as another steed smashed into the soil. "It looks fun," she said sarcastically, but deep down, she longed to play.

A full season had passed since her birth, and her short, bent wing had grown strong enough to carry her weight. She'd taught herself to fly, practicing alone in the canyons, and then she'd surprised her sire with a solo flight over his head. Instead of being angry, he'd been impressed. And yesterday he'd agreed to let her join flight school with the other yearlings. Rockwing wanted her to be strong for their upcoming migration to Valley Field, and today would be her second lesson.

Just then the instructor, a bay stallion named Hedgewind, glided over the trees and landed in the valley. "Formation, students!" he brayed, folding his wings.

Shadepebble trotted toward him with Ashwillow and the other yearlings. They lined up behind Hedgewind in angled rows.

"Ready?" he neighed, but he asked the question without enthusiasm. Hedgewind had been assigned to teach flight school after their last instructor was struck and killed by a lightning bolt. But much to his students' disappointment, the retired warrior preferred grazing to teaching.

"We're ready!" whinnied the yearlings, buzzing their wings.

Shadepebble rattled her feathers too, but her heart oozed dread. She was the slowest flier in Mountain Herd due to her mismatched wings. Yesterday the year-lings, who'd been flying since birth, cruised easily behind Hedgewind while Shadepebble had flapped madly at the end of the line.

Hedgewind must have remembered her difficulty from the day before because he glanced over his shoulder and said, "Someone needs to keep an eye on the little one."

The yearlings jerked their heads toward her, and Shadepebble ducked as though she could avoid their stares.

"You're not *that* slow," Ashwillow whispered.

Shadepebble flattened her ears. "Oh, thanks."

"I didn't—"

Hedgewind's eyes fell on Greenblade. "You, yes, the red roan. You stay with Shadepebble and make sure she doesn't fall behind like she did yesterday."

Greenblade rolled his eyes and left the front of the line to meet up with Shadepebble in the rear. "Hey," he said, studying her stunted wing with a skeptical eye.

She swallowed and her ears grew hot. "Hey," she answered back.

Greenblade flexed his wide, strong wings, twisting them to reflect the sunlight. "When I fly, I give off a pretty big wake. If you draft off me, you'll keep up, no problem."

As Shadepebble moved to Greenblade's right flank, the other fillies shuffled their hooves and glared at her with envious expressions. But Shadepebble relaxed. With Greenblade by her side, she had nothing to fear.

As the yearlings prepared for takeoff, Shadepebble closed her eyes and listened to their vibrating feathers. Her heartbeat thrummed and her breathing quickened. Then Hedgewind whinnied the signal, and the yearlings galloped into the sky. Shadepebble was catapulted forward on Greenblade's flowing wake, just like he'd promised.

As the pegasi ascended, the trees shrank below Shade-pebble's hooves. Even with Greenblade's help, she had to pump her little wing faster than the longer one to reach the flight school's cruising altitude. As the stout yearlings coasted in unison in front of her, she finally fell into their rhythm.

Hedgewind led his students through a dark cloud, and Shadepebble opened her mouth to taste the mist. "Where are we going?" she wondered aloud. They were coasting farther and farther from Canyon Meadow, heading west toward the old Sun Herd lands. She shivered, thinking of Star, the black foal of Anok. Her sire had won a great battle against Star and his guardian herd, but the black foal had escaped and formed River Herd. Now he had the power of the starfire, and he could be anywhere. Shadepebble scanned the clouds, feeling uneasy.

"Hedgewind is taking us to the Vein," said Greenblade.

"Why?" she asked, surprised. The Vein was the neutral territory between herds. It was supposed to be safe, but it was outside Mountain Herd's territory. With Star on the loose and the rumor of a Blue Tongue plague killing steeds in the north, Shadepebble didn't think her sire would want her leaving the Blue Mountains.

Greenblade glanced over his wing at her, lowering his voice. "There's untouched grassland in the Vein; that's why he takes us there."

"But he's supposed to be *teaching* us, not eating. Does my sire know about this?"

"Is there anything your father doesn't know?" huffed Greenblade. "Anyway, the Vein is safe enough."

"But the black foal? The plague? Times are not what they were."

"Yeah, well, it's better than starving. Our territory is picked clean. Be sure to eat during your breaks, and don't worry so much." He drew his neck into a tight, round arch. "I'll protect you from whatever comes."

Ashwillow had drifted closer to Shadepebble, and she stared at Greenblade so hard he turned away. "Wow," she mouthed to Shadepebble, her eyes riveted on the roan colt.

But Shadepebble's gut looped at his words. Greenblade might be large and powerful, but he was also young and not a battle stallion. His hooves weren't sharpened. She glanced at Hedgewind's hooves—they weren't sharpened either. She took stock of the school. They were flying *away* from the safety of the mountains under the protection of one apathetic teacher. None of them was safe! She decided she would speak to Rockwing about this as soon as they returned.

After flying for a while longer, Hedgewind signaled the group to land. Shadepebble glided to an animal trail, stubbed her front hooves on the landing, and somersaulted through the slushy snow. She rolled to a halt in front of Hedgewind.

He shook his mane at her, seeming annoyed. "We're practicing flying circles today," he said. "But Shadepebble will practice landings."

Everyone stared at her again as she pushed herself up and brushed off her knees with her wings. But Shadepebble was more irritated than embarrassed because she was actually quite good at flying circles. Her little wing and small size made it easy for her to spin tight patterns. She might have impressed her friends today—shown them that she was good at something—but Hedgewind was right; her landings were in dire need of improvement.

She watched the yearlings lift off and fly overhead, making large and small circles, flying faster and faster. Their feathers flashed in the rising sun, and their hooves split apart the clouds. Hedgewind neighed tips to them from the ground, between mouthfuls of grass.

"Lean into your turns.

"Did I say to slow down? Open your ears, yearlings. You need to build your speed before the turn.

"Stop watching your friends! Your body follows your muzzle. Point your nose where you want to go, not at what you want to look at.

"No! No! Tuck your legs. You look like a herd of flying squirrels."

Shadepebble flew to the tops of the trees and then back down, practicing landings over and over again like a weanling.

"You're breaking too early," said Hedgewind. "Wait longer, let the ground come to you, then flare your wings and glide down. Land on your back hooves first."

She nodded and tried harder.

As the day went on, Shadepebble noticed that Greenblade was correct about the foliage in the Vein. It was more plentiful here than in the mountains. Between her crash landings, Shadepebble snuffled through the patchy snow and stuffed her belly with juicy plants.

Midmorning, Hedgewind whistled for them. The yearlings descended in slow circles and touched down softly in the wet pine needles around their teacher. Shadepebble glided to the forest floor, flared her wings, and braked at the last second. She landed with a loud grunt, but she didn't fall.

"That's enough for today," Hedgewind said to the group. "We'll practice sprints on the way home. Pair up and take turns racing each other." He pointed at Greenblade. "You stay with Shadepebble."

The big yearling nodded and trotted to Shadepebble's side.

"I'm sorry you got stuck with me today," she said to him.

He nudged her shoulder. "Hey, it's all right. I don't mind."

She flicked her ears, feeling grateful but also sad. It seemed unfair to have two weaknesses: a stunted body and a stunted wing.

Ashwillow had paired up with a filly named Bright-leaf, and the pair swooped toward Shadepebble and Greenblade. "Brightleaf and I will race you two home," said Ashwillow. "I know a nest that already has eggs in it. They're warm and fresh. The first one back to Canyon Meadow gets to eat them."

"You're on," whinnied Greenblade. But he didn't need the temptation of raw eggs to lure him; everyone knew how much he liked to win.

Ashwillow gazed up at him, her eyes glowing. Shade-pebble nickered, knowing that her friend didn't care if she won or not; she just wanted to chase Greenblade. She took a breath, feeling content. The news that some birds had already laid eggs was good. It meant they'd have a warm spring. And so far, the black foal hadn't conquered the herds or sought revenge on her sire or Mountain Herd. Maybe everything would be okay.

"Let's go home," brayed Hedgewind. He galloped into the sky, and the yearlings lifted off behind him.

But Shadepebble was tired from the day's lessons. "You guys race," she said to her friends. "I'll be right behind you." She cruised at her own pace, watching the action ahead. Greenblade turned several times to check on her, but she encouraged him to have fun. "Faster!" she neighed. "Ashwillow is catching you!"

Before she knew it, her friends had shrunk in the distance and a cold chill settled in her heart. Everyone had passed her by.

Then she heard flapping wings behind her and felt immediate relief. "So I'm *not* the last one!" She turned to see who it was, and then sharp teeth gripped the base of her tail, yanking her backward. White fur flashed in the sky. Blue-gray feathers floated around her. Hot pain shot down her back.

Shadepebble screamed and twisted around. A huge, furry white stallion had her tail clamped between his teeth. A long, jagged scar divided his face in half. His golden eyes pierced her like sunrays.

She fluttered her wings, trying to pull away from him. Six more stallions surrounded her. She guessed by their size and coloring that they were from Snow Herd.

Far in the distance, Hedgewind turned and saw her clutched in the stallion's jaws.

"Help!" she whinnied. Her sharp cry sent a flock of sparrows darting out of the trees.

But her teacher hesitated.

Ashwillow and Greenblade whirled around. Hedgewind trumpeted orders to his students. "It's a raid! Fly home!"

Greenblade ignored Hedgewind and rocketed toward Shadepebble, followed by Ashwillow.

Meanwhile, Shadepebble thrashed and kicked the huge white stallion in the chest. He grunted and tried to reposition his grip on her. In that second, Shadepebble fell out of his mouth.

She balanced her wings, pushed down on the air, and surged toward the clouds.

"They're after you!" neighed Ashwillow. She and Greenblade flapped harder, closing the distance between them.

But the golden-eyed stallion was faster. He and the six others chased Shadepebble into a massive cloud. She tried to hide in the mist, but their huge wings scattered the fog. She flew a tight circle, darted behind them, and then dived toward land. She was small and they were big; maybe she could lose them in the trees.

Four stallions plummeted after her.

Greenblade and Ashwillow arrived and attacked the other two, but the furry steeds dwarfed the yearlings. A gray stallion kicked Greenblade in the flank and sent him spinning into Ashwillow. Her two friends fell toward land.

"This is neutral territory!" Greenblade neighed as he tried to regain his wings.

Shadepebble understood what was happening—this was a kidnapping! "Don't let them capture you," she whinnied to her friends. "Fly home. Tell Rockwing."

Ashwillow and Greenblade hit the ground and bolted away on hoof to get help.

Shadepebble dropped into the forest and angled through the trees. Her agile body narrowly dodged thick branches and wide trunks. Melting snow dripped off the leaves and onto her back. Shadepebble pinned her ears and concentrated.

The white stallions flew above the forest and peered through the leafless branches at her. She realized her mistake. The trees would have slowed them down had they flown as low as she, but instead they glided above the woods, unencumbered. Three stallions passed her, four slowed and stayed behind her, and then all seven crashed through the branches and surrounded her.

A yellow-feathered, gray pegasus shoved her with his shoulder, and Shadepebble tumbled headfirst onto the ground. She lay in the pine needles, fighting for breath. Her foreleg bled where it had scraped against a rock. But she was the filly of an over-stallion. She would not cry out. She stood up and faced her captors.

"You hurt her," scolded the pegasus with the frightening scar.

"So? We can't return to our territory with just one filly—especially this one." The gray stallion nodded toward Shadepebble's stunted right wing. "Let's snap her neck and get out of here before Rockwing comes."

The golden-eyed stallion examined Shadepebble. "No. She's healthy. Let's keep her."

Shadepebble guessed he was the leader.

"But—"

The white stallion rocked back and flared his wings, threatening the other. Shadepebble memorized the leader's blue-gray feathers and the long, ragged scar that ran from his forelock to the end of his nose. When her sire came for her, this stallion would be the first to die.

"But Twistwing will be disappointed?" continued the agitated pegasus. "Our orders are to bring home *strong* yearlings to replenish the herd, not one runt filly."

Shadepebble let out her breath, relieved. These stallions didn't know who she was, which meant they wouldn't try to use her to control her sire. They'd only caught her because she was slow, not because she was special. She shook her mane—normally that would not be a comforting thought.

"And you think Twistwing will be *less* disappointed if we bring home no yearlings?"

The annoyed pegasus held the gaze of his leader for a long time. Finally he lowered his head and shrugged his wings. "You're the captain."

The scarred stallion turned to Shadepebble. "I'm Clawfire," he whinnied.

She stared at him, saying nothing.

"We're taking you north. Follow us or we'll carry you. Try to escape and we'll hunt you down. You're a Snow Herd filly now. Accept your fate. You will never return to Mountain Herd."

They lifted into the sky, and Shadepebble followed because she didn't want to undergo the indignity of being carried like an over-tired foal. As they flew, she tried to gather her thoughts. She hadn't heard of a raid or a kidnapping since the black foal had received his power in Canyon Meadow one moon ago. The herds had all lived in relative peace—until now.

But why raid Mountain Herd? Her sire was the most feared and respected over-stallion in Anok. At least that's what the elders claimed during the evening story time in

Canyon Meadow. And she'd seen the dread in the eyes of these seven warriors when they worried about Rockwing showing up.

She glanced at the first ridge of the Blue Mountains. Soon Hedgewind and her friends would arrive in Canyon Meadow and inform her sire about the kidnapping. Any moment now, he'd crest that ridge and save her. Any moment . . .

Clawfire followed her gaze and seemed to read her thoughts. "They should be after us by now."

The yellow-feathered stallion lashed his tail. "Rockwing won't risk a war over a runt."

Clawfire considered his words. "You're probably right," he said. "That's good news for us." He led the group out of the mountains. They coasted north as the sun peaked overhead. They flew all day, and as soon as it was dark, Shadepebble let her tears fall. There was no sign of her sire coming to save her, not as far as she could see. And she knew why. It was because Hedgewind was a coward! He was hiding, she guessed. He was afraid to tell her sire what had happened. But when Rockwing found out that Hedgewind had abandoned her, he'd execute the stallion and save Shadepebble. She glanced behind her at the dark horizon, which was empty.

She longed to tell these Snow Herd stallions who she was—just to see the fear on their ugly faces. But she wasn't ready to give up that information yet. There was a chance they'd kill her on the spot or try to use her to control Rockwing. But if they made it all the way to Snow Herd's territory, her sister would figure out who she was quick enough.

Petalcloud had lived with Snow Herd for many seasons, but a messenger had informed her when Shadepebble was born. Petalcloud knew she had a tiny spotted sibling with one short wing and pale-pink feathers—and Shadepebble was probably the only yearling in Anok who fit that description. And Shadepebble couldn't wait to see Clawfire's face when Petalcloud revealed her identity. Then this scar-faced captain would understand that he had brought home more than just a short, malformed filly—he had brought destruction to his herd! Rockwing would stop at nothing to get Shadepebble back.

It seemed that, for better or for worse, war had returned to Anok.

The journey to Snow Herd's territory lasted eight days. Shadepebble's captors were tense and watchful until they crossed over their southern border. Each day of the journey, the scarred, golden-eyed stallion named Clawfire had made sure Shadepebble had enough water, food, and sleep. She'd drafted off his large wake, at his insistence, and this had helped her travel so far, so long, without her small wing cramping.

Now they cruised over the snow-covered tundra that was the same shade of gray as the sky. Shadepebble had no idea if they were flying high or low until she spotted a tree or a boulder or anything that lent her eyes perspective. The cold air burned her lungs, and she believed she'd freeze to death if she stopped moving. In the eight days of travel, she'd not spoken a single word to her captors.

Clawfire landed them to graze on fresh lichen. "We'll arrive at Snow Herd's winter valley today," he told her.

Shadepebble legs weakened at the news. Her confidence had eroded the farther they'd flown. Her herd was so far away, her sire's army had not appeared as she'd expected, and she guessed Petalcloud would be angry when she saw Shadepebble. Her older sister had made it clear that she wanted nothing to do with her Mountain Herd family.

Clawfire was watching Shadepebble, and he misread her concerned expression. "Don't worry," he said. "Snow Herd will accept you. You're one of us now."

Shadepebble squared her shoulders with his. "I'll never be one of you." She spat the words, her first in eight days.

"But you're here. You have to accept us."

She pinned her ears. "No. I don't." Stealing weanlings and yearlings was common in Anok. Most young steeds acclimated to their new herd, and some even went on to become warriors and leaders. But she was no ordinary yearling. She was the daughter of an over-stallion.

Clawfire kicked at the snow. "The sooner you decide to get along, the better. I'll allow you a few days to adjust, and then you'll start flight school with the rest of our healthy yearlings."

Shadepebble reeled. She'd been so sure she'd be rescued by now that she hadn't given much thought to the Blue Tongue plague, but she was about to face it. Or had she already? Her thoughts raced. What if one of these seven stallions was carrying it? Maybe this was why her sire hadn't come for her? He couldn't risk exposing his entire army to the plague, could he? Not with Star roaming Anok, gathering more followers.

She glared at Clawfire with new understanding. This captain was a devoted and loyal stallion who was following orders and trying to save his herd from extinction. A stallion like Clawfire was an asset to his herd—but he and she were on opposite sides. "I want to go home," she said.

Clawfire's hard golden eyes softened. "I'm sorry; that's impossible."

Her wings drooped. "You'll be sorrier when you find out who I am," she said, unable to stop herself.

He startled. "Who are you?"

"You'll know soon enough."

The stallion exhaled, his breath forming a burst of steam. "Come on, we're almost home."

The group kicked off and flew toward Snow Herd.

Shadepebble was glad to be flying again because flapping her wings kept her warm. They soared over a frozen lake and spooked a herd of large deer-like creatures with massive antlers. There were thousands of them running together. "What are those?" she asked in surprise.

"Caribou," said Clawfire. "And they will rip you to shreds if you get near them."

"I won't," she whispered. Soon an incredible mountain range appeared on her right, rivaling the Blue Mountains in height and breadth. Its surfaces were frosted with bright snow from the peaks to the bottoms. Ahead was a valley, and the snow there was well trampled, revealing green moss and dark bogs. Shadepebble saw a white bear standing on its hind legs, another herd of deer-like animals that Clawfire called elk, and a pack of wolves slinking across the tundra.

She noticed that the creatures were unafraid of the winged shadows of the pegasi. In her territory, even the black bears scooted for cover when pegasi flew overhead.

"There's Snow Herd," said Clawfire, taking a long, proud breath.

Shadepebble followed his gaze and saw hundreds of light-colored pegasi with pale feathers. Pregnant mothers grazed in a large group, yearlings played a game nearby, a band of warriors exercised overhead, and a collection of seriously ill steeds gathered far from the others.

A large ocean bay encroached inland from the sea. The water was not frozen, and it glistened in the cool sunlight. The wind was strong, and it pushed the fog toward the mountains. Clawfire whistled to his herd, and Shadepebble's gut twisted. Soon she would see her sister.

As they approached, a small envoy of pegasi lifted off and met them in the sky. "One filly?" said a magnificent red dun stallion.

Shadepebble guessed this was Twistwing, the angry captain who'd left Sun Herd and joined Snow Herd when Icewing had given up his power to follow Star. Twistwing had quickly taken advantage of the plague-stricken, leaderless herd and battled four contenders, one at a time, for the position of over-stallion. He won all four battles and sent messengers to the other herds informing them of his new status.

"Yes, just one filly," answered Clawfire.

Twistwing examined Shadepebble's wings. "What's wrong with her?"

"She's healthy," said Clawfire defensively.

"She doesn't look healthy," said Twistwing. "She's rangy and skinny."

"She's flown for eight days, and she's shivered off most of her weight," he explained. "But she's strong, and quite agile."

Twistwing huffed and ushered them to the ground. The Snow Herd pegasi stopped grazing to stare at her. Instead of the ferocious steeds she'd expected, she saw that their eyes were sad and defeated.

Then, out of the grouping of warriors, a gray mare emerged, and Shadepebble sucked in her breath. She'd never met her sister, Petalcloud, but she knew instantly that this was she. Their mother, Birchcloud, had described Petalcloud to perfection.

The mare approached with a carefree and brazen

expression until she spied Shadepebble. Then she pointed and choked on her words. "What is *she* doing here?"

Twistwing lashed his black tail. "You know her?"

"Yes. Her name is Shadepebble, and she's my sister."

The watching Snow Herd steeds lifted their heads, murmuring in fear.

"That's Rockwing's filly!"

"Clawfire has brought death to Snow Herd."

"No, death is already here!"

Twistwing rattled his feathers. "You captured Rockwing's filly!" he bellowed at his captain. "We can't fight the Mountain Herd army in our condition. You've killed us, Clawfire!"

Clawfire looked horrified, and even Shadepebble felt pity for him. The six stallions under his command edged away from him. "I didn't know who she was," said Clawfire. "I'll . . . I'll return her."

"Return her?" Petalcloud snorted. "The deed is done, captain." She glared at her sister. "Did anyone from Mountain Herd see you take her?"

"Yes," said Clawfire. "Several yearlings and her flight school instructor."

Petalcloud paced, and Shadepebble studied her. The stories about her sister were true; she was stunning, more beautiful than any mare Shadepebble had ever seen. Her feathers looked as soft as the spring velvet on a buck's antlers. Their violet color was bright and pure against the backdrop of the snowy mountains. Her winter coat was so dark it looked almost black, and her silver mane and tail shone like spider silk. She was well muscled and taller than most Mountain Herd mares. Here in the north, she'd grown a thick hide that masked her sparkling summer coat, but it was sleek and smooth, like the pelt of a baby seal.

"We can't keep her," said Petalcloud. For all her sister's warm beauty, Petalcloud's eyes were as cold and harsh as the north.

"Please let me go," whinnied Shadepebble. "I won't tell Rockwing who captured me. I promise."

Petalcloud tossed her glistening mane. "He already knows." She made a show of scanning the horizon. "But it's interesting he's not here."

"Please," said Shadepebble again. "Think of our dam. Birchcloud can't lose another foal. It will kill her. Let me go. I'll say I escaped."

"You . . . escaped?" whinnied Petalcloud. "No pegasus would believe that." She rolled her eyes over her sister's body. "I heard about your . . . defects . . . but I had no idea they were so pronounced. It's hard to believe we're sisters."

Shadepebble gasped, and her eyes tingled with hot tears. Her sister was evil, that's what everyone said when they weren't admiring her beauty. She hadn't wanted to believe it; but now that she was here, she understood why they said it, and questions sprang from her tongue. "Why did you leave our mother?" she asked. "You were her first live foal. Birchcloud misses you." Shadepebble wiped her tears. "And your colt, Frostfire, is killing himself trying to please Rockwing. He's so lonely. How could you have traded him"—she peered at the frozen north—"for this horrible place?"

Twistwing and Clawfire tensed, unsure what to do about the arguing mares.

Petalcloud rocked back on her hooves like she might strike Shadepebble. "*This* horrible place?" she neighed. "You're deluded, Shadepebble. It's Mountain Herd that's horrible. Birchcloud loved me, I know that, but Rockwing didn't even see me!" Fury twisted Petalcloud's composure. "How could I live with a sire who hated me for being female? I might have been his first living foal, but I was his nineteenth disappointment—and you're the twentieth!"

Shadepebble fluttered her pink feathers and shook her head.

Petalcloud took a long, calming breath. "Everyone

thinks I left my family because I wanted power. They're wrong. I left because I was *invisible*." She stamped her hoof, and snow splattered her leg. "Rockwing is not going to rescue you, Shadepebble. You can get that out of your head right now."

Shadepebble stood shivering; her sister's claims stunned her. Was it true? Would her sire let her go without a fight? Was she just another disappointment? She glanced south. A band of strong warriors, flying an urgent rescue mission, should have caught up to her by now.

Clawfire interrupted. "If she's right and Rockwing doesn't want her, then we're safe. We can assimilate her into the herd."

"No," neighed Petalcloud. "I said my sire wouldn't *rescue* her. I didn't say he wouldn't *avenge* her. Trust me, he'll punish us for taking what's his. Rockwing will come, probably this summer. We're weak, and the other herds won't stop him once they hear we stole Shadepebble. We have to disown ourselves from this now."

Twistwing sighed. "And how do we do that?"

Petalcloud pointed at Clawfire. "Banish him. We'll claim that Clawfire went rogue. That he's stealing yearlings to start his own herd."

"Went rogue?" neighed Clawfire, stunned. "I'm your

captain, Petalcloud. I've fought in six wars. I was born here." He looked from his lead mare to his over-stallion.

For the second time today, Shadepebble felt pity for the unlucky stallion. He'd made a huge mistake when he plucked her out of the sky.

All the gathered pegasi held their breath as they waited for Twistwing's decision. Finally the over-stallion spoke. "You're banished, Clawfire."

The captain's warriors immediately trotted away from him, leaving Clawfire and Shadepebble standing alone together. The rest of the army, which had landed to listen, also turned their backs on him.

"You're no longer a Snow Herd pegasus," said Twistwing. "You are a phantom, a ghost. Leave now with your stolen filly and don't come back. Your life is in your wings."

Shadepebble watched as all of Snow Herd turned their backs on Clawfire and walked away. Several mares broke into loud sobs, but they didn't look back. Shadepebble marveled at her prior words to Clawfire. She'd told him he'd be sorry when he found out who she was, but she hadn't expected this. Banishment was worse than death.

Clawfire faced her, his eyes empty. "Let's go," he said in a harsh whisper. He turned, and she followed him. For better or for worse, their fates were now tied together.

On the third day of their banishment, Shadepebble and Clawfire flew low over the sparse trees toward the north-eastern Vein. "Where are we going?" she asked him.

"I don't know yet," he muttered. "Just away from Snow Herd."

The climate grew harsher, and Shadepebble hid her misery and her tears. The terrain was flat and drab. Each day was the same as the last, and she couldn't tell if they were moving forward or flying in endless loops. But Clawfire flew with surety and led her farther and farther north. His thick, furry hide kept him warm. Her sleeker pelt did little to protect her.

Soon Clawfire landed them next to an oval pond and struck the icy surface with his hoof, breaking it and revealing the water underneath. "Drink," he told her. Up close, she noticed his golden eyes were flecked with amber.

Shadepebble scowled at him, but drank. The cold water shocked her teeth and went down her throat like fire.

"Spring is coming," said Clawfire. "Everything will warm soon and you'll feel better."

She whirled around, pretending to ignore him. Claw-fire was considerate for an enemy, always trying to help her and soothe her. It drove her crazy because she wanted to hate him.

"Let's move on." Clawfire kicked off and cruised low over the snow. "There are no herds east of our territory," he continued. "So I think we can fly higher now without fear of being spotted. Keep up." He pushed down hard on the wind and lifted himself into the foggy clouds.

Shadepebble flapped madly, her short wing doing twice the amount of work as the longer one, but she kept up with him. Clawfire chose an altitude that was high enough to coast on strong winds, but not high enough to encounter the dangerous jet streams. He settled in a northeastern tailwind, and Shadepebble drafted off him. As far as she could see, the world was frozen and white. Her sire would never find her here.

When evening came, Clawfire dropped to the base of a mountain range that had appeared out of the fog. It was also white save for several dark-gray exposed cliffs and crevices. The leafed trees were bare amid the needled trees, looking like upright skeletons. Shadepebble coasted in to land beside him; but her exhausted wing failed to slow her, and she crashed into Clawfire's flank.

He wrapped his blue-gray wing around her back to steady her.

Shadepebble kicked him in the ankle. "Don't touch me."

He folded his wings. "I thought you needed help."

"Of course I need help," she said. "I've been kid-napped—by you!" She lifted her head and whinnied for her herd as if they might hear her.

"Shush!" Clawfire said, trying to cover her mouth with his wings. "You'll draw predators."

Shadepebble bristled, holding his stare.

He tossed his gray forelock out of his eyes. "Why didn't you tell me who you were when I took you?" he asked.

"What?" Shadepebble's mind reeled at the change of subject. "Why would I?"

"No herd wants to anger your sire. If you'd told me, I'd have let you go."

She paused, knowing she shouldn't talk to him at all. Rockwing had taught her that foreign steeds were danger-ous and cruel—all of them. She couldn't trust Clawfire. She clenched her jaw, thinking. But this captain had not been cruel to her. And now he was banished. He'd lost his herd, his rank; he'd lost everything.

Her pity for him returned, but she knew better than to indulge it. Still, there was no one else to talk to, so she answered him. "At first I assumed you knew who I was, that you were kidnapping me to control my sire. By the time I realized you didn't know, I was afraid to tell you for the same reason—that you'd use me against Rockwing or kill me on the spot." She glanced mournfully at the desolate tundra. "I never thought it'd go this far."

"Something must have happened to stop him," said Clawfire. "You're his filly. He'll come for you."

"Hah," she snorted, suddenly unsure. "Well, he hasn't, has he?" Her eyes slid to her stunted wing—it made her slow, but did it also make her unlovable?

He noticed the look she gave herself. "Maybe you're better off," he said. "Your sire has a . . . reputation, and it's not a good one. Many of the steeds we've taken from Mountain Herd have thanked us."

She gasped. "My sire is *good*; he keeps us safe. And I doubt any Mountain Herd steed ever *thanked* you." She rattled her feathers. "Just let me go, and I'll fly home by myself."

"I have considered that," said Clawfire, folding his wide wings, "but it's not safe to travel that far alone. I've decided to take you to River Herd."

"What! Why?"

"Star is the most powerful pegasus in Anok now. He can return you or keep you, but either way, you'll be safer with his herd than with me alone."

"No. I don't trust Star," she blurted. "He tried to kill Rockwing."

"Hmm," said Clawfire, narrowing his eyes. "I remember that the other way around."

Shadepebble stamped the snow. "Don't talk to me."

The days were short in the north, and Shadepebble and Clawfire often traveled in the dark. She was dozing now, after flying half the night. Clawfire stirred and stretched his wings. Then his body tensed and he woke her.

She startled. "What is it?"

"Look," he said, pointing above them.

Shadepebble raised her eyes. Bright, floating colors danced above her, dashing and streaking and lighting up the sky. A thrill ran through her belly. "What is that?" she asked, forgetting she was angry.

"It's our Ancestors," he answered. "They're flying in the golden meadow. You can't see their bodies, but those streaks of light are their colorful feathers."

"Can we fly up there and see them closer?" Shadepebble was wide-awake now.

"Sure, but they're like rainbows. We'll never reach them."

"I don't care," she breathed.

"Let's go." They kicked off together and flew into the

dark sky. Clawfire barreled ahead of her and flew a loop just for fun.

He's playing, she thought. The adults in Mountain Herd never played.

Shadepebble watched the speeding colors of her Ancestors' feathers, and she wondered if they were Clawfire's Ancestors too. "Do the pegasi from all the herds live in the golden meadow together?" she asked.

"Of course. In the end, we're all one big herd."

Shadepebble followed him up, higher and higher. She soared in a loop with her head tilted back so that she spied the base of her tail. The world spun until she was facing the ground. Dizziness confused her, and she broke her loop, stalled out, and fell.

"Lift your muzzle," whinnied Clawfire.

She did and she righted herself.

"Let's land before we start sweating," said Clawfire. "It's not safe to sleep with wet hides."

He swooped toward the glittering snow and landed, making a white puff of powder. The mountain range stood behind him, a magnificent sentry against the wind, and Shadepebble saw for the first time the harsh beauty of the north. She made a perfect landing beside him.

Clawfire folded his wings and gazed at her; his eyes

appeared yellow in the moonlight. "You fly well."

"Thank you," she said, not expecting a compliment. Shadepebble listened to her heartbeat in the snow-muffled silence. "I feel like we're the last two pegasi in Anok."

"We might as well be," answered Clawfire.

Shadepebble fell asleep under the attentive guard of the golden-eyed, scar-faced stallion and grudgingly realized something: she didn't hate him.

The following morning, Clawfire woke her with a hard shove. "Storm!" he whinnied, pointing his wing toward the horizon.

Shadepebble shifted her eyes and saw what looked like a wall of snow coming toward them. She lurched to her hooves. "What do we do?"

"We have to find shelter. Now!"

They galloped across the frozen tundra. The wind whistled and blew their tails forward as they raced in the opposite direction of the snowstorm.

"There!" neighed Clawfire. "We'll shelter behind that clump of boulders."

He led her to an arrangement of large rocks at the base of the mountains. The huge stones leaned against one another and were taller than Clawfire. He used his hooves and wings to dig into the snowdrifts against the base of the natural shelter. Shadepebble trotted next to him and helped. The snow flurries crossed the tundra toward them, the wind stung their tender muzzles, and the pale sun vanished behind dark clouds. "Hurry," she cried.

"Done," he said, and he pulled her into the little nest they'd dug. The huge rocks leaned over them, giving them some protection from the wind and falling snow. Clawfire tucked in next to her and folded his wings over their heads, making a feathered cocoon. Soon their breath warmed the pocket of air, and Shadepebble stopped shivering. "Are you warm enough?" he asked.

"Yes," she answered. It would have been so easy for Clawfire to abandon her and let her die in the north. Each moment he spent with her meant doom if her sire's patrols spotted them together. Instead he risked his life to take her to Star, where he thought she'd be safe. But would the magical stallion turn her away? "What makes you think the black foal will accept me?" she asked. "If he's peaceful, he won't want to risk angering my sire."

"You're right, Star is peaceful," said Clawfire, "but he's not afraid of Rockwing, or any stallion. He has the starfire now. Your sire is the one who should be afraid."

Shadepebble startled. "Is that a threat?"

Clawfire nickered. "Why are you so suspicious, Shade-pebble? Don't you believe that some pegasi *want* to live in peace?"

"No, I don't. Foreign herds are always attacking my herd, for no reason. My sire works hard to protect us."

"For no reason?" sputtered Clawfire, shaking his head. "Do your elders teach *any* pegasi history?"

"Of course they do," she huffed. The wind blew around them with such force that she had to raise her voice. "Each night they describe the attacks we've endured and how my sire won the battles. He's a legend."

Clawfire sighed and stopped talking.

"What's wrong?"

"I won't speak against your sire," he said, drawing closer to her as the storm gained strength. "It's clear you admire him."

"That's right," said Shadepebble. She stared at Claw-fire's blue-gray feathers that sheltered her. *I won't speak against your sire*—what did that mean? Her thoughts swirled. She'd already realized that Rockwing was wrong about one thing: not *all* foreign steeds were awful, vicious killers; Clawfire was proof of that. And if *her* herd had captured the foal of an over-stallion, they'd have killed it immediately, for their own safety, of course. She shook her head. Suddenly that seemed cruel.

Was it possible that *her* herd was the violent one? That foreign pegasi attacked them because they'd been provoked? Suddenly she had to know more. "Will you teach me pegasi history?" she asked Clawfire. "Perhaps . . . I haven't heard the whole truth."

Clawfire nodded. "I will," he said. As the storm raged around them, Clawfire told her stories about battles, ancient and new; about past kidnappings and raids; about her sister, Petalcloud, coming to Snow Herd; about the over-stallions of Anok; and about her sire, Rockwing. He answered her questions with forthright honesty and spoke about all the herds' traits, both good and bad.

When he was finished, two days had passed, the storm was over, and Shadepebble was starving, not just for food, but also for more truth, because she believed Clawfire. The Mountain Herd elders' stories had always followed the same patterns: evil steeds attacked and the mighty Rockwing conquered them and saved Mountain Herd. She hadn't realized it at the time, but the elders had not ever represented the points of view of the other herds. Why would foreign pegasi attack them for *no reason*? In hindsight it didn't make sense, but now it all clicked into place. "I might be a little suspicious of strangers," said Shadepebble. "But I also want the herds of Anok to live in peace." She and Clawfire stood and shrugged the snow off their backs.

"Then River Herd is where you belong."

She noticed that Clawfire winced when he folded his wings across his back. He'd held them over her for two days, and she guessed they ached terribly. "What about you?" she asked. "Will you stay with River Herd and Star?"

He lowered her muzzle to hers. "No. I've hurt you enough, Shadepebble. I was wrong to think you'd be grateful I kidnapped you. I won't stay where you have to see me each day."

Shadepebble's throat tightened, and when she looked up at his scarred face, she saw a friend, not an enemy. "No, Clawfire, I'm okay now. And if Star wants to unite us, then I think you belong with him too. Please don't go away."

He looked relieved. "You're certain?"

She nickered. "I'm certain."

Clawfire and Shadepebble continued their travels, flying south and looking for River Herd. The two friends glided comfortably together, chatting and sharing stories. Spring was swift in the north, and each day since the storm had ended was longer than the last. Clawfire was shedding, and his hair blew off him in white chunks as he flew.

On the morning of the third day, Shadepebble noticed a change in the terrain. "Where are we?" she asked.

"We're leaving the Ice Lands now," said Clawfire. "Those are the Hoofbeat Mountains." He nodded toward the jagged range on their left. "And I haven't seen any signs of the River Herd steeds."

They cruised a wing length above the snow and passed the Hoofbeat mountain range. A massive forest rose ahead. "Is that the Trap?" asked Shadepebble. She'd heard about a forest in the north that was so dense that a pegasus could not fly out of it.

"Yes, and look—hoofprints!" Clawfire sailed forward.

Shadepebble pinned her ears and gave chase, making a game of catching him, and passing him.

The Trap was just ahead, and Shadepebble wanted to see it. When she reached the tree line, she rocketed into the dark woods. "Catch me," she whinnied, leaving Clawfire behind.

"Wait!" he neighed.

Shadepebble slowed and landed gently in the snow.

The branches interlocked overhead, blocking the sunlight. Steam poured out of her mouth like smoke, and with dismay she realized she was sweating. Clawfire had warned her to keep her coat dry in the north.

"Shadepebble?" he nickered in the distance, sounding worried.

She kept silent and flexed her wings, excited for him to find her. The forest was surprisingly warmer than the open tundra.

Ah, there he was! She inched forward, thinking to sneak up on him.

"Please don't hide," neighed Clawfire, his voice rising.

She was about to call out to him when her mane tingled and terror washed through her. She smelled the hunting predator before she saw it. *No!*

Shadepebble bolted just as sharp claws raked down her flank. She screamed in pain. Then a heavy force slammed into her and knocked her onto her side. A rumbling growl shook her rib cage. She twisted her head and was face-to-face with an ice tiger. Its lips curled back, showing long, walrus-like fangs that were chipped and stained yellow. Its blue eyes bore into hers.

The tree branches rattled, and Clawfire appeared, charging toward her. The cat halted midbite and hissed at the stallion. He kicked the tigress in the head, rocking her back.

As the weight of the cat shifted, Shadepebble rolled to her hooves and bolted. Glancing up she saw that she could not fly out of the Trap, but she was small enough to fit between the trees. She lifted off and cruised just over the pine needles, picking up speed.

The tigress ran away from the big stallion and galloped after Shadepebble. Its huge paws thumped the soil.

Clawfire chased the cat.

Shadepebble hurtled between the trees. Branches stung her chest, and hot blood flowed down her hind flank where the ice tiger had ripped into her. Clawfire's hooves strummed the forest floor. He whinnied to get the cat's attention. But the ice tiger was catching up to Shadepebble.

"Face her," Clawfire ordered.

Without thinking, Shadepebble whirled around and faced the cat. It skidded, halting a wing length away from her. Clawfire sprang and kicked the cat's black-and-white striped flank. The tigress hissed, looking from one pegasus to the other, confused.

"Go!" neighed Clawfire to Shadepebble. Then he leaped up, aided by his wings, and dropped onto the cat. He sank his teeth into her back. The great feline twisted toward him.

Shadepebble shrieked and bolted. Tears flooded her eyes. She had to help him. She turned back and saw the tigress shoving Clawfire around like he weighed nothing. No, Shadepebble couldn't help him, but maybe she could draw the cat away. "Come and get me!" she whinnied.

She galloped out of the forest and kept running. Sobs racked her sides. Her flank throbbed where the ice tiger had clawed her, but she didn't yet feel the pain.

She cantered south, confused and terrified, and then she halted, sliding across the snow. She looked back. The cat hadn't followed her. "Clawfire!" she whinnied. He didn't answer. She imagined the strong stallion in the jaws of the tigress. Her mind screamed, and her heart broke. She didn't care if it was stupid; she was going back to help him. "I'm coming!" she whinnied.

Then Shadepebble heard a tinkling crack. Her ears pricked. She recognized that sound. She'd heard it each time Clawfire kicked holes in ice so they could drink the water beneath it. Her gut lurched and she looked down. Tiny fractures spread out from her hooves. She was standing on a frozen pond, and the ice was cracking.

She spread her wings, about to fly off it, when the surface shattered. She crashed through the ice layer and sank into freezing water.

Shadepebble kicked hard for the surface and bumped her head on unbroken ice. She was trapped! She flipped over and kicked the ice with her hooves, but only managed to puncture small holes.

Her lungs burned from the effort of holding her breath and fighting for the surface at the same time. Her heart pounded so hard it hurt. *Calm down,* she thought. *Look for the hole you fell through.*

She scanned the bubbly surface. Large chunks of ice floated to her left. She swam toward them, using her wings and legs. She reached the hole and swam up, sucked a huge mouthful of air, and then went under again. She battled back toward the light and got her head free, took another breath. She tried to climb out, but the ice broke around her, making a larger hole. Instinctively, she whinnied for help even though she was alone.

Her legs slowed as the cold seeped her strength. She thought of Clawfire. They were both going to die here in the north. She drifted under the water and imagined her pink feathers streaking across the sky in the golden meadow. Her body went limp and she sank.

Then a black stallion, his face marked by a huge white star, appeared above her, hovering over the pond.

She twitched, shocked. It was the black foal of Anok.

"Relax," he instructed as her head emerged.

He plunged his head into the icy water, grabbed hold of her wing, and slowly lifted her. She struggled.

But after a moment, she obeyed and stopped fighting. Star's dark eyes were brilliant and full of concern, and the oddest feeling overcame her; *I'm safe. Everything is going to be okay.* And then she passed out as the black foal dragged her out of the water, slid her onto the solid ice, and pulled her to shore.

When Shadepebble woke, it was nighttime and she was surrounded by young pegasi. She stared at them, wondering if she'd died. Her body was warm and free of pain; but when she looked at her flank, she saw three neat scars, the healed claw marks of the ice tiger. But how was that possible—the wound had been fresh?

"You're safe," said a chestnut filly with aqua wings. It was the black foal's friend, Morningleaf.

"When am I?" Shadepebble asked, confused.

The young pegasi explained to her that they'd found her drowning in the pond earlier that day and that Star had healed her. "The black foal?" Shadepebble asked them. "Where is he?"

"He's right next to you," said Morningleaf. Her amber eyes were bright, and her tone was soothing and kind.

Shadepebble turned, saw Star, and blinked. He was large for a yearling, and the golden starfire crackled across his hide. "You healed me?"

Star nodded.

"Do you know who I am?"

"I do," said Star. "You're Rockwing's filly."

Her eyes bulged. "Yes. My father conquered your herd and tried to have you executed."

The black yearling exhaled in a long breath. "I know that, Shadepebble."

She gasped. "Of course—I'm sorry. . . . I just don't understand why you saved me. You could have let me drown and had revenge on my sire. I'm his last foal."

"Yes, I know that too."

Shadepebble stared at him for a long time. Everything that Clawfire had told her about the black foal seemed to be true. But she had to be certain. She lowered her head and said in a whisper, "My sire believes you'll claim Anok and destroy us. Is that true?"

Star pawed the ground. "It's not true, Shadepebble, but you can believe what you want." He gazed south, toward her homeland. "I've healed you; you're free to go."

She gaped at him. Star could easily force her to stay or try to use her against her sire, Rockwing, but instead he'd healed her wounds and was letting her go. Shadepebble shook her head, and her fear vanished. "Can I stay, for a while?" She'd been on an incredible journey and learned that her sire had told her many lies. She needed to rest and think.

The pegasi agreed to take her request to Star's council of supporters, and she told them about Clawfire. Soon Star sent out two patrols to look for the ice tiger and signs of Clawfire. But after hours of searching, they found nothing.

"It appears your captain escaped the ice tiger," said Star. "But we didn't find him."

Shadepebble nodded, and her heart filled with hope. If Clawfire had escaped the tiger, then he was alive, maybe hiding or injured but alive! She didn't know how or when, but she believed she'd see him again. And when she did, she'd thank him for rescuing her from the storm and the tiger, and from Mountain Herd.

Shadepebble hadn't believed foreign pegasi could live in peace, but Clawfire had shown her it was possible. The future was brighter because of it, and she made a decision. Shadepebble would not go back home, not ever. She would follow Star.

Read on for a sneak peek

at the final adventure in this first arc of

THE
GUARDIAN
~HERD~
SERIES

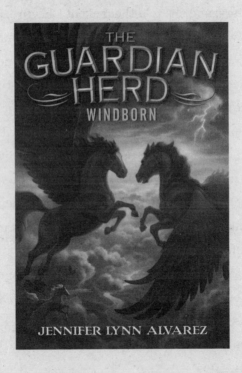

1

TEARS

HEAVY CLOUDS MASKED THE NIGHT SKY, AND cold drizzle collected on Star's feathers as he flapped through the mist, soaring straight up toward the moon. He was searching for the end of the massive cloud layer that blocked his view of northern Anok. Where was his herd? They had just been celebrating the defeat of Frostfire's Black Army at their camp in the Trap. Star was content. He'd used his starfire to heal his friends and his enemies, and the herds that had been hiding from Nightwing the Destroyer were finally united and working together. Star's ultimate goal of bringing peace to Anok had seemed imminent.

But then the cries of an injured pegasus had lured

Star deep into the woods. He'd found Frostfire's mate, Larksong, lying alone beneath a tree, groaning and bleeding. This mare was Nightwing's ally, but Star took pity on her, using his starfire to heal her and her unborn foal. And then guilt had driven Larksong to confess an awful trick: "Run back to your herd before it's too late," she'd whinnied. "Petalcloud did this to me. She beat me and left me here, to lure you away from your friends."

Petalcloud was the leader of the Ice Warriors, an army she'd formed to kill Star and win the favor of Nightwing. Petalcloud had abused Larksong in the hopes that Star would do exactly what he had done: abandon his friends.

Right after Larksong's confession, a flash of silver light appeared from the way Star had come. Then he heard a loud explosion, like lightning striking a thousand trees at once. He'd galloped back to the scene of the celebration only to find ashes covering the ground, a giant hole blasted through the ceiling of branches that sheltered the Trap, and emptiness where his herd had been reveling. Star knew instantly that Nightwing had been there. Perhaps since Frostfire's Black Army and Petalcloud's Ice Warriors had failed to capture Star, Nightwing had changed tactics and decided to capture Star's friends instead.

But where had the ancient stallion taken all of them?

Star burst into the clear sky above the clouds. Bitter cold slowed his blood, and screaming winds pierced his sensitive ears. He flew in a circle beneath the glittering stars, sucking at the sharp air and driving it into his burning lungs, but there were no pegasi here.

Frustrated, he pinned his wings and nose-dived toward land, hurtling through the wet clouds, which felt warm after the heights, and rocketing toward the Trap. He pulled up just before hitting the trees and then roared across them, his hooves skimming the branches, his eyes hunting for any sign of Nightwing or his friends.

Star landed back in the forest, and the pine needles swirled around his hooves. He held perfectly still and listened, his ears swiveling madly, trying to capture any sounds of wingbeats or hoofbeats, or the bleating of the newborns. But there was nothing, just forlorn silence and the wet smell of fog. If his herd was not in the sky and not in the Trap, then where could they be? Star galloped back to the place where Nightwing had blasted the huge hole through the thick canopy of branches.

The area was burned black. The shock of it had not left Star. He felt sick and dizzy, baffled and scared. Many steeds had died; the ashes told the story, but not all—Star held on to that hope: *not all*!